EVEN IN DARKNESS

Further Titles by Lynn Hightower

THE PIPER*

The Sonora Blair Series
EYESHOT
FLASHPOINT
NO GOOD DEED
THE DEBT COLLECTOR

The David Silver Series
ALIEN BLUES
ALIEN EYES
ALIEN HEAT
ALIEN RITES

The Lena Padgett Series
SATAN'S LAMBS
FORTUNES OF THE DEAD
WHEN SECRETS DIE

* *available from Severn House*

EVEN IN DARKNESS

Lynn Hightower

This first world edition published 2013
in Great Britain and 2014 in the USA by
SEVERN HOUSE PUBLISHERS LTD of
19 Cedar Road, Sutton, Surrey, England, SM2 5DA.
Trade paperback edition first published in
Great Britain and the USA 2014 by
SEVERN HOUSE PUBLISHERS LTD.

British Library Cataloguing in Publication Data

Hightower, Lynn S. author.
  Even in darkness.
  1. Murder–Investigation–Fiction. 2. Women television
  personalities–Fiction. 3. Recluses–Fiction.
  4. Suspense
  fiction.
  I. Title
  813.6-dc23

ISBN-13: 978-07278-8351-3 (cased)
ISBN-13: 978-1-84751-499-8 (trade paper)

All Severn House titles are printed on acid-free paper.

Severn House Publishers support the Forest Stewardship Council™ [FSC™],
the leading international forest certification organisation. All our titles that
are printed on FSC certified paper carry the FSC logo.

MIX
Paper from
responsible sources
FSC
www.fsc.org   FSC® C013056

Typeset by Palimpsest Book ᴾ
Falkirk, Stirlingshire, Scotlan
Printed and bound in Great Br
TJ International, Padstow, Cornwall.

For my magical, outrageous, steel magnolia mama – Joyce – who always knew I was going to be a writer.

ACKNOWLEDGEMENTS

To Robert, my husband, and Alan, Laurel, and Rachel. Rebecca, Brian, Katie, Isaac, David, Arthur, Wes, Arnaud & Julien.

To my agent, Matt Bialer, and Lindsay Ribar and Stephanie Diaz at Sanford J. Greenburger.

To Sheila Williams.

To Kate Lyall Grant, at Severn House, and Anna Telfer, Michelle Duff, Piers Tilbury.

If I take the wings of the morning, and settle at the farthest limits
of the sea
Even there your hand shall lead me, and your right hand shall
hold me fast.
If I say, 'Surely the darkness shall cover me, and the light around
me become night,'
Even the darkness is not dark to you; the night is as bright as the
day, for darkness is as light to you.

Psalms 139: 7–12

ONE

W hat brought me out of my dreams?

I think at some level I became aware of dark things. Something restless beneath the supposed serenity of a life I lived moment to moment. I liked to think I was free. That my past was the least important thing about me. But the universe is a thing of checks and balances, and your shadow follows.

There are times I think the Dark Man will be the source of my salvation, but there is never any doubt that he is a curse. My curse. If I had the chance for a lifetime do-over, I would never have gotten into the evangelism business. It is easy to forget what a dangerous job religion can be.

Caroline Miller is missing. Along with her daughter, my granddaughter, Andee Miller. Andee, whose eyes, the shape of her nose, the way she has of tilting her head to one side when she does not quite believe you – these things she gets from my son. Thus from me.

The Dark Man is back. And I know it is the Dark Man who has taken them.

Seven years ago, Caro was married to my son. Seven years ago, Caro killed my son. Seven years ago, I was a witness for the defense at her trial, testifying fervently on her behalf just before my . . . I believe the euphemism is *breakdown*.

Those days seemed full of the kind of events that happen only to other families. At times like that, nothing feels normal. Perhaps by that I really mean *right*. There is no question that the things that happened to us, to all of us, were not right.

I am awake again, to my life. Present in the moment. Seven years of winter, functional but frozen, hiding and hibernating, aware, but not afraid. If I miss anything about those years, it is that one thing. Not being afraid.

You might think seven years of drifting would pass slowly, but the time flowed like water draining out of the tub when you want to linger in the bath. I could sit and stare at a blank wall for hours, meditating like a wizened monk. The rapture of true meditation comes easily to me, and feels like a guilty pleasure. I find it seductive and addictive – surrendering to the wall.

It has been fourteen years since the Dark Man first approached me – a man squeezed by a mystifying welter of darkness and will, conflicting with revelation and light. There are times that I wish he'd gone through with his plans, and not let me stop him.

The Dark Man is a sociopath. I don't know his name, but I will, and soon. I'll get the name along with everything else. The FBI is trying to find him. So is every deputy sheriff, news reporter and vigilante in the state. He is the man of the moment, guilty of crimes that turn the strongest stomach.

And the only person who knows how to find him, is me.

TWO

I woke that morning at five a.m., I really can't say why. It could have been the significance of the date – the seventh anniversary of Joey's death. But I had never woken so early any other year on this day.

I lay quietly, alone of course, my mind straining, body sluggish. I rolled over and looked at the clock. Five twenty-two. The alarm would not go off for another hour. I remember wondering if I was up so early because of the energy supplements I had taken. Caro had sent them to me. The perfect formula for people who suffer from low thyroid. Caro eats organic, and is on the cutting edge of homeopathy. She often sends me things. They often do exactly as she promises.

And that was it. The only unusual thing. Until the mail came.

Marsha brought it in. She always does when she's here, which is more often than she should be. I think she is lonely. She is the kind of mean-spirited person other people avoid, myself included, even though she is my cousin. She hides her unkindness beneath a layer of treacly voice tones and faux jokes – the refuge of many who say things that are unpleasant. *I was just kidding. Can't you take a joke?*

I think she is aware how much I dislike her going through the mail. It is one of the reasons she does it, to annoy me, to have power over me, and also because she is obsessively interested in every detail of my life.

She is the accountant for Joy Miller Ministries, not the secretary, so technically the mail is not her province. As I work out of my home, some of the mail is business oriented, and some of it is personal. She goes through my things, too, upstairs in my bedroom, through my closet, my makeup drawer, my jewelry. I wonder if she knows that I know.

I often think of firing her. But she is loyal *to the cause* (her words, not mine, as the cause is me, or rather, my ministries) and I don't pay her as much as a new accountant would cost. And the ministries are winding down. I don't take in very much these days. The heyday of cable television and continuous revivals and preaching gigs are like the memory of a woman I once knew very well, but have lost touch with. It doesn't seem like it could ever have been *my* life. My cousin Marsha stays employed through the benevolence of my inertia, plus she keeps the IRS off my back.

She stands in the foyer of my house, studying postmarks, holding envelopes to the light. She seems unconcerned that I am standing right beside her with my hand out. She frowns over a thick brown envelope marked personal.

'What's this?' she asks. Her eyes are hungry.

I just smile and take the mail. Why do I smile?

'Do you want me to come in tomorrow, Joy? I've got a hair appointment at ten. Sorry, but it was the only day Rena had free.'

I don't believe her. Her schedule is six hours, nine to three, Monday, Tuesday and Wednesday. Of course, I am not her only client. I'm just the one foolish enough to put her on a salary instead of an hourly rate.

'Just come in afterward and stay late,' I say.

Marsha is already headed out the door, but this stops her and she looks at me over her shoulder. 'Stay late?'

I nod.

'*Oh?*'

Even then, before I opened that brown envelope marked personal, something inside me was waking up.

As soon as Marsha is gone I kick off my shoes. This is part of the Monday, Tuesday, Wednesday ritual. Get rid of Marsha, get rid of shoes.

Outside, my dog Leo is barking. I will wait until he is quiet before I bring him in. I cannot go out while he is barking, because that would give him the message that barking is a good thing – barking gets results. Leo is four-teen months old, a lean eighty-three pounds, and I am still training him.

I tear the envelope open. The return address is *my* address, though I didn't send it. My name and particulars are printed on simple white labels, and the word PERSONAL is stamped in two inch red letters. On the back, another red stamp says PHOTOS – DO NOT BEND.

Inside, I find a stack of four by six color photographs. There are three sets, clipped together with oversized black binders.

The top picture shows a man standing behind a pulpit. He wears a suit and his hair is combed and gelled into an under-stated pompadour, which immediately makes me tag him as a Southern Baptist. One of those sticky white labels has been stuck along the bottom of the picture, obscuring the back view of a packed and attentive Sunday morning congregation. Printed on this label is a name. THE REVEREND JIMMY MAHAN.

Mahan. *Jimmy* Mahan. I know this name.

We were in school together. He was two years behind me, working on a religion degree.

I bring the picture close and squint. I recognize the name but not the man. If I know him, if he is the Jimmy Mahan I used to know, he is changed or I've forgotten his face. He has a girth on him and though it is hard to tell from the picture, he looks like one of those red-faced men who sweat. And indeed in the next picture he has taken out a handkerchief to mop his face. Different suit. This one grey. The first navy blue.

He is playing golf in the next shot. I don't recognize the golf course but the terrain reminds me of South Carolina, maybe Georgia. Pine trees, needles in sandy soil. His shirt is Kelly green, short-sleeved, and he wears white shorts, which seems less than wise. His pompadour is higher here, and he does not seem to be sweating. Early spring, sunny and cool.

The next shot disturbs me. Mahan is asleep in a brown recliner, mouth open. There is the arm of a matching recliner and an elbow in the corner. A woman? His wife? The shot seems intrusive. I wonder who took it and how. Why.

The next picture up sends rivulets of shock tingling down my spine. I hear a voice, my voice. *Oh God. Oh shit.* My heart is pounding. I sit down on the floor.

I am suddenly remembering something about Jimmy Mahan. How they used to call him 'the mouth that roared'. He was skinny then, a medium sort of height, as I remember. Quick-moving, loud-talking, a laugh that used to echo in the hallways. People would roll their eyes and say his name. Fondly. Or with irritation. Usually with irritation.

I cannot find the skinny guy with the big laugh in this picture. But the man with the pompadour and the tear-stained face looks oddly brave, braver than I would be with my head jerked back, my neck exposed and a gun jammed hard to my throat.

I am propelling myself backward, scooting on the floor until my back is against the wall. I draw my knees up and look at the next picture.

Mahan's throat has been ripped open, a piece of something like pink pipe cleaner sticking up, and if I had not seen the gun in the other picture I would have thought that Jimmy Mahan had been attacked by some animal, a lion or a wolf, something that had ripped his throat out in a death-lust frenzy.

This one has a label. THE REVEREND JIMMY MAHAN, AFTER DEATH. There is writing on the back of the picture, in green ink, bold, like a Sharpie.

HE CHOSE US IN HIM BEFORE THE FOUNDATION OF THE WORLD, THAT WE SHOULD BE HOLY AND BLAMELESS BEFORE HIM. IN LOVE HE PREDESTINED US TO ADOPTION AS SONS THROUGH JESUS CHRIST TO HIMSELF, ACCORDING TO THE KIND INTENTION OF HIS WILL.

I am experiencing a strange double vision. Part of me seems to be viewing myself, huddled against the wall, staring at these pictures. The other is studying this final shot – Jimmy Mahan's face splashed with Jimmy Mahan's blood. There is nothing left of his chin. His hair, parted on the left, has flopped over one eye. One dead eye. And I remember this – that Jimmy Mahan was vain about his hair. I remember how he used to wear it long, and toss his head back, thin white wormlike fingers pushing the hair from his eyes whenever he answered a question in class, or made a point in discussion.

There are more pictures. There are two more sets.

I realize that Leo is quiet now. I should go and get him, bring him into the house. I should call the police. Although if the police are coming, maybe I should leave Leo out. He will jump on them and bark and he is scary-looking, despite his teddy bear heart, but he's been out too long as it is, he's probably thirsty.

He barks again, as if he knows I am thinking about him. I can't go now, not until he is quiet, but I can't leave him barking, he is no doubt disturbing the neighbors. I can lock him in the bathroom while the police are here. It will only be a problem if one of the police officers needs to use the bathroom, but that would be unprofessional, wouldn't it? Maybe I should vacuum the living room before they come, because Leo sheds, he sheds a lot.

I scream. A long scream that hurts. Why did these pictures come to me? Who sent them? Who put *my* address in the top left corner, and my address in the center, as if I'd sent this packet to myself? I scream again, but I don't feel better.

Who?

Why?

And why me? Me? Me? What did *I* do?

Is this some sort of a confession? The televangelism used to pull in the nuts, but those days are over, nobody remembers. I don't know anybody who would do something like this.

Except, wait. Maybe I do.

THREE

Leo knows I am unhappy. A dog always knows.

I wonder absently why I live in this house. I don't *like* this house, I never liked this house. My husband, fourteen years dead – he's the one who picked this house out, this is the house that *he* wanted, and more house than we could afford in those days. In any days, really. I've been house poor most of my life. Why do I still live here after all these years?

There are two more sets of pictures. It surprises me that I have not at least given them a quick glimpse. I have as much human curiosity as anyone else. Maybe more.

But what I want to do is throw them all away. Burn them. I don't want their presence in my space, and even as I have this thought I feel a sense of guilt, as if I am betraying Jimmy. These glimpses I have of his final moments make me feel defiled. Death is intimate and I do not want to witness this private montage of the end of his life.

I stumble back into my shoes and trudge down the carpeted hallway through the kitchen and to the back door and in my head I list everything I hate about this house. The layout, for example, is too much like a rat warren. I want openness and tall ceilings. And I don't like carpet, I like wood floors. Old ones, not too shiny, covered in the patina of scuff and scratches, worn with life but ready for more. I like old houses and tall ceilings, homes designed when architects still held sway, instead of the way they are built now – contractors piecing them together like a toddler with a small selection of blocks. Random thoughts to fill my head, a way to push back the images of pictures I never wanted to see.

I stare out the window of the kitchen door and for once I catch Leo unaware. He is snuffling through the monkey grass that rings the white birch tree, and I see from the way he jerks his head up and backward that he has rooted up yet another garter snake. They love the long grass but they do not love Leo. He noses them up for the evident pleasure of watching them glide swiftly out of reach, a puzzled but satisfied light in his teddy bear eyes. I have never seen Leo harm any living being, with the exception of flies, which he can snap right out of the air, but to the cats, dogs, snakes and neighbors that are the focus of his affectionate enthusiasm, he is an object of terror. Lean and athletic as he is, a still-growing adolescent of fourteen months, he weighs eighty-three pounds and stands twenty-seven inches high at the shoulder. He is thirty-eight inches long, not counting the fifteen inches of tail that will take out any low-lying coffee cups. His coloring is unusual – black and tan feathered with silver, without the standard black saddle markings common to most German shepherds.

Leo's feet are monstrous and he has yet to grow into them. I think, with pride and uneasiness, that he will not reach full size for yet another year. His ears are long, upright and pointed, and his face is solid black, and when I take him for walks, people cross to the other side of the street.

I am sitting on the couch again, and Leo, who has raced through the living room three times, slopped water out of his bowl on to his 'shirtfront' of fur and into a line of puddles on the kitchen floor, has suddenly caught my mood. He trots close, winds his way around the chair and coffee table, which he has knocked two feet off kilter, and sits on the rug that is now wrinkled and curled sideways. He lays his head sideways in my lap. My off-white cargo pants soak up the water that dribbles off his muzzle and I feel the thunder of his heartbeat against my leg. He offers me consolation by bringing me his third favorite toy, the beloved 'chip monkey' – now headless – and it sits on my knee, the fur sticky with dog spit. I pull Leo's ears and scratch behind them, feeling the hardened lump of fur where a neighboring cat has swiped at him, drawing a copious amount of blood.

I left the pictures on the coffee table. I reach for the second set. One hand on Leo's head. One hand on the pictures. I think of the dreams these photographs will bring me.

Now Gloria I do recognize, with a dread that makes me feel weirdly hollow through the knees, and it is good that I am sitting down. In the first shot she is standing on the steps of her church in the traditional black robes trimmed in purple, a good Presbyterian assistant pastor. I used to envy her having a church of her own. I could not get one, so I went into televangelism, and by the time I was offered my choice of positions, I didn't want them anymore. In an echo from the past, I hear the familiar introduction, *Joy Miller, a preacher without a pulpit*, the way pulpit would become *pull-pit* in a drawn out southern drawl.

Gloria's hair is mostly grey now, and it is cut short. Like me, Gloria Schmid got a degree in religion. Unlike me, she began with the intention of 'keeping her place' in the church – an obedient female, she would focus on counseling, though if ever a woman was born to preach, it was Gloria.

Hanging out with me, in the days we were students together, was politically incorrect in a big way and she took flak for it. I have been both credited and vilified for convincing Gloria to preach. In those days, a woman in the religion business didn't take the pulpit, she captured it, like changing lanes on the 405 in Los Angeles.

Like all of us, she's changed dramatically since school. For Gloria, there is weight, grey hair and more than the hint of a double chin. That air of disapproval I remember about her still emanates from the muddy green of her eyes or maybe I am imagining it. She certainly disapproved of me – disapproved, competed, judged, took me on as a project, tried to save me, reported on me to our professors and, years later when my cable show became a hit, followed in my footsteps.

There is a student hierarchy, in seminaries. We are categor-
ized, and there is a pecking order. I have heard that when Billy
Graham was in seminary it was thought he would not amount
to much.

The most admired student among my own classmates was
good old Elwood Shipley, who professed to having been a
heroin addict who slept under the I-65 northbound bypass until
he awoke one day with a religious tract in hand that turned
his life, as he used to say, *right side in.* The peckerwood
accent, the Howdy Doody freckles and Opie of Mayberry
sprouts of reddish brown hair gave him a *so uncool he was
cool* credibility and he spent his off-study time saving endan-
gered souls at the top of his lungs.

The professors loved him. Even when he was exposed as
the son of well-to-do physicians, a boy who'd gotten a brand
new Corvette at the age of sixteen, and a boy who had never
been addicted to anything except being the center of attention,
they still loved him. He just confessed his sin of lying and
begged them to join hands with him as he knelt in front of
the whole student body to beg for God's forgiveness and
direction.

I cannot see in the picture of Gloria Schmid if she still
wears the tiny pearl earrings she wore every day in school.
She always wore pantyhose to class, skirts and uncomfortable-
looking polyester blouses, and flat, square-toed shoes that just
looked odd on her long chunky legs.

There were times we banded together, as only women can
when drowning in a sea of men. And others when we were at
each other's throats, as only women can be when drowning
in a sea of men.

I was 'the albino', Gloria was 'the frump'. Most female
students had a derogatory nickname, supplied by a small cadre
of small-minded male students we ourselves nicknamed 'the
frat pack'.

It is true that my skin is very pale, almost bluish. I think if
I were ever foolish enough to try a tanning bed, they would
have to give my money back. I am slim and tall and got my
first bra more from desperation than need; I wear a minimum
of makeup and have always dressed plainly. If I have a style,

you'd call it stark. My face is sharp and angular, my nose broad. I am intellectually adventurous, if physically frail. In high school, my looks never earned me a place on the cheer-leading squad, but I was the hands down choice to play Joan of Arc in the senior play.

It was unfair as well as unkind to label Gloria a frump. She was merely conservative and formal. Where I am androgynous, she is Rubenesque. In a physical sense, as a woman, Gloria would be a sonnet. I would be a haiku.

Leo whimpers softly, head burrowing deeper into my lap. 'Be easy,' I say. Not sure which of us I am trying to reassure.

She has children. Gloria. I lost track of her, but I know that she married. In the next picture, she's hugging a boy of about sixteen. He is reluctant enough that he is clearly hers. She got married way after I did, waited sensibly to establish her career before she had kids. The boy looks like her, minus the air of disapproval. He has evidently just lost a soccer game, from the looks of his mud-streaked uniform and the glum aura of his teammates. No doubt a public hug from Mom made it better.

He is caught exchanging looks with his father, who stands behind Gloria, a tall, broad bear of a man with a pewter grey crew cut, and something of a military bearing. I wonder about this boy, bracketed between a minister mother and military father.

And then it hits me that the minister mother may be dead now and I move through the next two pictures.

Just like the sequence with Jimmy Mahan, these pictures follow a pattern. Subject at work. Subject at play. Subject with family. Subject moments before death.

Oh, Gloria. All of those times I hated you, I admit it; I see your eyes now and am filled with such compassion that it feels like love. How stupid we were, way back when. What a waste it was, all that anger and angst. I would not wish this on you in a million years. I would take it off your shoulders if I could. If I could have been there to hold your hand, Gloria, just to hold your hand, let you feel the warmth of another human being, to give you something – some connection when you were so afraid. I see such fear in your eyes, I would do that for you Gloria, I would.

It is not a weak thing to be frightened. But to see Gloria in so much fear makes my throat so tight that trying to swallow makes me give off a dry sort of choke that makes Leo raise his head.

Gloria is ravaged just like Jimmy Mahan. Throat torn open by a bullet, and the blood and bits of flesh that hang beneath her head, the bib of red that runs down the front of her silky green blouse, strike me as pornographic in the perverseness of the violence.

I put my head in my lap. Feel Leo snuffle my ear with his nose.

The next set of pictures. These. These are even worse than the last. I recognize him right away. Darrin Lane. He is thin still, hair no longer that baby fine pale blond, but now a taupe silver, like champagne, with sun streaks of whitish blond, no doubt earned while building schools in the hot African sun.

In spite of the other pictures that sit in my lap, I still have hopes for Darrin.

He's not like the other two. He was a skinny country boy from Western Kentucky, outspoken in the confident way of people who are not used to hiding behind words. He arrived at school with little experience and less regard for the way speaking your mind on matters spiritual can make you vulnerable to the piranha-like pounce of religion students who are as loud as they are narrow.

Darrin was just so normal. No ax to grind, and a quiet calling he'd rarely mention. He was a boy of compassion, and for Darrin, compassion was an action, not a feeling or idea. It was what he did and why he did it.

The pecking order of wannabe religious leaders is established by those who talk the talk. Not Darrin. His good works were as private and habitual as brushing your teeth and changing your underwear.

Nobody much knew what he was up to, in school. He did not get a lot of attention. I knew because I gave him rides when his pickup truck was in the shop, and I never took the gas money he tried to give me. I had generous parents. I did not need the crinkled dollar bills and pocketful of quarters that he offered. Darrin was the kind of guy, if he had a dollar, you had a dollar, which meant he was usually broke.

I go through the pictures methodically. It's one of those juvenile things. Hold your mouth just right, crank once and then the car will start. Only now it is curl your toes and don't breathe and Darrin will come out of this one alive. Go through the pictures one at a time, fifteen seconds apart, and Darrin will be OK.

Whoever this is – and I think I know who, I'm afraid that I do – he sent me these pictures with an agenda. But maybe even he could see that Darrin Lane is different. This man – this Dark Man if he is who I think he is – you can't tell what he will do. He can surprise you. There is a reason to have hope if it's him.

The first picture is vintage Darrin. Sitting outside behind a rough wood table under the trees. It's spring, because the trees are just beginning to bud out. Darrin sits on the side with about ten other people. Looks like breakfast – I can see bacon and a metal coffee pot. Darrin is in his element there at his addiction rehab boot camp for at-risk adolescents, twelve to seventeen. It is just like him to be sitting along one side with everybody else, instead of at one end or other of the table, leading the pack.

I'm sure Darrin is not the only adult there. But all I can see in this first shot is Darrin himself, chin in his hand, listening to a boy who has a pierced eyebrow and lip, spiky black hair and his hand in the air. The boy, fourteen maybe, looks intense, and huddles in a grey hoodie in a way that makes it clear it's a source of comfort, habit and warmth. Darrin's eyes are narrowed. It makes me remember that about him – how good he was at listening, how attentive he was, how connected.

The thing about Darrin – he's a safe place in an unsafe world.

The next picture shows him hiking. He's third in line. I get the impression of a pretty big group – maybe twenty – all going single file up the side of a mountain. The trail is steep and the girl at the head of the line has turned back to look over her shoulder. She is sweating, her hair plastered to her neck, and she has a serious look, like she is counting heads. If the well being of the group rests upon her, which might well be the case, that would be Darrin's style. To trust. To give responsibility. To let people accomplish things on their own so they can revel in the way that doing well makes you feel good. She cannot be staff; she looks barely twelve.

Regret rises inside me, pressure mounting like an oil well about to blow, and I wonder how Darrin's program was going. How he related to his charges – did he save their souls? Set them on the path of self respect and sobriety? I know he was particularly concerned with addictions and people in thrall to that brand of hell. I know he felt most rehab programs fell short, that you had to find a way to deal with the darkness that drove the addict as well as the addiction. He used to spout statistics on the success versus failure rate of different programs. The high failure rates worried him. Actually kept him up at night. He said the problem had to be in most part the programs themselves. If they were any good, why didn't they work? Why assume the addict failed the program when it was clear, from the failure rates, that the programs failed the addict?

Like a lot of things, many of them precious, Darrin slipped through the fingers of time, fading from my life a little bit more every day. I wish I had not let him go.

But I did. If he was still alive – please, please – if he was still alive I would reconnect. If I could have that second chance.

The *please, please* dies on my lips when I flip to the next photo.

Darrin is sweating hard, his hair gone dark and wet, and his right eye is swollen shut. He put up a fight. Of course he did. Kentucky boys don't just lie down and die.

But he did die. Just like the others.

FOUR

The note says there are two reasons I should not go to the police. It is much in the style of kidnappers who tell their victims not to go to the authorities – when of course that is exactly what they should do. Still, it sticks in my mind – *two reasons*?

I'm not so sure what this means, but the usual threat concerns family. My family is Leo, my dog, Caroline, my DIL (daughter-in-law) and Andee, my granddaughter. Some people do not count dogs. Which leaves Caro and Andee. Two reasons?

I check my watch. Three p.m., and they are on Central time. Caro will not be off work until four thirty, five thirty my time. Too early to call. The best time to catch her is that pocket of opportunity between dinner and bed, when she and Andee curl up together on the couch. Andee is allowed one hour of television every day. If she uses it up during the afternoon, they curl up together and read instead. Andee has chocolate milk. Caro a glass of red wine. There is nothing the two of them treasure so much as the time they spend lost in their books.

If this packet is from who I think it is, one of those reasons could be that I owe him my life. But that would only be one reason, and he mentions two.

They never cover this problem in the movies. But I've always thought that in real life, as in now, it would not be unusual for people *not* to be able to figure out the cryptic demands of the weird and deranged. It is like trying to figure out the tax code – ripe with trouble and retribution and a perverse logic that is clear only to the perpetrator. I can't get through the daily crossword in the newspaper, so how am I going to figure out the hazy demands of a sociopath?

I need to hear Caroline's voice.

I pick up the phone, knowing I am way too early, but unable to help myself, and, as expected, catch the voice mail. This is a comfort, but a small one, a sense of business as usual that

I cling to. Caro will be home from work in three hours. It should be OK to wait that long before I call the police. In case she and Andee are the two reasons.

Which seems likely, considering the significance of the date. I tell myself it could be a coincidence. For *him* to know the date, he'd have to have been keeping track of me. I don't like to think of him keeping track of me.

And keeping track would not be difficult. My son's death was media fodder off and on for eighteen months. Maybe Joey's death is one of the reasons, the second. Which means my husband's death, fourteen years ago, is reason one, and my son's death, seven years ago, is reason two. Tragedy comes to me in seven-year cycles, like locusts. Which means that my card has come up again.

I have fallen asleep with Leo's head on my foot, my neck sloped sideways in an awkward slant that makes me ache when I wake up. Leo, whose head is also slanted sideways, does not seem to ache. He blinks his sleepy eyes at me, watchful, perhaps, to see if I am going to cry. I have overslept. It is too late now to be calling my DIL.

Caro answers on the first ring. She sounds breathless, not like her usual self. On the other hand, today is after all the seventh anniversary of the day she shot and killed Joey, her husband and my son, in self defense. Always the thought comes to me – if only she had not bought a gun. Followed as always by the next thought – would he have killed *her*? I love my son as much today as I did the day he was born. I miss him every day of my life, and, considering who his father was, he turned out better than he should have. But he had miles to go and years of evolution ahead of him. He just didn't last long enough.

It is wrong to blame Caroline, who was five months pregnant that day and on her way out the door and the marriage. In all fairness to me, it was undoubtedly my testimony that influenced the jury to acquit. The average jail time for a woman who kills her husband in self defense is twenty-five years. Men who kill their wives average seven.

I know I did the right thing, saying what I did at the trial.

I know that Joey, for all of his faults, genuinely loved Caroline, and I know he would not have wanted her to go to jail, and knowing all of these things I still cannot think of what I said without feeling knotted up inside.

I see Joey in Andee's eyes and some of her mannerisms, and though Caro and I try to stay in touch, it has always – no surprise – been awkward between us. She lives in Fort Smith, Arkansas now – just a place she stopped on her way to California, the vague destination of people who are breaking tries with their past. Andee got sick on the way, and they stayed where they landed for a few days, Caro too wise and kind a mother to push a sick toddler on a cross country trip in that rackety Jeep Wrangler she drives. They met some nice people, she found a little bungalow to rent, a job in a local bank, and she felt good there. She stayed.

Caro seems happy enough in Arkansas, where she says the state motto should be *it's not as bad as you think*. Sometimes I think she is homesick, but I don't blame her for leaving Kentucky. If she'd stayed here in Lexington, she would have been defined by the worst day of her life. She told me that she wanted it to be the *least* important thing about her, not the most.

Sometimes I dream that it was I who killed Joey, not Caroline. I raised him, after all. He was my only son. And while I consider Andee and Caro my family, to all points and purposes, it's just me and Leo.

'Hey, Caro, it's Joy. I'm sorry to call so late.'

'Oh, hey.' Caro is a well brought up southern girl, and she is well mannered enough to sound glad to talk to me, but my voice is clearly not the one she was expecting to hear.

'Did I wake you up?' I ask.

'No, no.'

Her voice sounds heavy, so it could be sleep or it could be something else.

'I was thinking you might call,' she says.

It can't be because it is the unhappy anniversary of Joey's death. This is the one day of the year that we never talk. I often wonder if she felt different, after. Killing someone, even in self defense, changes you, this I know. But you never quite feel like you're supposed to feel. You never react the way people think.

'Mrs Miller, did you get anything funny in the mail today? Icky funny, I mean?'

Icky funny. That was one way to put it.

'I did.' My voice broke. I wasn't expecting that. I had called to see if *she* was OK. She and Andee. But it hits me that there is never anyone to call and see if I am all right, and I am pathetically grateful for the kindness I hear in Caro's voice.

'Me too. Mrs Miller, I'm sorry, this has got to be hard for you.'

All these years, and she still calls me 'Mrs Miller'.

'Did you get pictures?' I ask her. My hand aches and I realize how tightly I am holding the phone so I make an effort to loosen my grip. Leo wedges his giant head into my lap.

'Pictures?' She sounds puzzled. 'Newspaper pictures, if that's what you mean. Copies of all the stories they ran, you know, after Joey died. All about my trial. My all time favorite headline . . . "Pregnant Shooter Jailed".'

Damn. Weird. 'Is there a postmark? Any kind of note?'

'The postmark is from Lexington, Bluegrass Station. And there's a weird note. It says "Retribution is yours, Caroline Staley Miller" and some other stuff.'

'And that's all?'

'Isn't that enough?'

'Did it come in a plain brown envelope with white sticker labels printed up on some home computer?'

'Yeah. It did.'

'And was the note torn off a yellow legal pad, and written in green Sharpie?'

'*Yes*. What did yours say? You got the same thing, right? About Joey?'

'Not exactly.'

There was no way to tell her easy. Unwise to tone it down. I read her the note that came with my package.

FOR THE PAST FOURTEEN YEARS I HAVE BEEN TRYING TO FIND MY WAY TO SALVATION. THE PATH ELUDES ME, AS YOU CAN SEE. I TRIED

OTHERS, BUT THERE SEEMS TO BE NO DENYING
THAT YOU ARE THE ONE. YOU ARE MY NATURAL
BRIDGE TO OVERTHROW THE PRECIPICE OF
ETERNAL DAMNATION. I WISH IT DID NOT HAVE
TO BE YOU.

LET'S KEEP THIS BETWEEN US, SHALL WE?
FOR TWO VERY GOOD REASONS. NO POLICE.
I'LL BE IN TOUCH.

'Jesus,' Caro says.
'I know.'
'This is . . . it's—'
'Terrifying. And it's got to be the same guy that sent the
newspaper clippings to you.'
'Do you have any idea who it might be?'
'No. Of course not.' When I lie, I do it well.
'Are you scared, Joy?'
'I am so scared it's not funny. For you, and for me, and for
Andee.'
'Are you all by yourself?'
I look at my lap. 'I have Leo.'
'Leo?'
'My dog.'
'Oh. Right.'
'And you? Are you and Andee alone? You're not . . . I mean,
I know you're seeing someone special.'
'Well, I still have Ruby.'
I smile. Ruby is a good dog. A big dog. A very *old* big dog.
'Sanderson's still living up in Fayetteville. Because of the
restaurant.'
'Oh, yes, Sanderson. And he works in a restaurant?'
'He owns it. I called and left him a message. He drives
down a lot of nights.'
'Good. That's good. Is he a good guy? Good to you and to
Andee?' Dumb question. She does not answer. 'I'm sorry,
Caroline, I'm not trying to be nosy. But I've wanted to tell
you for a long time that I hope you'll find a really great man
to share your life with. Someone who will love you and Andee

like you deserve to be loved. Who will be better for you than
Joey was.' Someone, I am thinking, who is really big. And
knows martial arts.

She still does not say anything.

'I'm sorry it took me seven years to tell you that, Caroline.'

'Thank you,' she says. Her voice is very small. 'Sanderson
is good to me. And he's nothing like—'

'Like my son,' I say flatly.

'I didn't mean—'

'I understand. Look, I don't really know what to do about
all of this, Caroline, but I'm not going to the police, at least
not right away.'

'I think you *should*, Mrs Miller. I'm not a big fan of the
police, you know that, but this is way too big, way too creepy,
for the two of us.'

Caroline is the kind of person who does the right thing –
except maybe the day she bought the gun, though her position
could be argued, and as a matter of fact I remember arguing
with the prosecuting attorney about it in court. But afterwards,
after she shot Joey, she did not run away. She called nine-one-
one. And the police, not overly sympathetic to my blood-
spattered five months pregnant daughter-in-law, put her under
immediate arrest.

Now her life is OK. She has a new man. No doubt they
will get married and he will be a wonderful father to my
granddaughter, the child Joey did not live to see. And while
I always knew this day would come, while I wish her well
– I do, really – I'm wise enough to know how the world works.
I'm afraid I will not be a welcome part of this family, that
Andee and I will not be allowed to stay close.

And Andee I would love all on her own, but she is also
everything good about my Joey. She looks like him and she
has his laugh and his ears, and she is what he could have been
without the dysfunctional demons that slipped so effortlessly
into our lives.

'I guess Andee's sound asleep,' I say, and I can hear the
echo of hope in my voice.

'She is,' Caro says.

I would not have let her wake my granddaughter, but there

is a part of me that wants the choice, the comfort of knowing I am that important. She has called me 'Nina' since she was a baby. A name she came up with herself. I want to hear her say my name, to talk a few minutes, to hear her voice.

'What are you going to do?' Caro asks.

'I honestly don't know. But stay close to your Sanderson, will you? Are *you* going to the police?'

She sighs. 'Just thinking about it makes me hyperventilate. But I don't think we have a choice.'

She says *we*. *We* are in this together. It makes me feel a little less lonely, but I'd rather she and Andee were safe out of it.

'It's late, Caro. Let's sleep on it and talk tomorrow. We're not going to solve it tonight.'

'OK. Goodnight, Mrs Miller.'

'Goodnight,' I say, but her voice is already distant and she hangs up before she hears me tell her to stay safe. She is a long way away, and getting further by the minute.

And I am so alone.

FIVE

I do not go to the police. The police come to me. The noise they make, the jackhammer of fists at my front door, brings me awake in pure panic.

Leo is barking. It's been said that the roar of a lion can be heard eight miles away in the jungle. In the subdivision, the bark of my Leo can be heard for ten.

I look out the bedroom window and see nothing but my backyard, the grass waterlogged from the rain that started before I got Leo out for his late night wee wee, where the two of us, dry now, were spattered with the initial onslaught of fat cold drops. I pull jeans over the white boxer shorts I wore to bed, and slide a fisherman's sweater over my white cotton tee. I run down the stairs, unfastening the baby gate at the bottom that keeps Leo and his youthful habits of destructive chewing and nosiness out of the upstairs rooms of the house. I would pay extra for a Marsha-proof gate.

I think as I run down the stairs that this house is ridiculously big for me and that I have been living here as a penance. Maybe I've been too lazy to move. Maybe I have thought I didn't deserve to. Maybe I'm letting Carl punish me, for what happened fourteen years ago.

I see blue lights pulsing. The intermittent throb shines through the green damask curtains in the living room. I don't like these curtains either. They are overly formal, keep out too much light, gather too much dust.

Blue lights.

Leo is frantic, running from the door to me to the window, and the hair stands stiffly in a stripe down his back, fanning out over his lean shepherd rump. He is intense in the way of GSDs on the alert, and he is young enough to be unsure what it is he is supposed to do, but sure he is supposed to do something.

I love him dearly and wish he would shut up.

'*Quiet*, Leo.'

He barks louder.

I hold his collar – it takes all my strength to keep him close – and with the other hand I open the front door. Now that it is too late, I realize I should have locked him in the bathroom off the hall *before* I opened the door. So far he has been determined to protect me from the garbage pickup men, the black lab one block over and baby strollers with wheels that rattle a certain way on the sidewalk. He does not feel I am in any danger from the occasional copperhead snake that wanders over from the creek across the road, and he's been known to nose them up in my direction, just like he does with the little grass snakes that like to slither through my yard. His intent is to play, theirs to slide confusedly my way for protection, and none of us are happy with the result.

I see a man and woman on my doorstep, both wearing business formal, and there is one uniformed officer at their back. I am aware that there may be more people out there in the front of my yard – I get the impression of more official vehicles than I can count on one hand, but Leo is on his hind legs, front ones paddling with the effort to break away from my grip and get down to the serious business of protecting me from the people trying to crowd through my door.

Both the man and the woman are talking to me; the woman, actually, is shouting, something about *the dog*, but my ears ring with the near painful volume of Leo's bark and I can't hear anything except *the dog . . . dammit*.

I wave at them, which can mean whatever it is they want it to mean, and put both hands on Leo's leather collar, which is stretching as much as leather can stretch. I drag him backward toward the bathroom. My wrists are already aching, as they have ached since I started leash training this dog, and pulling him along backward is a new trick that gives me a little bit of leverage as it tips him off balance. He flips sideways – that's a new one too, but we're right in front of the bathroom door now, and I shove him inside, telling him to hush, more a wish than a command, and shut him in. He continues to bark and scrabble his toenails against the door, and I know he is adding a new layer of nail tracks to join the other ones that travel up and down the panel of wood. More paint flecks on the floor. I can't see them, but I know they are there.

'Leo. Quiet. Now.'

A small whimper then a sad yelp, and silence followed by a tremendous thud. Leo is lying down.

The man and woman in business suits and a deputy sheriff are in my living room. Different faces, but the same sort of crew that stood there seven years ago to the day.

'The dog is safe,' I tell them, trying to catch my breath. I nod toward the bathroom door. 'He's still in training, that's all.'

'No kidding?' the woman says.

The sheriff nods in Leo's direction. His bullet-shaped head is shaved to a fine blondish crew, his uniform neatly ironed, and he affects the posture of the alpha male, shoulders square and confident.

'I used to work K-9. Shepherds can be the best dogs in the world, but you need to get him in hand, ma'am. That one looks like he's not going to stop until he achieves world domination.'

'You must be a dog whisperer. It's like you can read his mind.' This from the woman in her tight navy skirt and snug little blouse.

I don't like her.

The man in the suit, also navy, seems off balance, thanks, I think, to Leo. He seems less than patient with our chit chat.

'Agent Russell Woods, FBI, and this is my partner, Agent Mavis Jones. And this is Deputy Sheriff Bernard Collins.'

I look at their official identifications, check names and faces against pictures, shake all the hands, while my heart beats faster and faster. I don't introduce myself. They know who I am, don't they?

'Ma'am, you are Joy Miller?' Agent Woods says.

'Yes, I'm Joy Miller. Is there some kind of trouble?'

Agent Mavis Jones narrows her eyes at me. 'You tell us.'

'Let me rephrase that, Agent Jones. What in the hell do you mean by beating on my door in the middle of the night and scaring me half to death?'

Agent Jones glares at me and it is Special Agent Woods who explains.

'Mrs Miller, we're very sorry to disturb you, but we got a call from the Little Rock office in Arkansas . . .'

This. Cannot. No.

'. . . regarding a Caroline Miller, age twenty-nine, and her daughter, Andee Miller, age seven.'

My ears are buzzing and my vision tunnels. I can see Agent Woods, his mouth is moving, but I cannot hear what he says. I am sliding away. There is no point to my life anymore. No point to me.

Someone is calling my name. *Joy. Joy Miller.* I am not sure I am standing up, but I'm not on the floor. Deputy Collins stands at my back, one arm around my waist, the terrible Agent Mavis Jones is talking talking talking and now I am sitting on the couch, and someone bends my head over my knees which makes my stomach jump and my vision go dark. It's like having fizz in your head. My nerve endings tingle like a toothache, and I take slow deep breaths like the voice tells me. Someone wraps me in something warm, a fringe of some material caresses my cheek. It is my fuzzy little pink throw that I bought myself for Christmas last year and keep on the couch even though it clashes with the maroon plaid loveseat my husband picked out years and years ago. I don't like the couch any more than I like the house, any more than I like the curtains, but the pink throw is soft, and that I do like. Especially now, because I am weirdly cold. Someone is rubbing my hands, and saying that they feel like ice.

It's OK to sit still, the voice says so, and I do for the longest time. After a while I smell coffee, the scent streaming in from my kitchen, and the female I don't like, she is beside me now. She hands me a mug of coffee. She's put it in the yellow mug, which used to be my favorite, but that was before I found the tall skinny lavender mugs on clearance at Target.

Mavis Jones' hands are trembling and she makes sure I have the mug safe in my grip before she lets it go. She is different now. Kindness under the hard edges. It's just a feeling I get, a connection from her to me. She has put half and half in my coffee, good for her, and sugar, lots of it, which I don't take but seems maybe like not such a bad idea. I have done that myself more times than I can count, gone into a strange kitchen and made hot coffee, filled the cup with hot liquid, sugar and cream. It is what you do when you are ministering to people who are going through a terrible trauma. Like a death in the family.

I take a sip. It is so hot, the coffee, but I am thirsty, my mouth is so dry it is painful, which I know is a sign of shock. So that's it, then. I'm in shock. I know all about shock from my previous life, helping people through the dark times that always seem to come up.

The coffee is good. Henry's Blend, Seattle's Best, the price will make you do a double take, I buy it at Kroger. Marsha leaves great battleship cans of Wal-Mart coffee on my kitchen counter tops, and I donate the Marsha-coffee to some lawyer friends downtown. They'll drink anything. I am a coffee snob. I can do a blind taste test and tell you the religious affiliation of the person who brewed the cup. God save us all from the Methodists.

My hand trembles and I put the yellow mug on the coffee table. There's a reason I shouldn't put it there. Something to do with Leo. But I don't see Leo, so I guess it's OK.

'Tell me what happened,' I say. My voice sounds tinny and weird. I catch a glimpse of my face in the ornate, gold leaf mirror that hangs on the wall across from the sofa. I look the way I used to when I was a little girl and carsick, and could see my weirdly blanched skin in the rearview mirror. The décor in this living room is so Holiday Inn – every item the result of a long drawn out argument with my husband, who is now dead. He should have taken it with him. All the furniture. This house.

Caroline now. She knows how to make a room work. She doesn't see what's actually in a room. She sees what a room can be. Did I mention that she makes buttermilk pancakes from scratch? In spite of all the health stuff and organics, she's still a lot of fun.

I feel talky all of a sudden.

'I'm sure you know that Caroline Miller is my daughter-in-law. I call her my DIL. She is an artist when it comes to decorating. After all this time, all these years and the things we have been through, would you believe she still calls me Mrs Miller?' I blink at Agent Woods and Agent Jones, and Deputy Sheriff Collins, all of whom are watching me like I'm their favorite soap opera. 'It's a southern thing. She has excellent manners. I often wonder if she said "pardon me" the day she shot Joey. Excuse me, that's just a little mother-of-the-dead-son humor.' I look at them. They seem appalled. 'Tell me what happened, please?' I stand up. 'What happened to Caro and Andee? Damn it, you tell me right now.'

I'm not quite sure what to do next, so I sit back down.

'They're missing,' Mavis Jones says. Quickly. She sounds apprehensive, and I hear how out of control I sound. I'd be apprehensive too.

'Missing?' I say. It's a question. 'Missing? Not *dead*?'

'Did you expect them to be dead?' Agent Mavis Jones sounds sympathetic, but off kilter, in the way of wily cops.

'A nine-one-one call came in from their neighbor at eleven eleven p.m., Central Standard Time, tonight, the neighbor reporting that he'd seen an intruder entering your daughter-in-law's house.'

Agent Woods leans toward me as he talks, and the matter-of-fact quality in his voice makes me feel better. Like everything is normal and under control even though I know it's not. 'The dispatch operator instructed him to stay on the line while they sent officers out to the scene.'

So it becomes a scene, I think, what once was a house.

'A few minutes later the operator heard shots fired, and was unable to get the neighbor back on the phone.'

Because he was dead, I think, because he was dead. 'He was dead?'

Agent Woods nods.

'Was it Burton Stafford? He and his wife live behind Caroline. They're her landlords, she rents her house from them. They look after Andee in the afternoons after she gets home from school, until Caro gets back from the bank.'

Woods hesitated. 'We can't confirm that pending notification of next of kin, but yes, unofficially, that is who it was.'

No yes, I think. No yes.

'Your granddaughter and your daughter-in-law were not in the house. There were clear signs of forced entry, but there was no blood. Nightclothes were found on both beds, the mother's and the child's. It looks like they were forced to dress. There were muddy footprints up and down the staircase. All the windows were open. So were the front and back doors. A large dog, identified by other neighbors as the Miller dog, Ruby, was found wandering in the backyard. She had glass in her paw, and it looks as if she was wandering back and forth between the Miller house and the Stafford house which sits directly behind. The storm door was broken at the Stafford house, we think by a bullet that went through the door and into the victim. Burton Stafford was shot twice, and his body was found by officers in the kitchen of his home when they arrived on the scene. There was meat, cheese, that kind of thing, out on the kitchen counters and a beer that was open but full. It looks like Mr Stafford was up making himself a sandwich, looked out the back door and happened to see an intruder going into your daughter-in-law's home. We think the intruder saw Mr Stafford standing at his back door. The porch light was on and he shot Mr Stafford twice and also shot out the porch light.'

'No witnesses,' I say, thinking what that means for Caro and Andee.

'Exactly. Mrs Stafford heard the shots, heard her husband cry out, but did not see the perpetrator. She's evidently wheelchair bound—'

'Degenerative arthritis,' I say. 'Just getting in and out of the chair is hard for her.' I think what it must have been like for Mary Stafford, lying in that bed, unable to walk. 'She didn't see anything?'

'No. But she heard. She heard her husband up and on the phone, and she called out to him. He came into the hall, very agitated, and told her he'd seen a man going into your daughter-in-law's house. She can't remember exactly what her husband said, but she got the impression the man was skinny, very tall, dressed in black. He either had dark hair or wore a watch cap. She wasn't sure.'

I am thinking that I would like to talk to her. And that her description of this man sounds familiar to me. He does have dark hair. He is tall. And slender, very slender. The Dark Man that I know.

Agent Woods clears his throat. He looks at Agent Jones and she looks back at him and shrugs, and a flurry of unspoken communication is passing between them.

Agent Jones cocks her head at me. She is perched on the edge of the couch and the way she is wiggling her toes in her shoes makes me think her feet ache and she's had a long day. I see from the pane of windows next to the front door that the sun is rising. It's probably around six thirty. On normal days, I might be waking up, or I might be lying still in my bed, never having slept. Or I might be sleeping hard, having been up all night but having finally dropped off, the way I often do, around a quarter to five.

Jones turns her knees in to face me. 'The Fort Smith Police Department does have someone in custody, a Sanderson Davis, but they expect to release him later today.'

'Sanderson Davis? He's Caro's boyfriend. He owns a restaurant in Fayetteville; sometimes he drives down after work and spends the night. He's not your guy.'

'No, we don't think so either. Evidently Caroline had left

him several messages on his cell phone, but his restaurant, Cloud Nine Bistro, was slammed last night, and he didn't get off until late. He got to your daughter-in-law's house around midnight, about the time the local police were trying to get things sorted. Being the boyfriend put him in the spotlight, but it looks like he'll check out. He did mention a message Caroline left him about something upsetting happening that day, and that she needed to talk.'

'Yes,' I say.

'Mrs Miller, the Fort Smith PD found an envelope full of newspaper clippings that had evidently arrived in the mail,' Agent Jones looks at her watch, 'yesterday, actually. The clippings concern—'

'I know about them. They're about Caroline's trial, when she killed my son in self defense seven years ago. Seven years ago exactly as of yesterday, if you didn't know the date.'

'Yes.' She looks intelligent and speculative and not at all sympathetic. And I suddenly see what they've been thinking.

'I didn't have anything to do with it. With Caroline's disappearance? Is that what you think?'

Woods turns his hand to one side, as if asking me to be reasonable. 'She did kill your son. And there's a note with that package of newspaper clippings she got. Did you know there was a note?'

'Yes. Caroline read it to me. Something about retribution, I don't remember the exact words.' I frown trying to remember, then look up. 'And if you read the articles or check it out you'll see that I testified on her behalf at the trial. Ask the local prosecutor. He'll tell you that I'm the main reason she got off.'

Deputy Collins shifts on the couch. I realize that they are bracketing me, Collins on one side, Woods and Jones on the other.

Collins clears his throat. 'I've brought Agents Woods and Jones up to date on what happened to your son, Mrs Miller.'

'Of course you have.'

'Including what was pretty common knowledge at the time – that you had some sort of breakdown, after the trial, and that pretty soon after that you quit your cable television show, and retired from your job.'

'What has that got to do with anything?'

The deputy won't meet my eyes.

Agent Jones doesn't have that problem. 'Mrs Miller, did you have second thoughts after you testified at your daughter-in-law's trial?'

'No.'

'You're sure that's not the reason you broke down afterward? And that ever since you've lived almost as a recluse?'

'It would make sense. I mean, it would be understandable. For you to feel that way.' Deputy Collins seems apologetic too, but I'm wary of sympathetic law enforcement officers. Those are the ones who get confessions.

Agent Woods is giving Collins a hard look and I have the feeling that he's not supposed to speak. But what he said makes a certain sense. And was it that far from the truth? The truth is complicated. Fluid.

'I did the right thing,' I say. 'It wasn't an easy thing, taking her side, but it was the right thing. I never regretted it, and I don't harbor any resentment toward my daughter-in-law for what happened. But don't take my word for it. Check the phone records. I called Caroline from here about an hour before the nine-one-one call. It's a fourteen hour drive from Lexington to Fort Smith. Even if I hadn't called her, I couldn't have been there tonight and made it back by the time you guys arrived on my doorstep.'

'We know that, ma'am,' Woods says.

'So what, you think I hired it done?'

'It would make sense,' Woods says. 'Seven years to the day.'

'Maybe. Except Caroline wasn't the only one who got a package in the mail yesterday.'

They perk up like hound dogs.

'Let me show you what came in the mail for me.'

SIX

I know things the FBI does not. I know what the Dark Man wants – redemption, grace, atonement. He did not tell me this in so many words. No. More convincingly, he told me by what he did; specifically by what he did not. The verse of scripture on the back of Jimmy Mahan's picture is not as obscure as it seems. It's one of many well worn, ill-used passages – summoned, perversely, by Calvinists on the weary old subject of predetermination. As if God decided who would and would not be saved. As if free will is just another myth.

It lets me know that the Dark Man has not found what he looks for.

I am not impressed by the folklore that surrounds serial killers – the opinions of forensic wise men, the FBI experts at Quantico. By the posturing novels, movies, television shows. By the average guy on the street, infected by all the above. Their pronouncements strike me as the simplistic renderings of narrow minds.

The popular notion that sociopaths are a form of being with no conscience and no regret begs the issue, which is that these beings are suffering. I don't hold with the opinion that the labyrinth of sadistic, violent acts they commit are the enactment of fantasies, like a child making mud pies in a ditch during the rain. That they do it because they can. I believe that sociopaths would have you think this. I believe it to be bravado and a con.

I base my opinion on the men and women I have counseled over the years, some of them sociopaths themselves, some of them living with one, some of them in the ministry. Religion is honey to evil. Normally cautious people let their guard down for the clergy. And, of course, my convictions are based on my dealings with the Dark Man, who could have killed me, but did not.

The explanation that someone so twisted does not suffer

because they do not have a conscience makes no sense. It is the conscience that provides the conduit to the perversities of their pleasure. A feeding trough for their evil. If they didn't know they were bad, it wouldn't be any fun. More to the point, it would not serve the purpose – protection. The question, the true question, involves remorse. And so often it looks as if there isn't any. But I think the lack of remorse functions like armor, that it builds the walls of self defense. To feel remorse would destroy that defense and the being inside as well. Some sociopaths, like the Dark Man, suffer for the choices they make, but inside them is a knowledge that if they make other choices, better ones, they will collapse and disintegrate, like the Wicked Witch of the West in *The Wizard of Oz*, oozing into a puddle of misery when Dorothy douses her with water. 'I am melting,' the witch wails. To those on the outside, like Dorothy, mouth open in shock, it is a revelation that the evil is a prop that becomes surprisingly fragile under the right conditions. Sociopaths are vulnerable creatures, trapped in a maze of impulse and pain, and every perverse pleasure is a twist in the heart. Pity them if you can, but fear them always. They suffer. They'll make you suffer too.

Right now the FBI forms its new task force to find Caroline and Andee, and enmeshes itself in the infighting that will rise as the new task force competes with the old. One looking for the kidnapper of my daughter-in-law and her child. The other trying to solve the brutal murder of three evangelists who happen to be classmates of mine. The connection intrigues them. Worries them. I am under suspicion. I have hired an attorney, Smitty Madison, who defended Caroline when she was on trial. Who got her off.

There will be great minds working. Much energy and many tax dollars will be expended. The personally ambitious and the genuine heroes will sweat blood and shed internal tears. No doubt the experts in Quantico will be consulted, as well as their pet forensic psychologists, and they will all look into the sociopath crystal ball, and scour the habitat of the sociopath. And while they do all of that, and I wish them well, I will go where a tortured man seeking redemption might logically have gone, fourteen years ago, when he made the decision to alter his path. A goal in which he has spectacularly failed.

I am thirty-five miles from my home, literally at the gates of the Abbey of Gethsemani, home to Thomas Merton, the great monk. It is beautiful here. A place to start a new life, or reflect on the old one until it too becomes new. The grounds are lush, the unreal fodder of postcards to anyone who has not learned to take the countryside of central Kentucky for granted. Not an auto parts supplier in sight, although there is a Toyota plant around somewhere.

The Abbey of Gethsemani has been put on notice to expect me. There are certain professional courtesies extended even to those like myself.

I drive up the curling asphalt path, noting the aged trees, the complex juxtaposition of old limbs and new. This is a monastery that looks like a horse farm. The kind of monastery you find in Kentucky or the south of France.

A twelve foot black iron gate stands open, and GOD ALONE is inscribed in stone. I hesitate before the gate, freeing the heel of my right shoe, which has become wedged in a crack between the flagstones. It is ten until two and someone is supposed to meet me on the hour. I expect that monks are punctual. Baptists, frequently, are not.

Caroline and Andee float like a mental screensaver of worry in the back of my mind. I want to storm the gates.

I hear a faint sigh and turn to see a man in trousers, soft-soled shoes and a coarse brown monk's robe standing on the other side. I did not see him approach, did not hear the sound of his shoes on the stones. He smiles at me, waiting, for what I do not know, but he, unlike myself, has an air of patience and centered well being. He is from India, his complexion dark, his skin rugged, his eyes so brown they look black. He beckons and I follow.

The monk leads me up a set of stone stairs, and along a paved walkway that skirts the grass. The abbey has four stories. We pass through a sort of lobby. His footsteps are quiet. Mine set up embarrassing echoes. The abbey seems deserted.

He heads down a hallway through an open set of double doors and into a spacious room with book shelves and tables, clearly a library. From there we pass into a narrower, darker hallway, and I follow, looking once, then a second time back over my shoulder until the monk turns right and waves me into a sort of library annex. It is beautiful here, with stone floors and a bank of windows all along one wall.

'Welcome, dear friend, I am Father Panatel.' The Indian inflection transforms his English into music and the calm in his voice brings the surprise of tears to my eyes. I want to tell this man how alone I feel. How afraid I am for Caro and Andee. I want to confide in him. I want him to tell me what is right, and what is not.

'Forgive the silence, before, but we are permitted to speak in designated areas only.'

Father Panatel shakes my hand and guides me toward two heavy, throne-like chairs. He settles across from me; we are in an open area of the room, away from a massive and intricately carved wood desk that sits along one wall.

The priest waits for me to talk. Begins when I do not.

'I understand you are something of a colleague. I confess that I was doing the watching for you on television, plenty many years ago.'

Plenty many indeed. 'I'm hoping you were a fan.'

He smiles at me gently, and I see that shiny look in his eyes, familiar still, that tells me he was, indeed. I know I should hold the look, summon the charisma, but my attention wanders through the room. I feel an odd hunger for this place, the walls deeply inset with shelves that are crammed with books. Every surface is pristine, dust free, the stone floors recently washed down.

The priest, to my envy, seems vibrant with happiness. I had expected someone sour with an air of depression, I'm not sure why.

'May I show you something, dear lady?'

'Of course.'

He goes to his desk, opens a side drawer. He moves quietly, easily, he is more comfortable here than I am anywhere. The drawer is deep, and he has to pull it all the way out. He reaches to the very end and tugs at something. A large tome, and my heartbeat picks up. It could be anything, here in this abbey. He brings the book to me, and as he gets closer I see that the pages are heavy, like cardboard, and bound with string, and my mind races from one possibility to another – some Catholic relic, some ancient text – only to see, as he gets close, that it is a garden variety scrapbook, a decade old, maybe two.

He sits with the book in his lap, and I see that he has taken care with this book, I see the edges of newspaper and magazine clippings.

Father Panatel turns the pages carefully, his attention caught from time to time. He looks up. 'Please, I am sorry, I have not opened this book for some time. I started it years ago when I first began to feel my calling to the church.' He stands up to show me a page. A newspaper article from *The Times*, titled 'Thomas Merton and the Abbey of Gethsemani'. 'This is the article that first brought me here. I was studying in Oxford, you know. From Oxford to Kentucky, USA.'

I return his smile. An outrageous journey – India, Oxford, Kentucky.

'Here, dear lady, this is you. This you must have to remember.'

He passes the book across to my lap. I turn it around and smile, just a small one. I shake my head. I have not looked at this in years.

The tag-line on the front cover reads 'Divine Joy', and that's my picture, there, on the cover of *Time* magazine.

The cover shot was a surprise. The initial notion of a mention in a national magazine was flattering and terrifying, but when we set it up there was no mention that I was going to be cover material. I think it was the picture, spontaneous and unexpected. A tiny stab of meanness from my husband that backfired and landed me right in the spotlight.

I had been running late, as I always was in those days, and when the reporter and photographer arrived, my husband, Carl, had kept them in the foyer with that pompous little speech, the one he always made to the media – that they were not to put him in their article for any reason. He longed, always, for the protest. The family angle was important, he thought. *He* was important – the man behind the woman. But this time, they did not bite. They were not interested in him, and they agreed immediately.

It made Carl angry, the dismissal. So he'd taken them through unannounced, opened the door to my office without knocking, and said in a mix of pomp and sarcasm 'The great Joy Miller' before he disappeared down the hall. Which is why they caught the great Joy Miller scrambling to clean up her office.

I remember how my cheeks had gone hot when I saw them in the doorway, their faces registering the hostility from my husband. I shrugged, shook my head and grinned at them, standing with my back to the wall, my arms open wide. Carl or no Carl, I was excited about the interview, flattered, speculating about the good it might do. I used to think like that, when I was very young.

The photographer, alert like the best ones are, crouched right then and there and took a candid photo.

The picture astounds me. I hardly know this woman.

Joy Miller, back to the wall, wearing a black tweedy skirt and pink sweater, arms wide, that trademark smile that was so full of love and *joy*; the office mess around her, which included a baseball jersey and cleats that had clearly just been dropped by her son, a basket with an ancient, deaf basset hound named Bella curled up inside, dog toys and chewies littering the immediate area, open books on the desk, and a half eaten chocolate bar on the file cabinet.

I scan the article, wincing as I read.

> Head high, eyes crinkled in a smile, right arm raised in a fisted thumbs-up that is her signature, Joy Miller starts every sermon with the same words. 'According to the dictates of the church where I grew up, it was decided that a woman should not preach.'
>
> At this point there is a cheer, drowning out the next words which tell how Joy Miller has been called by God and no man will stop her. It seems that no man will. The Joy Miller Ministries brings in over three million dollars a year, and that figure is expected to

double in the next two. She takes a modest salary, and the rest of the money is deposited into a foundation account that is earmarked for the Joy Miller Ministries causes – a women's shelter, a 'home' for troubled teens, community food pantries, scholarships for deserving students, no-kill animal shelters and funding for training search and rescue dogs for law enforcement. Her staff is minimal, consisting mainly of her cousin Marsha who handles the bookkeeping, temporary workers who are hired as needed, and numerous church volunteers. The lion's share of the load rests on the shoulders of Joy Miller herself, and there is no question that this woman puts in a long day. In addition to her television ministry, she is inundated with speaking engagements and meetings with charities who would like to have a piece of the Ministries' pie, as well as the detail and grind of working with the foundation board. She reserves fifteen hours a week to counsel the members of her 'tele-congregation,' and yes, she's a member of the PTA.

If the women love her dearly, the men love her more. She is pretty, sweet and fresh as a Georgia peach. She is confident without being cocky, and she is no man-hater. The man who follows Joy Miller has the double pleasure of being thought open-minded, compassionate and appealing to women.

Joy Miller seems to appeal to everyone, except the hard liners. A married woman with one child – a stay-at-home mom until she heard the call. She understands marriage, parenting, stay-at-home-mothering, and working moms. She stands for the sanctity of marriage, of staying together no matter what, of taking that tough road and where it can lead.

Joy Miller thinks monogamy is exciting.

Time received a record number of letters about that picture, and with the exception of one man who clearly thought that Joy Miller was a disgustingly deficient housekeeper, most of the letters were cheers and jeers from the same old weary divide – how shocking, a woman who wants to preach. The article got it wrong, a lot of it. I never said monogamy was exciting. At least I don't remember saying that. And I had 'the calling' and went to seminary before I got married, before Joey was born. But the man who was upset by my untidy home – he had a valid point. I was way too busy to be a good housekeeper, in those days. As is often the case with women, the three million I pulled in annual donations paled beside the question of whether or not my toilets were properly scrubbed.

I look at Father Panatel, and see the look I know very well. I am a celebrity in his shiny eyes. He will answer my questions and keep my confidence, and he would do so, church or no church.

'Thank you, so much, for showing this to me. I'm incredibly flattered, to be in your book.'

He leans toward me. 'I just want you to know you are with a friend. For you to please, just be free to talk here, dear lady.'

There is a calmness about him that makes me ache, and I want to lean on this man. I will have to watch myself, not to tell him too much. My photographs – good reminders there – are in the hands of the FBI, but the memories are easy to conjure. They slide in and out of my mind.

I clear my throat, compose my thoughts. What to tell – what to hold back?

'First, let me thank you for meeting on such short notice.' I fall back on the southern courtesy do-si-do. 'As I said on the phone, I wanted to ask you about someone who I think was a visitor here, on a retreat, roughly fourteen years ago. Which I know is a long time. But the Dark Man is the kind of visitor you would remember.'

I give the date once again, a date that stays in the back of my mind. 'He would have come alone, without making previous arrangements. He would not fit in. He would not be overly concerned with your rules. He might smoke cigarettes in places he is not allowed to smoke. He has a way about him. A feeling. He is the kind of man you would hesitate to cross.'

Father Panatel shows me a furrowed brow. 'It is a strange thing to be asking, I think, if I can remember a man from fourteen years ago.'

I feel the hot flash that means my cheeks are going red. 'This man makes you afraid, Father. Being around him can make you afraid.'

Father Panatel leans back in his chair and frowns at me. 'When I got your call, dear lady, and you made so clear the urgency of this matter, I did go back over my notebooks. All through the years I keep a spiritual journal. So I am able to go back and see what I am writing then, in that particular period of time. As it happens, it was a significant period for me as well. And this feeling of discomfort and fear you speak of, this most definitely brings someone to mind. It makes me think I know the one. You are so correct when you say he makes the impression. If it is the same man, I remember him very well.'

Father Panatel rubs his chin, and the ripple of disturbance that invades the calm gives me hope. The Dark Man has been here. He would leave this wake of discomfort.

'I remember him, I'm thinking, and I remember the other, as well.'

'I don't understand, Father. What other man?'

'One of our postulates. A man named Jathan Sandbone, who has befriended this man you talk about, this Dark Soul Man. They left together, at the end of the retreat, on their way from here to Salt Lake City.'

'Why Salt Lake City?'

Father Panatel nods. 'Sandbone was taking him to our sister abbey. But after we have talked on the phone, I am trying to find Sandbone, and there is no luck. It would seem that neither of them arrived in Salt Lake City. And Sandbone was never seen again, from what I can tell due to checking. Of course, he could have dropped away. Some do. But I would not have thought it of him.'

I dig my fingernails into the palms of my hands. 'Do you have a name, Father, something in your records?'

'I can find nothing but what I have already in my memory. That Sandbone referred to him as Paul.'

'Paul? That's it?'

'I do not think this was his real name,' Father Panatel says. 'I believe it was to be a new name, and a new start.'

'Of course. Saul, the criminal. Paul from Damascus.'

'Yes.' Father Panatel laced his fingers together. 'Sandbone was a good man. How would you say it? That he was *true*? He had much of the life experience, and he was compassionate. This other man, Paul, as we called him, made many of the brothers uncomfortable. Every one was relieved when Sandbone tucked him under his wings.' Father Panatel looks at my face. 'This is the expression, yes, dear friend? Under his wings?'

'Close enough.'

The priest gives me a steady look, but there is a light in his eyes. I am thinking that he knows his slang is off kilter, and enjoys making fun of himself. 'And do you have dealings with him now, this Dark Soul Paul? It occurs to me, dear lady, that if Paul had no luck finding what he was looking for with us, he might go elsewhere in his search. And it worries me that Sandbone left with him, and did not return.'

This is my chance, I see it, I could tell this man everything. I am too close to this business, too weighed down in worry. He would be objective. He would be wise.

'Do you think that it is this Paul who may be responsible for Sandbone's disappearance?' he asks.

'Just that it would not surprise me, Father.'

'I remember how Sandbone was good to him.'

'Yes, Father. But with a man like this, who is searching for spiritual redemption, there is a risk in becoming his spiritual advisor. He might tell you things, and then regret the telling. He might have certain expectations. He might be disappointed when they were not met.'

Father Panatel nods, and in his eyes I can see understanding, and worry. Somewhere I hear the faint tread of footsteps. The sun streams in through the windows and lights the motes of dust in the air.

'There is something else you wished to say.' Panatel sounds sympathetic, but he watches me.

My throat feels sore. 'Everything that I tell you puts you at risk.'

'Nothing you say will go further than this room.'

'I would ask you to tell me your memories of this man, and, for your own sake, not ask me any questions.' I find I have tucked my hands beneath me.

Father Panatel has been in the business long enough to know there is quite a lot I wish to say, and he waits me out, a technique I have used myself.

'This man. This *Paul*. Before he came here, to your abbey, he came to me.'

'Ah. I wondered if that might not be so. There is more?'

'Much more,' I say. 'But nothing I can discuss without putting other people, not to mention you, in danger. I know how that sounds, how dramatic, but it's true and I would ask you to keep my confidence on this.'

He looks at me for such a long time. I am tired and worried and I wonder if I should say more, but I feel, strongly, that I may already have said too much.

He leans toward me. 'I would like there to be more for me to do than the telling of old stories, dear lady, for I think you are in need of some help.'

I scoot to the back of my chair, keeping my knees together and my ankles crossed. I hope I do not look as uncomfortable as I feel. My ears are tuned now, to the rhythm of his speech. I am ready for once upon a time.

'Fourteen years ago I was still just a student, you must understand. I was here on retreat as well. I was very interested in Thomas Merton, as I am a follower of this man. You are familiar with this Thomas Merton?'

'I am. I studied him in seminary.'

He nods. 'I was present for two weeks of retreat, and my time ended on the same Friday afternoon that it did for Mr Sandbone and Mr Paul. He has made quite the impression, Mr Paul, what you call the *sore thumb*. He did not seem to know the ways of religion, and he broke many rules, many rules.'

'For example?' I ask. Looking for anything.

'Please understand this, dear lady. A retreat is a place apart to entertain silence in the heart and listen for the voice of God. To pray for your own discovery. This man, Mr Paul, will speak without any thinking. He does not say much, but his time for speaking is very misjudged. He is lodged next to Mr Sandbone in the retreat house and each guest has a private room with a bathroom. The others here did not know what to make of Mr Paul, and it is clear that he had no notion of expectations. He was conscious of the self and felt the odd man out. Mr Sandbone took him in hand – is that the expression? Took him in hand?'

'Depends on what you mean by that,' I said.

'What I mean is that the good Mr Sandbone is the constant companion of Mr Paul, and if they are talking more than is expected late at night in their rooms, no one is complaining, because Mr Paul has them all feeling unsettled. But they are noticing, yes, Mr Paul and Mr Sandbone are very much noticed.'

'Did you overhear any of their conversations? Or did anyone else overhear them and make any kind of comment you recall?'

'My dear friend, I was listening for the voice of God, not the back and forth between two men who did not have the courtesy and respect to follow the rules. But there was one night when I was awakened by the voices and the smell of the cigarettes. The walls, you see, are very thin. I admit to you I was quite annoyed by it and thought to complain. I was disturbed by their noise and their disrespect.'

'What did you hear?' I say.

The priest lowered his head. 'It would seem that Mr Paul has led a life of great violence.'

'I see.'

'That is what I have heard. Sandbone himself is a veteran of war, and this creates between them a sort of empathy. But mostly it is Paul who is talking. He says that he has committed acts of actual murder. It was a thing most chilling for me to listen to, because he speaks with such a way that is matter of fact. Mr Paul said that most of the killings were for monetary gain. He spoke again and again of internal transformation, saying he wishes not to kill ever again, but is unclear how to make that stop. There seems to be a fear that if he changes into a man of good, he will die. He spoke over and over of the dangers of morality, as if it is some kind of curse. He is asking for God to show him the way. How to become another, but still be safe.'

Father Panatel looks out the window. 'You would think that I would feel pity for such a man. But I was young then, and quick to condemn. I felt Mr Paul was looking for something, but not looking, if that makes sense at all. I could not find it in my heart to feel sad for him, not at that time in my life.'

I nodded. I understood. Only too well.

'You should know that I did have conversation with Mr Sandbone on the afternoon of departing. Mr Paul had gone back to his room to look for a keychain he had bought from the gift shop, and their car is packed for leaving.'

'So there's no question, then, that they left together? You saw this?'

'I saw the preparations being made. I told Mr Sandbone farewell, and I am with my own bags packed, waiting. He asked me if I needed transportation anywhere, he knows I am a student. And I told him that such has been taken care of by the abbey. He asks me where I am to go, and I tell him that I am on my way to take a plane for India. I ask him what are his own plans, and he says he is on his way to the Shepherds Of The Land, which is a monastery begun in Utah by monks from this very abbey here. He has spent his six months there as a postulate, and is ready to begin his two years as a novice, after which he will take a temporary vow to bind him to the monastic life for three years. He says that Mr Paul is interested in becoming a postulate, and I can tell you, dear lady, that I must have looked surprised. Mr Sandbone, he puts a hand on my shoulder, and he calls me son. That is a thing in America, yes, for a man of some years to call a young man son. And he says to me something that I was always to remember. He says "Mr Paul has a past, my son, but also he has a future."'

Sandbone's words seem to generate a sort of presence, and we both sit quiet for a while.

'Sandbone was a brave man,' I say finally. 'But foolish. Men like this Dark Man. I'm not sure they *can* be saved.'

I can see it in Father Panatel's face, that in spite of the

optimism of certain passages of scripture, he has struggled with the very same thing 'Do you really believe that, dear lady?'

It's a good question. *The* question, as a matter of fact.

'Let's say it is my *fear*, Father Panatel, that they cannot.'

SEVEN

My cell phone rings on my way home from the seminary. I pull to the side of the road. I am distracted and it takes all of my concentration to drive.

'My name is Mrs Hunter, Melissa Hunter, and I'm with the Sebastian County Humane Society. I was told to call this number for a Joy Miller.'

'I'm Joy Miller. I'm sorry, who did you say you were?'

'Mrs Melissa Hunter. With the Sebastian County Humane Society.' She sounds like an older woman, and easily annoyed. 'We understand that you are the contact in regard to a golden retriever mix named Ruby—' I hear the rustle of papers, '. . . a dog belonging to a Caroline Miller?'

'I . . . yes. Is Ruby there with you?'

A pause. 'She's in our kennel.' There is disapproval in her voice, as if I have accused her of the impropriety of having the dog sit with her at her desk. 'This dog was brought in and left here by the police.'

'Right. Right, of course.'

'We'd like to know what you want done with the dog. Do you want her to go up for adoption, or do you want to pick her up?'

'Oh, no, I'll come and get her. I – do I need to come myself? Can I have someone pick her up for me?' I was thinking of Sanderson. Caroline's Fayetteville boyfriend.

'Umm . . . well, this is unusual, but I've got instructions here in the file that say that the dog can only be released to you. But really, if you want to fax me a signed authorization—'

'You have instructions? In the file? Who gave you the instructions?'

She makes a noise of exasperation. 'Let me look at this here. It says . . . evidently we had a phone call from someone in the family. They said it had been arranged for you to pick the dog up. They left your number and—'

'Yes. Yes, that's fine. I'll be there as soon as I can.'

'We close at five.'

Automatically I check the clock on the dash of my car. It is three thirty and it will take me fourteen hours to drive to Fort Smith if I make the usual stops.

'I'll can't be there until tomorrow. But I'll get there as soon as I can. Is she OK? Ruby?'

The woman's voice changes. 'Actually, I checked on her myself this morning when I was reviewing her arrangements. I understand that she has not been eating. When I saw her she was curled up at the back of her cage, and she did not look well. She's quite elderly, isn't she? I'm wondering if she has arthritis meds or something she might be needing.'

I have a flash of memory, of watching Caro give Ruby her pills. 'I think she does, come to think of it. I'll stop at my daughter-in-law's house and pick them up. And I'll be there as soon as I can.'

'Excellent. Ruby will be waiting. And if something comes up, and you won't be able to get here, you'll be sure to let me know?'

'Of course. But I'll be there.'

I flip the phone closed. A car with oversized speakers blows past, and the pulse of music makes me jump.

A phone call from someone in the family? Instructions for me to pick the dog up? Caro's dog. Andee's dog.

The FBI will be watching my mail. They are probably monitoring my phone. The Dark Man is getting in touch.

I stop by the house to pack a bag and make arrangements for Leo. Marsha's car is in the driveway and she has parked up near the front door, blocking the garage. I don't want to tell her where I am going. It is impossible for her to keep a secret.

I walk into the house, and she meets me at the door.

'There you are. I've been looking all over for you.'

She has had her hair done. It has been shellacked to her head, and she is wearing a forest green silk blouse, and khakis. One hand is balled in a fist at her throat.

'Here I am. Why are *you* here?'

'I work here, remember? I had a hair appointment, I mentioned it yesterday. You *told* me to stay late. But listen, Joy. The FBI has been to my house. They told me about Caroline and Andee. They – Joy, do you realize they think you might have had something to do with that? I tried to tell them how ridiculous it was.'

'Thank you for that.'

'But what's going on?'

'It's complicated. All I know is that Caro and Andee are missing, and they have to check everybody out.'

'Has there been a ransom note?'

I hesitate. 'No, not yet.'

'Those agents – and by the way, that Mavis Jones agent girl is such a bitch. But they said you got some pictures in the mail. They showed me the envelope and asked me if I'd seen them. I told them it was part of my job to get the mail, and that I'd brought the envelope in myself. I remembered it. Giving it to you. And then they wouldn't tell me what it was all about. Joy, what was it?'

'Pictures, Marsha. You don't want to know.'

Her mouth opens wide. 'Pornography?'

'Of crimes.'

'What kind of crimes?'

'Murders. Executions.'

'*Joy.*'

'There were three of them, three people. Pictures of them shot in the throat. All of them evangelists I went to seminary with.'

'Did you say—' Marsha puts her hand out as if to break her fall. Her face has gone chalk white.

I take her elbow and lead her to the couch. Caroline and Andee have been kidnapped, and it is somehow tied into the execution of three evangelists that I used to know, and I am suspected of being involved. Collapsing in the foyer is a personal best for Marsha – in circumstances such as these how else will she be in the center? She will offer to help, then come unglued, that will be the pattern. Whether or not she will actually be of any help will be a matter of chance and caprice.

But she is quite capable of crashing to the floor, and much too heavy for me to lift. I need to shut this down. I guide her to the couch and when she resists I admit I am a little bit rough, but I'm in a hurry. The Dark Man has instructions for me in Arkansas. I need to pick up Caro's dog.

As soon as I get her settled, Marsha doubles over and there is a film of sweat on her upper lip. 'You said "shot in the throat". You're sure? The FBI, they told you that?'

'They didn't have to. I saw it in the pictures.'

She lifts her head. The pupils of her eyes have gone huge, black holes that crowd the blue irises into the thinnest of circles.

'Joy. Oh, Joy. I am sorry. I am *sorry*.'

I don't want to feel sorry for Marsha, but I can't help it.

She grabs my arm with both hands, and her fingernails dig into my forearm. 'I can't believe this is happening, I just can't believe it—'

Her voice is going up octaves, an opera of distress, and she starts breathing faster and faster.

'*Marsha.*' I peel her hands off my arm, see that her nails have left red and purple dents and in two or three places drawn tiny dots of blood. Marsha and her damn claw manicures. I wrap my pink fuzzy throw around her shoulders. 'Deep breaths,' I tell her. 'I'll be right back.'

I smell fresh coffee from the kitchen, which makes one less thing I'll have to do, and I glance back over my shoulder. Marsha's head touches the tops of her knees, and she has wrapped her arms around herself and is crying softly. Almost, I go to her. Almost, I put my arms around her with real affection.

And then with a flash of memory comes a sliver of resentment. This is the same Marsha who took me to the ER with a red hot appendix four years ago. The same Marsha who held up my admittance because she wanted to look at the list of

ER doctors on duty before she would let them take me away, the same Marsha who sobbed like a baby when I snapped her head off and told her to let it be. The same Marsha, soothed by emergency room nurses and admitting clerks who ran to get her hot coffee and a comfortable place to sit while I writhed in agony. And somehow, as only Marsha can, my cousin had turned my emergency into a personal soap opera, starring none other than poor little Marsha herself, doing her best for her cousin, who rewards her with brutal unkindness and hurts the tender feelings of her heart.

Right. Coffee. A glass of water. And I'll be on my way.

But the phone rings while I'm pouring the coffee, and I wipe my hands on a dishtowel and head for the office extension. Marsha, miraculously on her feet, moves like a racehorse at the starting bell, and she's picked it up before I've taken more than three steps.

It is a relief to hear how calm her voice is. She's OK now. One cup of coffee and I'll go.

I hear her mutter something, and the clack of her shoes in the hall.

'Joy?' she says, appearing around the doorframe.

I am already shaking my head and mouthing *no*.

'It was the FBI. They need to talk to you. They want you to go in to their office right now and answer questions. They want you *immediately* – they said it's urgent.'

I blow air out of my cheeks, not sure what to do. 'Are they still on the phone? Are they waiting?'

She shakes her head. 'I stalled. I told them you weren't expected until tonight, and that I'd already tried to get you a little earlier, but that you weren't answering your cell. I set it up for you to go in first thing in the morning, but they made me promise to try to get you in their office today, if you happened to call and check in.'

I frown at her, not understanding, and she puts a hand on my arm.

'Joy, the things they were saying when they talked to me. Earlier, when they came to my house. They asked me for a sample of your handwriting.'

'Did you give it to them?'

'Well, sure. Because they said it was to rule you out. But now that I think about it, it worries me. You need to get a lawyer before you talk to them. Don't go down to that office alone.'

EIGHT

My trip to Arkansas is on hold till I talk to the FBI.
The conference room is too hot. The carpet is thin and grey, and I sit behind a large, rectangular, faux wood-grain metal table. There is no window in the room. There are scuff marks on the off-white walls.

I know better than to talk to anyone in law enforcement without an attorney. The reality of my experience in religious counseling is no different from most other professions, in that my university course work could fall under the double heading of *inadequate* and *bad joke* compared to the real life details of the job. I often felt inadequate; I often was. But if nothing else, I was well versed in the axiom that good things happen to bad people, bad things happen to good people, and innocence is no defense against being proven guilty in a court of law.

One cannot underestimate the importance of a confident attorney with a strong presence, and Smitty Madison is exactly that. He grated on my nerves the first two times that I met him, but his ability to annoy people is just one of many traits that I have learned to treasure.

He sighs, checks his watch and winks at me. Standard operating procedure, his look seems to say, and he pats my hand, which is trembling. We have done our prep work. Preparation is one of Smitty's strengths and, obvious as it seems, the majority of attorneys I know tend to wing it. It is the one quality that makes the difference between mediocre and excellent representation.

We don't talk. Smitty has warned me in advance to stay quiet in the interrogation room, having learned, in the past, that there might be people listening in, even making recordings. We have discussed the adversarial attitude of the FBI, but Smitty seems to feel it is standard procedure, and assures me that Caroline's boyfriend in Arkansas is likely getting it worse. My reputation, such as it is, means they will handle me carefully. My ministry funnels significant money to several local causes, including the funding of search and rescue dogs for the Kentucky State Police K-9 Unit. So I am surprised when Smitty leans close and speaks to me in a low tone.

'I don't like them keeping us waiting like this. It's not how you treat family. They're probably annoyed you brought a lawyer.'

I used to value Smitty's honesty but just now I wish he'd shut the hell up.

I haven't told Smitty everything. I've withheld from him as well as the FBI. I tell myself to stay the course, but part of me wants to turn everything over to the professionals.

If I give the Dark Man everything he wants, will he return Caroline and Andee? It is foolish to trust a sociopath. And yet . . . I am the one person still alive who knows that his yearning for redemption is genuine.

The door opens and the noise startles me, even though I have been expecting it this last twenty minutes. Smitty pats my hand again. I understand for the first time the psychological advantage law enforcement holds, and why the innocent confess.

Agent Russell Woods surreptitiously checks his fly as he comes through the door. He slaps a thick file down on the table, and I jump. The clack of women's shoes echoes in the hallway, and Agent Mavis Jones scoots in through the partially open door.

Mavis Jones is an unexpected vision. Slender in a deep plum pencil skirt that reaches two inches below her knees, proper in a black silk Oxford-styled blouse. She has very good hair – brunette with auburn highlights, brushed back from her wide forehead, cut to hang thickly and just graze her shoulders. Her face is perfectly symmetrical and her skin positively glows. How is this possible in the FBI?

I remember what Smitty told me – all the gossipy details,

divulged to make the agents seem vulnerable and human and me feel strong. Mavis Jones has a slow metabolism and restricts herself to eleven hundred calories a day, except when her work frustrates her – then she gets up in the night and eats bread. If she eats more than three pieces, she is careful to throw it all up. And I already know Russell Woods obsessively checks his fly. I have no confidence in this man and woman, who arrived on my doorstep with bad news and accusations the night my girls were taken away.

Woods and Jones sit across from us, and exchange little nods with Smitty. He gives them a curt good morning. Smitty has told me that in spite of the rumors he does not think Woods and Jones are having sex. They are competitive with each other, very different people with similar, high ambitions, and they keep each other's secrets in an uneasy balance of truce and struggle. If the balance of power shifts, there will be no loyalty, and as partners they are an edgy match. There are rumors that Jones consults tarot cards for every case, but Smitty says the story came from an unreliable source.

Mavis Jones realizes she's left the door open, and shuts it softly while Woods switches on the recorder and officially reads me my rights. Woods pauses and looks over at Smitty, who does not disappoint.

'I'd like it noted on the record that my client, Joy Miller, is here voluntarily, and is anxious to do whatever she can to aid this investigation. That she is extremely worried and suffering from anxiety about the safety of her granddaughter and daughter-in-law, Andee and Caroline Miller. And that she would appreciate every consideration as a concerned member of the family.'

I listen to this and I like it, and I wonder why it is that people hate lawyers. There is nothing better when you need a hired gun.

'So noted,' Woods says.

They are dancing – Woods, Jones, my own attorney, Smitty – following rhythms and doing the steps they have all done before. They know each other. They work together. To them this is a job. To me it is my life.

Woods begins with routine questions – my address, my

whereabouts on the day that Caro and Andee disappeared. Do I know of any threatening phone calls, any enemies, anything out of the ordinary, before the package of articles arrived? Do I have enemies, stalkers from my days on television, who might be involved?

But I have been out of the public eye for many years. I have little or nothing for them. Nothing to satisfy that edge in their voice. Smitty frowns at his watch.

Woods smiles like a predator. 'Mrs Miller, tell me about your relationship with your daughter-in-law, Caroline Miller. Would you describe it as cordial?'

'Yes.'

'Close?'

I hesitate. 'Yes.'

'How often do you talk to Caroline?'

'Once in a while.'

'Every day?'

'No.'

'Every week?'

'No.'

'She answered the question, Agent Woods,' Smitty says. 'They were close. They were cordial. Sometimes they talked on the phone.'

'Did you talk to her once a month?' Woods asks.

'Maybe.' This is making me uncomfortable.

'Maybe?'

'Every two or three months.'

'Every two or three months. And this is a relationship you describe as close?'

Woods makes me nervous. He has the by-the-book ferocity you find in the IRS, and the arrogance that comes with working for the government. A man like Woods has rules instead of ethics, and he will send you to jail, innocent or guilty, so long as the paperwork pans out.

I lift my chin. 'Yes, that's right.'

Woods stares at me and earns an intense glare from Smitty. Woods shrugs. 'Have you ever visited your granddaughter at her home in Arkansas?'

'No.'

'And they've lived there how long?'

I look at the ceiling, doing the numbers in my head. 'Andee was about two and a half when they left, so roughly five years.'

'So in five years you've never gone to Arkansas to visit?'

'We've made plans a few times. It never quite worked out.'

'How many times?'

'Maybe . . . I think three. Three times.'

'Why didn't it work out?'

I shrug. 'Things came up. Her job. Sometimes mine.'

'It doesn't sound like either of you were trying too hard.'

I bite the tip of my tongue. If it isn't an actual question, and it has nothing to do with the kidnapping, Smitty told me not to reply.

'Mrs Miller, a young woman and her daughter, *your granddaughter*, are missing. They were taken from their home, from their beds, by a man who did not hesitate to shoot and kill their neighbor just because he got a glimpse of him from the back kitchen door.'

Agent Jones pulls a notepad close and starts writing something. I wonder what it is. I wonder if I am supposed to wonder.

Woods opens the file and takes out a stack of pictures. He lays two of them down, rotating them in my direction.

One is a photograph I have at home on my dresser – Andee's school photo from last year. She is wearing a black jumper and a purple and white striped shirt, and I smile because it's an outfit we bought together on a shopping trip. We had lunch afterwards, at McDonald's. We got cheeseburgers for Ruby, her dog. There was one of those traveling amusement parks in the mall parking lot that day, and we rode the Carousel and the Spider, which made us both sick.

The next shot is a wedding picture. Joey and Caroline – young, happy, blissfully unaware. I have packed those pictures away, the portrait that hung in the upstairs hallway, the eight-by-ten that used to be displayed in the living room, the three-by-five on my desk. Whatever you say about my son, he is breathtakingly handsome in a tux.

I think how innocent they all look in their pictures. How anything could happen to them, and often does.

'Why are you crying, Mrs Miller?'

I use a knuckle to wipe a tear from my cheek. When I go home today, I'm going to take those pictures out of the box in the attic and put them back up again.

Woods puts two more pictures on the table, snapping the edges and pushing them close. The first shows a man on his back and a dark stain that runs like syrup from beneath his body to the edge of a refrigerator. The toe of the man's right foot points south, resting a few inches from a storm door. The bottom glass is fractured where the bullet went through.

The second picture is a close-up, skillful or lucky. You can see the destruction of the man's left eye, now a dark, blood-crusted hole.

'Do you recognize this man, Mrs Miller?'

'No.'

'This is Burton Stafford. Shot two times through the head. Once from a distance, once close range. He was in the kitchen, making a sandwich.' Woods reminds me of Jimmy Mahan, snorting fire and brimstone from the pulpit. He stabs the close-up with his finger. 'Mrs Stafford was in bed at the end of the hallway when this happened, Mrs Miller. Just a few feet away. She *heard* the shots. She *heard* her husband cry out. She *heard* him fall. She *knew* there was an intruder in Caroline's house, because her husband told her about it while he called the police.

'Think about that. Mary Stafford spends *her* days in a wheelchair. She can't get out of bed by herself. So she has to lie there. Afraid. Not knowing if her husband is dead or alive. She can't go to help him. She doesn't know if the killer is in the house, if he's coming for her too. And she can't run away. All she can do is hide under the blankets, and wait.'

Woods is good. He looks at me with such intensity that I feel guilty, as if all of this is my fault. I want to be forgiven. I want to make it stop. If he offered me absolution and understanding I would say whatever he wanted to hear.

Woods leans across the table, maintaining eye contact. 'Anything you know. You have to help us. This man is dangerous. The longer Caroline and Andee are gone, the less our chances are of finding them alive.' He taps Andee's picture with a fingertip and it's all I can do not to snatch the picture away. '*Help us.* I know you know something.'

'I've told you everything I can think of that might help.' Does he know that I'm lying? Is that why he is so intense?

Smitty scoots to the edge of his chair. 'Agent Woods. Please either sit back down or move to the other side of the room, but stop leaning over my client.'

Woods rears back like he has been slapped. He begins again, taking me through everything – my conversation with Caroline. The death of my son. The pictures of Burton Stafford. Then he moves to the three dead evangelists. Did I know them?

Yes.

Had any recent contact with them?

No.

Question after question, like playing scales on the piano, up and down the keyboard. Woods and Jones listen carefully, waiting to hear a wrong note.

Smitty purses his lips, checks his watch yet again, and holds a hand up. 'Let's wrap this up. Mrs Miller has answered all of your questions and told you everything she can to help. I am now calling an end to this interview, at—'

'One more thing.' Agent Jones has not said a word until now, just scribbled on her notepad, listening hard, watching my every twitch. It all seems to have significance – when I cross my legs, when I close my eyes. She knows I am picking at the sleeve of my jacket before I do.

'*What?*' Smitty says.

'I'm trying to understand.'

Of the two, I think Jones has the conscience. She will be dangerous if she thinks you are guilty, and her opinion will depend upon her instinct and maybe the cut of the cards. She will be impervious to the influence of co-workers. She thought I was guilty the night she came to my door, but she has doubts now, big ones. I wonder what the cards have shown her. It does not bother me that she uses them – in fact, I find it encouraging. It is an indication that she worries about the life and death decisions that permeate her world.

'Look at it from our viewpoint.' From her voice and the look in her eyes, the way she curves her body toward mine,

I believe she really is trying to understand.. 'Your son is murdered by your daughter-in-law – your only child, who, from all reports, you were devoted to. And yet you take Caroline's side during her trial? Now maybe it's the right thing to do, and maybe it's not. But still. He's your son, and he's dead, and she shot him.'

I've heard all this before. I have no regrets. Not after watching Caroline, pregnant and swollen with child and tears, put her head on her mother's shoulder and sob out her grief. Not after sitting beside Caro every day, during the recesses of the trial, lending presence and support. I sat to her left, her mother to her right, and she clutched both our hands.

Outsiders never get it. They don't want to hear any of the *good* things about Joey. They don't understand how Caroline could have shot him dead in self defense, and mourned his loss the next day. But I understood. Her mother did as well. I remember the things she told Caroline because there were times when I felt she was talking to me. *A boy who learns from the kind of father Joey had grows up with certain consequences, but they do not absolve him from responsibility for what he does. You will always miss the good parts of Joey and, even more, you'll grieve for the man he could have been.*

'Mrs Miller? I asked you a question.'

'Maybe you could ask it again.'

'I was talking about your daughter-in-law's trial. About afterwards, when you had your breakdown. When you were hospitalized.'

'I was *not* hospitalized.'

'Are you saying you did not suffer some kind of breakdown?'

'Not at all. I suffered the kind of breakdown that tears you into a million little pieces. The kind of breakdown that happens when your child dies.'

Agent Jones looks ready to offer me sympathy and tea. 'Maybe. Or maybe it was the kind of breakdown that happens when you spend months helping the woman who killed your son.'

'Where are you going with this?' Smitty says.

Jones shakes her head at him. 'Don't play dumb. I think

your client is a severely conflicted woman. And I think this kind of conflict is a kind of pattern in her life.'

'What on earth are you getting at?' I say.

Smitty gives me a warning look.

Mavis Jones leans back in her chair. There is something like a smirk on her lips. 'Tell me about your cousin, Marsha Dewberry.'

I'm aware that Smitty is tensing up beside me and I have the peculiar feeling that everyone in this room knows something I don't. But I cannot imagine that even the FBI cares about the private and petty irritations between my cousin Marsha and me. Do they really want to know that my mother made me hang out with her year after year because Marsha never had many friends?

Mavis Jones flips through the file, finding what she wants suspiciously fast. 'This is from Caroline's diary.' She clears her throat.

'"Thursday, nine p.m. Never in my life could I have imagined how lonely marriage can be. I know Joey loves me. I used to think that if two people cared for each other they could work things out. Now all I know is that he and I are fighting every single day and nothing I do seems to help. Getting him just to listen or talk to me is impossible. He's always tired. He comes home, eats dinner and watches television until he falls asleep. Those are the good days. The other ones he's spoiling for a fight. I try to understand in terms of Joey's childhood. Joey never gets worked up over the stuff his dad did to him, but he obsesses over the way his father treated his mother. Then he turns around and does the same thing to me. I know Joey feels guilty about his dad's affair with that cousin, Marsha, who has always worked for his mom. They were actually doing it on the living room couch one afternoon when he came home from school. His dad made him swear not to tell his mother, but I think she already knew. I think his mom was going to divorce him, and that's why his father killed himself. Some kind of twisted—"'

'That's enough.' Smitty does not even raise his voice. There are tears dripping down my cheeks and I realize I am on my feet. I think I was going to run out of the room, but Smitty takes my arm. My mind is like a Rolodex of memories as things begin to fall into place.

'You people are out of your minds.' Smitty stacks his papers. Clearly, we are done, and leaving with dignity. 'None of this has any bearing on Caroline and Andee Miller's kidnapping. If this kind of unprofessional nonsense is any indication of how you're running this investigation, I have serious concerns over your ability to find my client's granddaughter. I will be making a formal request to have both of you taken off this case. You can expect the paperwork in twenty-four hours.'

'You can leave if you want,' Mavis Jones says, 'but it doesn't change the facts. Your client is betrayed – first by her cousin and her husband. Then by Caroline.' She looks over at me. 'You stand beside her after she murders your son, and it breaks you. You stop the cable show, you live like a hermit. And she doesn't exactly include you in her life, does she, this daughter-in-law you stood up for in court? Not a lot of gratitude there, that I can see. So you crack. You've had enough.'

Smitty's voice is cold and hard. 'If you're making an accusation—'

'How do you explain the newspaper articles about the trial arriving in Caroline's mail on the anniversary of Joey Miller's death? How do you explain the Lexington postmarks? How do you explain Caroline and Andee's disappearance that very same night?'

'What about the pictures my *client* got in the mail? What about the three dead evangelists? You going to tell me that's not connected, or are you telling me she killed them too? Because you know damn well she didn't. You know because you don't have a motive, or a shred of physical evidence. You've got a missing child and her mother, and another evangelist—' now *Smitty* is pointing at me '—in peril. Oh, and two incompetent investigators.'

'It's not too late,' Mavis Jones tells me, and she is so calm that you would think Smitty and Woods weren't glaring at each other over the conference table, close enough to mingle sweat. 'You can stop this whole thing. Tell us who you hired to do it. Stafford is dead, but stop this now. Help us bring Andee home safe, and we can work something out. I promise.'

My knees are like jelly. 'Who have you people been talking to? Who says these kinds of things about me?'

Mavis Jones opens her mouth, but I never do find out what it is she is going to say.

'This interview is at an end.' Smitty pulls me away, and I follow like a lost child. Like any good attorney, Smitty knows to shut things down when they really get interesting.

NINE

S mitty and I are silent as we ride the elevator down from the offices of the FBI – he is tense and unhappy, and I am almost too shaky to walk. He keeps a hand on my elbow, and leads me to my car. Physically, he is not the sort of man to turn a woman's head. Roundish of figure, heavy eyebrows, brown hair, straight and very short. His eyes are a sort of muddy brown. But Smitty Madison has presence, intellect, and a can-do attitude. Born, raised and educated in Chicago, he has honed his edgy intolerance of southern mannerisms and cultural courtesies to a vague, impatient stoicism, though I've heard him refer to dealings with local lawyers as a 'pokey party'. Abrasive though he might be, he is protective and attentive to women, and during the single years between his first and second marriage he was hotly pursued.

It rained while we were in the building; the pavement is dark in patches, and it's cloudy out, and cool. Smitty looks at his watch like he wants to kill it and walks with fast, jerky steps.

'Look, I'd like to talk about all of this, but I need to be in court at one, and I'm barely going to make it as it is.'

I grit my teeth. I understand that Smitty is busy and on the run, but it does seem to be a habit of attorneys to disappear when things get sticky. I point to my Jeep which is parallel parked on Main Street. 'This is me. Look, I know you're in a hurry, but I want a quick run down on what you think went on in here.'

Smitty nods, and I wait for him to tell me that all is well, in spite of the intensity of the interview, and that I have nothing to worry about. He hesitates, rubs the bridge of his nose.

'Looked like an ambush to me.'

I brace my legs and rest a hand on the hood of my aging Jeep Cherokee, which I immediately regret because the cold metal is wet and gritty with dirt.

'Joy, do you remember in our phone conversation yesterday, when we talked about trial defense and finances and levels one, two and three?'

I nod at him. There's a weird buzz in the back of my head.

'You need to know that you're at level two.'

I bite my tongue and frown very hard. I need to pay close attention and I really don't want to cry. My voice goes all husky and deep.

'You really think it's that bad?'

Level two means a thirty thousand dollar retainer. It means Smitty will do everything he can to prevent my indictment, and if that is not possible, he will orchestrate my arrest and try for bail. Any left over monies will constitute a down payment on the one to three hundred thousand I will need for him actually to represent me at trial.

I don't have that kind of money. It would take my house and all of my retirement and even then it would be a close-run thing. But Smitty had covered that as well. 'If something unforeseen develops,' he had told me, 'it's going to come down to some kind of nutcase with a religious obsession. It will have roots in your ministry, like an occupational hazard. So you will go to the board of your ministries and get them to foot the bill. And they will. It's the Joy Miller Ministries. And you're Joy Miller. Everything stands on your reputation.'

Smitty puts a hand on my shoulder. 'Joy, listen to me. Caroline and Andee are mysteriously kidnapped on the anniversary of Joey's death. Three evangelists you were in seminary with have been executed. There is one common denominator in all of this, and that common denominator is you.'

'But—'

'Just listen. You had, in your possession, pictures of the executions of the evangelists. Pictures that had to have come from the killer. Both the package of pictures you received in the mail and the package sent to Caroline have Lexington postmarks.'

'But I have an alibi. There's no way I could possibly have—'

'They're going on the premise that you paid to have it done.'

I take a step backward. 'Like I hired a hit man? That's ridiculous.'

'That's right, it is, but that's where they're heading. I need to find out if they've got anything else.'

'But how bad is this, Smitty? Are they going to put me under arrest?'

Smitty takes some time to think the question over. He squints his eyes tight, which means his mind is in high gear. 'You're not without influence, Joy. You're a well known religious leader, your ministry is known for its good works and contributions to the community. And hit men don't just fall out of trees. They're going to have to connect you up with the actual killer, or they're not going to have a case. You don't know any professional killers, do you, Joy?'

'No,' I shake my head. 'Of course not.'

Smitty is thinking out loud. 'If I were them, I'd be looking at people you counseled, people in your congregation. Crazies drawn in by your show. I'm surprised they didn't ask for a handwriting sample, but they will. Look, let's be prepared for three things. Turning over the records of your counseling clients—'

'I can't do that. Those files are confidential.'

'. . . a sample of your handwriting.'

'They got one already. From Marsha.'

He stares. 'Why didn't you tell me?'

'I forgot.'

His expression tells me that this sort of thing has happened with clients before, and he still doesn't understand it. But he recovers quickly and moves on.

'I want you to agree to a lie detector test.'

'*No.*'

He puts a hand on my shoulder, and his voice is soothing.

'We got somebody who can coach you through it, Joy. We'll use our people, not theirs.'

'I don't trust those things. I'll be nervous and that will screw it up.'

He hesitates, gives me a second look. I recognize the lawyer-sidestep, that little dance an attorney does when he thinks the client may be guilty of something. The legal profession is almost as judgmental as mine.

'How about we discuss this when we have more time? I've got to be in court.'

'Fine.'

Smitty gives me a second look. He hears the edge in my voice, and he's been in Kentucky long enough to know that when a southern woman says *fine* it's code for *fuck you*.

He takes two steps backward. Gives me a little wave. 'I'll give you a call.'

I know I've given him something to think about. I didn't mean to.

TEN

Traffic is heavy for a Wednesday, which means that as I sit daydreaming and the traffic light turns from red to green, I am pummeled with a cacophony of horns. The people behind me have places to be. I'm content right where I am. I don't want to go home.

True tragedy can be measured by the scars of those of us who are left behind – the sleepless nights, the loneliness, the memories, good and bad. I used to think I had caught things in time. That Carl's death, however tragic, had freed my son and me from the darkness that my husband always brought in his wake. And I think we came close, Joey and I. I was not blind to the uneasy ripples – all those years with Carl had affected us both. It wasn't until afterward, and the things that happened with Caroline, that I understood my mistake – that standing between your child and a bad parent is never enough. That the damage had already been done.

I have always believed that Joey would have turned the corner – if things had happened differently, if the entire ugly mess could have functioned as a wake up call and a chance to heal. If he had not come home from work early that particular night, if he'd survived the gunshot wound, if I'd had the brains to boot Carl out of our lives from the very first moment I saw how dark he was, and felt that first flood of despair.

Those days have stayed distant, and in time a wall of fog slowly settled in my mind, acting as a barrier, dividing the bad times from the now.

But fog is nothing more than mist. It drifts. And images come to me as if someone is flipping a Rolodex of days gone by, with a live-wire clarity that *puts* me there, and every detail is revealed.

It is the old police file that worries me.

I can see the kitchen clock in the back of my mind, the face reading three a.m. I was wrapped in a worn pink terry-cloth bathrobe, drinking coffee and thinking. I had to have a story. I needed a story before anything else. Lying to the police would be like public speaking. Know your subject matter, but don't over-rehearse, and stick as close to the truth as you can.

Even though I was expecting it, the ring of the doorbell sent a feeling like electrical fizz jingling along the small of my back.

There were two police officers on the front stoop, both male, burly in their black leather jackets, an intimidating amount of equipment on their belts. The one who spoke first was older, early forties, trim. His shoulders were straight, his posture correct. He had grey hair cropped very close.

'Is this the Miller residence? Could we come in, please, ma'am?'

'Of course,' I said. I sounded worried. Who wouldn't? I waved them into the living room.

The older officer, Calhoun was his name, opens a notebook. 'When was the last time you saw your husband, Mrs Miller?'

I take a minute to get control of my voice, which wants to

go high and tight. 'I would appreciate it very much, officer, if you would say whatever it is you have come to say.'

'Ma'am, your Jeep Cherokee was found in the parking lot at the lodge at Natural Bridge State Park. A man's body was found on the rocks beneath the bridge. We think this man is your husband, Carl Miller, and we think he may have jumped to his death.'

I open my mouth, close it. Take a step backward. 'There must be some mistake. This doesn't make any sense.'

Calhoun looks like he's in pain. 'He was seen by one of the housekeepers heading up the trail alone around dusk. She states that he was alone. And there was no sign of a struggle. We believe your husband made a point of waiting until it was almost dark, so he could be sure there would be no one else up on the bridge. He was not registered as a guest of the lodge. We think it's likely that your husband chose to end his life.'

'We'll need someone to identify the body,' the younger officer says. 'You may want to have a friend or another relative take care of that, or come with you at least. The remains are not in good shape.'

Unexpectedly, I scream. I'm not sure which of the three of us is more surprised. The tears come easily after all. I never needed to worry.

A female officer is immediately called in for backup, proving that even the bravest men fear emotional women. They also call my friend Barbara James. I will learn that Calhoun questioned Barbara in great detail. That she confirmed that my son Joey had been at her house the last two nights. She told them I had been terribly distraught the night I dropped Joey off. She gave the opinion that our marriage was in trouble, and that I was planning to divorce my husband. She felt that the impending divorce would have affected Carl's state of mind greatly.

Barbara James was with me when I went to identify the body. She held my hand and waited beside me in the hall. We stood in front of the viewing window, just outside the refrigerated unit where what was left of my husband Carl lay motionless on a metal gurney. A woman in green hospital fatigues waited for my nod before she unzipped the heavy plastic baggie that was used to transport the body from the mountain to the morgue.

It is here, at this moment, that the first weight settles over me. It is the first time Carl's death actually seems real. His head is smashed like a rotten pumpkin from his long and terrible fall. The coroner's report will note massive internal injuries, a broken pelvis and shattered left femur. He will rule the death a suicide and the jointly owned life insurance policy, no more than six months old, will not pay a death claim on a suicide because the requisite two years have not passed.

But the suicide ruling suits me. I did not want to profit from Carl's death.

'That is Carl,' I tell them, and Barbara pulls me away. She leads me to the car and helps me when I fumble awkwardly with the seatbelt, telling me that Carl undoubtedly died upon impact and swearing that he did not suffer, lying through the night with his head smashed, his bones broken, bleeding from the inside out. She is kind. The possibility that Carl suffered should affect me, but does not.

I stare out the window at the familiar landscape of my town, and fumble for the sunglasses in my purse. I know that things will get better. My son and I will not only survive, we'll be better than we've ever been. And though I will never escape this curious heaviness that sits like a ring of dread around my heart, the shock will fade, like it always does, and Joey and I will feel normal again. I will find contentment in my work, in being a mother to my son. If I've lost a treasured part of myself, I accept it as a pretty fair trade. In every tragedy, one gains experience and completes a predestined lesson. I've certainly learned what my priorities are, and that there is nothing I will not do, or sacrifice, to do what is best for my child.

Even when it means doing the smart thing, instead of the right one.

ELEVEN

It surprises me, pulling into the driveway, finding Marsha is still at the house. It does not surprise me that she has parked so I cannot get into my garage. She is on the phone when I go inside, her desk piled with papers, my Rolodex in the middle of the mess. Leo barks and runs in circles, and Marsha gives me a look.

'Put him out, will you, Joy? I can't hear myself think.'

Leo sits suddenly, knowing there will be no petting until he does, and I stroke his ears, and study my cousin. For the first time in a long time, I really look. She waves me away, preoccupied and industrious, and fury rises inside me like helium. I put Leo outside.

Marsha's dirty coffee cup is on the counter top, along with a spray of coffee grounds, an open package of Pecan Sandies and a dirty, coffee-stained spoon. She has left the carton of half and half out, and when I put it back in the refrigerator, I find it warm to the touch. I wonder how long it has been sitting there. Has it gone bad – should I throw it away? As always, Marsha leaves these tiny messes behind. I throw the spoon across the kitchen and into the sink. The amount of noise it makes is absurd.

'Yes, yes, I'll tell her. Thank you, Brice. I'll wait for your call.' Her tone is syrupy, like it always is when she talks to members of the board. I am her boss, but they cut the checks for her salary. Marsha rounds the corner, patting at her hair, which is still in place from the day before. She must use a lot of hairspray, and sleep very carefully in her bed.

'What on earth is all the noise in here, didn't you see I was on the phone?'

'*You*,' I say.

Marsha's mouth hangs open. She breathes heavily, chest rising and falling, and the pink drains out of her cheeks. 'What in the hell is up with you?'

I head out of the kitchen to the living room, and she follows me, calling my name over and over and asking me what's wrong. I glance into the fake gilt mirror, then turn around, because I don't like the look of my face. I stand with my back to the ugly faux cherry console, another example of Carl's execrable taste.

'I spent over three hours with the FBI this morning.'

Marsha is in her stooped-forward stance, which means she is thinking instead of posing. 'But why are you mad at *me*? Look, you're not angry that I gave them that handwriting sample, are you? They said it was just a formality, and I figured it would be OK. I thought it would get them off your back.'

She chatters on and on about the sample, and how she knew I'd want her to cooperate so the authorities could bring Andee and Caro home safe. I wait for her to wind down, and eventually she is silent. She stares at me, unhappy, but she finally stops talking and is still.

'We covered a lot of ground this morning, Agent Woods, Agent Jones and myself. And Smitty was there, of course. Three straight hours of questions takes you everywhere. The here, the now and the past.'

Marsha looks at me sideways, genuinely bewildered.

'They had Caroline's diary. Agent Jones found it amusing to read it out loud. Just a couple of stupid pages where Caro oh-so-casually mentioned how hard it was on Joey to walk in on his father when he was cheating on his mother. Especially when the other woman was Cousin Marsha, and they were doing it on the living room couch.'

Marsha's mouth opens and closes, and she looks around the living room like she has dropped something tiny on the floor. She sits finally, on the edge of the couch, stands back up like she's been burned, and moves to a chair.

Her voice is oddly soft. 'I thought you knew.'

'Why? *Why* would you think that?'

She slides deeper into the chair as I cross the room and stand over her.

'Do you think I would have kept you around if I'd *known* about it? Do you think I'd still give you this *job*? I'd have drop kicked your butt to the curb, which is what I'm doing right this minute. Do you hear me, Marsha? Do you understand?'

At this point, anyone within five square miles can hear me. She starts to get up, but I'm not through with her yet.

'Just answer me, Marsha. How could you think that I knew?'

She takes a breath, and tears cascade down her cheeks. Her nose is starting to run. 'Carl *told* me you knew. I didn't believe him until you came to me about the money.' She whispers so softly I have to lean closer to hear. 'You remember, Joy. You came to me about the eleven thousand that was missing and asked me to cover it up.'

'Until I could pay it back.'

'Yes. Until you could make it up.'

'And I paid every last cent of it back, didn't I, Marsha?'

'Of course you did.'

I take a breath. 'I can't believe how stupid I was. *You* helped him take the money in the first place, didn't you? You probably wrote the checks yourself.'

Marsha is shaking her head, twisting the end of her turquoise blouse in her hands. 'No, no, no, it wasn't like that. He took the money out himself and he forged your signature on three different checks.'

I have to sit down right away, but I don't want to sit on the couch any more than she does. I wind up on the ottoman at her feet.

Marsha inhales and exhales, and stifles a shuddering sob. 'Carl had it all set up so that if anybody found out about it, the blame would go on you. But I caught it. I know your signature better than I know my own. *I* told him he'd have to pay it back. I threatened to go to the board over it, and he said if I did he'd tell them about the affair and I'd get fired. I told him to go ahead. I wasn't going to help him embezzle from the foundation. The board might *fire* me but they'd put *him* in jail. He warned me. He said I'd create a scandal that would end the ministries. I could see his point, so I told him I would talk to you and you could decide. That's when he said that you already knew.' She looks up at me. 'I'm the one who told you the money was missing in the first place, don't you remember?'

'Of course I remember. What I don't recall is you saying anything about sleeping with my husband.'

'I was going to tell you. But when you came back to me and asked me to cover it up, and said you'd pay everything back, I figured Carl had told you everything, just like he said.'

'How long were you having sex with Carl, how long?'

'A few weeks, that's all.'

'That's enough. Look, I have to go out of town. You can clean out your desk and get your personal things next week. I'll give you a call when I get back and we can settle up your pay and all that.'

Marsha's face is red, her eyes wide and streaming with tears. 'Don't you understand that Carl used me to get to the *money*? He thought I'd go along with it, *with him*, but I *didn't*. I'm a *victim*, just the same as you.'

'Not quite the same.'

'But where are you going? Have you found out something about the kidnappers? Don't you want me to keep Leo?'

'No, Leo is going with me.'

'*Joy*. At least wait till Andee and Caroline come back. You need me.'

I am shaking my head. 'No. You're exactly what I don't need. You were easy prey, Marsha. It was obvious to Carl, just like it is to anybody with a brain, that whatever I have, you want. So be it. I don't want you near me, ever again.'

Marsha lifts her chin. 'We're family, Joy. I've worked hard on this ministry a lot of years. You can't just throw me away.'

I say nothing. Waiting for her to leave.

'You'll change your mind. When you're not so mad, you'll see. This is not who you are.'

I shake my head at her. I don't know who I am anymore, so how can she?

TWELVE

The drive from Lexington to Fort Smith is an agony of tedium. I drink coffee and chew gum and listen to NPR until I am suicidal over the state of the world. By midnight I hit Memphis, and it's all I can do to make it off an exit to a hotel.

Leo and I are on the road again by six a.m., and by noon we're rolling into Fort Smith.

It's a smallish town. I frown over the directions I have printed out from MapQuest. It takes me twenty minutes and two wrong turns before I find Caroline's place. Her Jeep Wrangler still sits in the driveway. I never came to visit them. I always meant to.

The flower beds in the front yard are carefully weeded, and next door the grass has been cut so recently I can smell the green. White Impatiens grow thickly in the window boxes. The yard is shaded by old trees, their roots like veins just below the surface, the grass so thin beneath that you can see the sandy soil, the pine needles.

The door is blocked with crime scene tape, an embarrassment in this gentle neighborhood. I have a key Caro sent me three years ago for a visit I never made.

The porch creaks when I walk across the warped wood planks. The beautifully arched front door is painted grey. There is a scratched brass mailbox hanging on the door and it looks empty. I wonder if someone is picking up the mail.

My key works just fine. I break the crime scene tape and walk in slowly, almost on tiptoe, absorbing the silence. There is a brass umbrella stand on the left, just behind the front door. The great room is cavernous, with high ceilings and worn wood floors. The furniture is simple, antique store bargains.

There is mud smeared on the staircase. Left by the intruder, I think.

The great room opens on to an octagonal dining nook, directly off the kitchen. There is a bank of windows, and a drop-leaf cherry table. This is the one she told me about, bought at the bargain rate of one hundred eighty-seven dollars. The surface needs refinishing. It is scratched and cloudy with abuse. A square of lace in the center covers the worst of the wear, and on top of that is an oversized rattan basket with old mail.

I sort through what is there. A car insurance bill, a flier from Lowe's, a bank statement from Arvest Bank. A newspaper lies folded next to the basket, the rubber band that held it tossed to one side. The *Arkansas Democrat* – dated the day Caro and Andee disappeared. I look through the back window and see where Burton Stafford took the privacy fence down between their backyards, giving Caroline and Andee access to the in-ground pool. Since then he had put up a gazebo and a swing set, and re-cemented the basketball hoop and tetherball pole the Stafford kids had used growing up.

The sound of a car horn makes me jump. It sounds very much like my Jeep. I go to the front door and look outside. Leo has scrambled to the driver's side and his front paws are propped on the steering wheel. He sees me looking and plasters himself against the window and whines.

I let him out and he races up and down the front yard, sniffing, moving in random patterns that no doubt make sense to him. A pudgy yellow-tailed squirrel chatters at him from its perch on the fence and he thunders across the yard. I head up the sidewalk to the porch. Leo appears instantly beside me, trying to crowd ahead. I block him until he sits, then I push the door open. Leo follows me in. He is full of curiosity and without inhibition. He circles the couch, runs into the dining nook, stops long enough to prop his front paws on the table and sniff Caroline's boots, then hops down and tears into the kitchen.

Ruby's doggie bowls sit neatly on a small braided rug by

the refrigerator. Leo sticks his head in the water and laps loudly. He dives into the stale kibble with rapture.

I walk softly. I would love to have a kitchen like this. The wood floors are in beautiful shape, the walls freshly painted, vanilla cream, and there are white plantation shutters on the windows. The counter tops are tiled, cobalt blue, and the stove is a Jenn-Air gas with a grill. There's a built-in pantry with glass doors, a deep red teapot on the stove, and the cabinets are white and spotless. A wood-burning stove is perched on a small brick hearth. The ceiling is bead board, painted white.

There is a wine bottle on the counter top. Australian Cabernet, Yellow Tail, three quarters full, the cork jammed into the throttle, a dried smear of wine on the tile.

The kitchen table is a small, perfect square. It's old wood, painted yellow, with three matching yellow chairs. A small pot in the center holds brown, crispy irises. I picture myself there, with Caro and Andee, eating toast and jam and eggs.

I have brought in my overnight case, the leather one. Leo has chewed a hole in the top. He is running free in the fenced backyard, finding trails to follow, sniffing at the trees for squirrel. I take my bag upstairs, avoiding the crusts of mud. The Dark Man has left them there like graffiti, marking his territory like a dog.

I pause in the hallway, looking into my granddaughter's room, feeling my breathing quicken and my chest go tight. The bed is unmade. She was sleeping right there, not six feet away, when the Dark Man took her away. I walk in on tiptoe, and sit on the unmade bed. I pick up her pillow, and I can smell the faint scent of her strawberry shampoo and the lingering smell of little girl. My knees begin to tremble; it is good I am sitting down.

Andee's bedspread is lavender with white unicorns. There are books on simple white shelves, the highest no more than three feet tall. The shelves hold the entire collection of Beatrix Potter books I have sent her, and a mishmash of stuffed animals, Barbie dolls, and stacks and stacks of puzzles. A blue plastic writing desk and matching chair are tucked in the corner, and on the inexpensive painted pine dresser is the rabbit lamp I bought when Andee was born. Next to the lamp is a set of Tinkerbell bubble bath, little girl makeup and perfume.

I want it to be her mother who woke her that night.

I stand abruptly, and shut the door. I hesitate in the hallway, then move to the edge of Caro's bedroom.

It's a large room, with a fireplace that for now is merely decorative, the chimney bricks crumbling beneath a thick coat of paint. Caro is saving for a gas insert.

The carpet is off-white Berber, streaked with mud like the stairs. Her bed is unmade. There is a crumpled duvet of white eyelet, sheets white with silvery stripes. There are four over-sized pillows at the head of the bed, and at least six small ones, lace, velvet, like a collection. I walk carefully, watching where I step, pausing in front of the nightstand. There is a picture in a silver frame of Caro and Andee, by a lake. I imagine my son in the photograph, his arms around them both.

A wine glass sits by the telephone, the dregs coating the bottom of the glass, dark and crusty, like dried blood. There is a book splayed on the floor, pages bent, jacket askew. I wonder what she was reading. I do not touch.

How long, I wonder? How long after she and I talked on the phone, till the Dark Man came to take her away? Was she asleep? Did she hear him come in? Did she get out of bed to check a noise, and find him waiting outside in the hall?

'Retribution is coming for you.' That was what the note had said and that was what had come true.

Caroline told me that she used to dream of footsteps – how she could read the whole of Joey's day and, more importantly, the night to come, in the sound of his feet on the stairs. Had she heard the Dark Man's footsteps that night?

I take my overnight bag and put it back in the car.

THIRTEEN

The Moran Memorial Pet Cemetery runs adjacent to the Sebastian County Humane Society in Fort Smith. It is less than four miles from Caro's house, but I spent over forty minutes finding it, even with the MapQuest directions.

I left Leo closed up in the hall bathroom because I did not trust him not to find something interesting to chew. I could not leave him out in the yard. There is not a gate latch on the market that he can't open.

I have his leash in hand, and I lock up the Jeep. Animal shelters upset me. My ministry contributes heavily to no-kill shelters.

From the outside, this one doesn't look too bad – a modern, boxy building, white with a dark roof. The strips of grass out front are neatly mowed. There is a statue of St Francis in the cemetery, and when I walk inside it is clean and open, with blond maple partitions, the counter tops covered in white Formica. You can hear dogs barking. You can see the animals because the walls are glass. Dogs on the left. Cats on the right. Just inside the corridor is the Donor Wall, honoring adoptions.

The girl behind the desk is bent over a computer and she wears the kind of scrubs you see in a vet's office, a sky blue background with pictures of kittens tumbling through the air. A poster lets me know that I can have my pet buried in the cemetery next door for two hundred and fifty dollars, which includes a funeral service, pet casket and small grey headstone. Cremation costs extra.

'Excuse me,' I say.

The young woman holds one finger up, absorbed in whatever it is she is doing with the computer. Her fingernails are trimmed short, and she has small, white hands. Her hair is pulled up high and tight in a ponytail, and no doubt the stack of textbooks near the computer are hers. Her nametag says 'Sharon'. She is much too young to be the woman I talked to on the phone.

'Is Melissa Hunter here? My name is Joy Miller, and I talked to her about picking up my daughter-in-law's dog.'

The girl turns away from the computer screen, eyes cloudy with other matters. She takes a moment to gather her thoughts. 'Mrs Hunter had a board meeting this afternoon, and she won't be back until tomorrow. Can *I* help you?'

'Yes. You have a dog here named Ruby who belongs to Caroline Miller, and there are instructions in the file for you to hold the dog for me to pick up.'

'Are you adopting the dog?' Sharon chewed on the edge of her thumb. She'd either been eating a cherry popsicle or was wearing lip gloss. Otherwise her face was sadly free of makeup.

'No, I'm family, I'm picking her up.'

Sharon returned to the computer, tapped on the keyboard, frowned, and tapped some more. 'I don't have any record of this. What kind of dog is it again?'

'Golden retriever, Irish setter mix. Elderly. She's big, probably over ninety pounds.'

More tapping, then a shake of the head. 'Sorry.'

My palms were sweating. 'Look. Mrs Hunter called me the day before yesterday. She said the dog was here. I've driven over fourteen hours to pick her up.'

Sharon squinted her eyes at me. 'You drove fourteen hours to get here? Where in the heck in Arkansas do you live?'

'I don't live in Arkansas.'

'You don't live in Arkansas?'

'My daughter-in-law lives in Arkansas. She lives here, in Fort Smith. Her name is Caroline Miller, the dog's name is Ruby, and Melissa Hunter said she was here.'

'Your daughter?'

'The dog.'

Sharon went back to chewing her thumb.

I took a slow breath. 'I'm absolutely positive the dog is here, and I'd be so very grateful if you'd find her.'

Sharon wrinkles her brow but goes gamely back to the computer, and her questions are brisk. 'How long has the dog been in the shelter? If it's over—'

'Three days, that's all.'

'And animal control picked her up?'

'No. There was a family emergency. The police dropped her off.'

'Oh. Oh oh oh. Now I get it. Hold on a sec.' Sharon went back to the computer keyboard, and I moved to the glassed-in wall to scan the dog cages.

'She won't be in there.' Sharon gave me a quick glance over her shoulder. 'Those are up for adoption. We keep the other ones in another room. Ah, OK. Here we go. It says I am to release the dog to Joy Miller. That must be you, am I right?'

I nod my head, but realize she's looking at the computer and not me. 'Yes, I'm Joy Miller.'

'I'll have to see some ID.' She gives me a quick look, sounding defensive. 'There's a fee.'

I sign forms and haul out my debit card. Sharon is surprisingly brisk with the paperwork, and comes out from behind the counter. I follow her, scraping one fingernail nervously along the tooth marks Leo has made in the leash. We go down a hallway that smells of antiseptic and enter a room with concrete floors and cages. This room smells of dog and desperation. Three slots down and I see Ruby, curled in the back of her cage. I focus on Ruby entirely and make no eye contact with any other dog.

'*Ruby.*'

She is ignoring the schnauzer in the next cage who is trying to get my attention. There is fresh water and a food bowl which is full of dried kibble. Ruby is technically awake but her eyes have an otherworldly look, as if she has gone away in her head.

'Ruby?' I say again, softly.

Sharon bites the tip of one finger. 'Are you sure you have the right dog? She doesn't seem to know you. Usually they get real excited when their owners come.'

I crouch down in front of the cage. 'Hey girl, hey Ruby. Remember me? It's Joy.'

Ruby inches forward and sniffs the finger I poke into the cage. Her tail begins to wag, and she rises painfully to her feet. She noses me through the wire mesh of the cage and whimpers. Her eyes brighten and the aura of depression disappears.

'Oh, hey,' Sharon says. 'There you go.'

She unlocks the cage, and I kneel down and hug Ruby, who licks my neck, my ears, my face. I try not to look at the dogs we leave behind, but they call to me, barking, whining. Ruby walks easily by my side, and I don't bother to attach the leash. She sticks to my left leg like Velcro, and when I stop at the front desk she leans against me and I stroke her head. Sharon is once more at the computer.

'Is this everything?' I ask.

'We only give the Welcome Kits to the adoptions.'

'No, no, I just was wondering if there was some kind of file or paperwork . . .'

I trail off. Sharon is busy, and Ruby is yearning for the door.

Ruby trots happily into the parking lot, but has trouble jumping into the back of the Jeep. She whines and circles the open hatch at the back, and the front of the car. I try lifting her, but she is monstrous heavy, and I finally open the passenger door up front. She props her paws on the seat. I lift her hind end, and she scrambles into the car. Teamwork.

I brush dog hair off my shirt and Ruby covers me with dog kisses while I reassure her that she's safe and will be going home with me. Caro's mother has irritable cats, and Ruby stays with me when Caroline and Andee are in town, so we're tight, me and Ruby. I open Leo's bag of pig ears, and hand one to Ruby who takes it gently in her mouth. Ruby has very nice manners. It took me a week to train Leo not to take my hand with the treat.

Ruby stretches out across the transmission and puts her head in my lap. She holds the pig ear in her mouth. We are on our way.

I watch for the nearest McDonald's. It is part of a secret tradition, during those visits to Kentucky, that the three of us, Andee and Ruby and I, have lunch at Mickey D's. Caroline has never asked me *not* to take Andee to McDonald's and I am not foolish enough to ask.

I feel better immediately, with Ruby by my side. She connects me to Andee and Caroline, and knowing she is safe and secure was worth the drive of seven hundred some odd miles.

Still, I am a little flat with the disappointment. Evidently I misunderstood the significance of the humane society call. I was so sure there would be some sort of message from the Dark Man, something to set things in motion so I could bring Caro and Andee home safe. I must be getting paranoid – seeing portents and messages in the turn of a breeze.

I am two miles down the road, absently stroking Ruby's neck, when I notice the loose stitching on her collar, a circular tube of leather like the one Leo wears. But I remember from last summer's visit that Ruby's collar was worn and soft and very loose, the same belt-like style that is the norm. This collar is brand new and the seam along the side is coming apart.

There is a McDonald's on the right two lights down the road. I pass through the drivethrough window and park, then wrestle Ruby for the collar while she noses the bag of food. I break the cheeseburgers into smallish pieces, and Ruby inhales everything except two pickles. Once all of the food is gone, each crumb of bun nosed out, and the wrapping sufficiently licked, Ruby moves to the other side of the car, making snout marks on the window.

There is a pair of nail scissors in my purse and I use them to snip the heavy threading that holds the collar together. As I work to unravel the stitching I see signs – nicks in the leather, a difference in thread from one section to the next. It's enough to start my heart pounding. I was right all along. The Dark Man is reaching out.

I have peeled two inches of leather apart when I see the edge of yellow paper rolled up in the leather tube. I use the scissors to tease it out. There are two sheets that have been torn from a yellow legal pad, probably the same pad as the original note that arrived with the pictures of murdered evangelists. And the writing is in green Sharpie.

I wonder if all of the notes were written on the same day. One for my package of pictures, one for Caro's newspaper articles and this one to lie in wait for me. Did the Dark Man switch Ruby's collar the night he took Caro and Andee away? Are there other notes out there, carefully placed, to guide me through his malevolent maze?

Can anything good come from doing exactly as he says? I don't know what else to do. The Dark Man will tell me what I want to believe – that if I obey, Caro and Andee will come home safe. It is hard to overestimate the power of hearing what you want to hear.

I unroll the paper. Like the other notes, the writing is in neat block letters.

THEY ARE ALIVE AND WELL. FOR NOW.

FOLLOW THE INSTRUCTIONS BELOW.

YOU WILL SEE THEM IN PERSON VIA WEB CAM.

DO NOT BRING IN THE FBI OR THERE WILL BE REPERCUSSIONS.

There are three paragraphs of instructions that follow, informing me that a laptop computer has been hidden in a box next to the chimney in Caro's attic. It is programmed and ready to go.

The second page has an e-mail address, a user name and a password. It is time, at last, for the Dark Man and me to talk.

FOURTEEN

The long-suffering Ruby snoozes in the Jeep, pig ear tucked beneath one paw, while I stop at the public library. The library is no more than a block from Caroline's bungalow – a large brick building, fairly new, across the street from a park that is shaded by old trees. A small train runs on a track that circles the park perimeter, with rows of seats for children who want to ride. Caro once told me that fifty cents buys two trips – undoubtedly the best deal in town.

The public computers are on the second floor, and I mount a sweeping split staircase. There are a handful of terminals available, only one in use, and I go to the work station that is the greatest distance from everyone else. I log on in what I hope is sufficient anonymity, and take the note pages out of my pocket, unfolding the second page that has the e-mail address. My user name is *Sanctuary* and my password is *Inspired*.

I am nervous. Whatever it is the Dark Man wants will not be in my power to give.

The library computers have a wireless connection, but the wait is an agony of slow. I chew my bottom lip. Two seats over a man settles in and begins habitually clearing his throat. Two women are whispering in the book stacks a few feet away. My account comes up, and I enter the password. It does not go through – my fingers are shaky. I enter the password again, slowly this time, making sure to get it right.

I have six messages. I am entreated to take medication so that I can satisfy any woman, enlarge my penis, buy cheap diet pills and consolidate my debt.

At last, though, is the message I look for and dread.

DEAR JOY MILLER,

IT HAS COME TO THIS – THAT IN ALL OF MY TRAVELS AND STUDIES SINCE LAST WE MET, I

HAVE FOUND NO ANSWERS THAT STIR MY SOUL – IF I CAN BE SAID TO HAVE ONE, AS YOU ASSURED ME I DID, FOURTEEN YEARS AGO.

I WANT YOU TO UNDERSTAND HOW HARD I HAVE TRIED. I HAVE READ MANY BOOKS, TALKED TO PEOPLE I HOPED COULD HELP.

THE DANGER, OF COURSE, IS HONESTY. ONCE THEY KNOW ME, THEY MUST BE ABLE TO HELP ME. YET NO ONE HAS HELPED ME. SO ALL OF THEM DIED.

AND NOW I WONDER. COULD THEIR FEAR – AND THEY WERE SO AFRAID – COULD THEIR FEAR HAVE CLOUDED THEIR MINDS? PERHAPS THEY NEEDED TIME TO STUDY AND REFLECT. BUT OF COURSE, UNDER THE CIRCUMSTANCES, THAT COULD NOT BE ARRANGED.

AND I DO NOT FEEL, UPON REFLECTION, THAT OTHERS TAKE MY SOUL'S AWAKENING WITH ANY DEGREE OF SERIOUS CONTEMPLATION. THEY CANNOT BE BLAMED. IT IS YOU, AND ONLY YOU, WHO KNOW THE VALIDITY OF MY REQUEST. YOU WHO WITNESSED MY FIRST ATTEMPT. YOUR LIFE THAT I SAVED.

IS THERE GRACE FOR THE DARK ENTITIES LIKE MYSELF? CAN THERE BE REDEMPTION FOR THIS STAINED AND ANCIENT SOUL?

I HAVE TRIED ALONE, AND FAILED, TIME AND TIME AGAIN. AND IN MY FAILURES TO BE GOOD, I DO EVEN MORE HARM.

I THOUGHT, UNTIL I MET YOU, THAT DARKNESS WAS MY DESTINY. I LOOK TO YOU TO SHOW ME THE WAY.

I HOLD YOUR HEART IN MY HANDS. THEY WILL
BE SAFE WITH THE PART OF ME THAT WANTS
TO DO GOOD. FOR THE SAKE OF ALL OF US, YOU
MUST SHOW ME THE WAY. THINK. REFLECT. AND
WE'LL TALK.

JUST YOU AND ME, JOY. DON'T COMPLICATE
THINGS BY BRINGING IN THE LAW. THINGS WILL
GO BADLY FOR ALL OF US IF YOU DO.

And my reply:

Dear Seeker,
Your situation is complicated. I will return answers after
research and contemplation.
Keep my girls safe.
Joy Miller

FIFTEEN

Special Agent Harris of the Arkansas FBI doesn't look
anything at all like Russell Woods, so that's one prevalent
theory shot to hell. All Feds don't look alike. But *think*
alike? That may be what started the rumors. Because Special
Agent Harris, a thin man with a brownish buzz cut, is looking
at me with an unfriendly face.

I am sitting opposite his crapped-over desk, which looks
like someone tossed forms, files and paper into the air and
let them drift randomly back on the top. Nevertheless, being
in an actual office is a step up from an interrogation room.

'Why didn't you inform Agent Woods of the dog situation
before you came out here?' Harris leans forward, elbows
on the desk. His head seems small for his body.

I lean back in my chair and cross my legs. Up until now
it has not crossed my mind to call my attorney, Smitty
Madison.

'Can we get past the *stupid* questions and move on to the ones that make sense? I'm not trying to antagonize you, Agent Harris, but we're kind of on the clock.'

He glares at me. I look over at the pictures on the walls. Harris is clearly ex-navy. He wears a wedding band, but there are no photographs of his family. Just a framed picture of the Destroyer he served on during his years in military service, no doubt near and dear to his heart.

Harris points a finger. I don't like people to do that, but I endure.

'Mrs Miller, are you aware of what's at stake here? I can have you arrested for obstruction of justice just for violating the crime scene.'

I hold my hands out. 'Let's get on with it, shall we? If you want to arrest me and put me in handcuffs, go ahead. I'd prefer to call my attorney first. I just bring that up because with handcuffs on it's going to be hard to dial.'

Harris sighs. 'Don't make things more difficult, Mrs Miller. Let's do it like this. You go and wait in one of the interrogation rooms. We'll make you comfortable; get you coffee, whatever you need. And I'm going to send somebody out to your daughter-in-law's house to connect up with the kidnapper on the web cast which –' he checks his watch – 'is three hours and some odd minutes from now.'

I lean forward. 'You read the note, Agent Harris. The kidnapper specifically asked for me and told me not to bring in the FBI.'

He places both palms on the desk, as if preparing to rise. 'You think? Most kidnappers ask for me by name.'

'How many victims have you gotten killed during your career, Agent Harris?'

He doesn't even look at me. Just crosses the room, stands patiently by the door, waiting for me to comply. 'I can have you removed, Mrs Miller, if that's what you'd prefer.'

'Do what you have to do. But you're not going to find that computer.'

He stands very still, eyes narrow. 'What makes you say that?'

'I'm just making a prediction, Agent Harris. I think when

you go up to the attic to find the laptop, it won't be there. But that's just an opinion.'

He moves back into the office and stands over me, bending close enough that I can feel his breath on my temple. 'Mrs Miller, I'm a compassionate man. So if you don't cooperate and hand that computer over immediately, and you cause the deaths of your granddaughter and daughter-in-law, I will personally escort you from your jail cell to their funerals.'

I push him gently away. 'That isn't going to work with me, Agent Harris. But I will negotiate with you. If you agree that I will be on the web cam making contact with the kidnapper, just like he asks—'

'You're not running this operation.' He inclines his head toward the door. 'This way, please, Mrs Miller.'

I stand. 'Go back through the photographs of the dead evangelists. Jimmy Mahan, Gloria Schmid and Darrin Lane. Tell me this man doesn't have a problem controlling his rage. At least consult Russell Woods on this. It's his investigation, from the Lexington end, he's got some insight into this guy.'

'Woods will agree with me.'

'If he does, so much the better. Because if you go this route, and the kidnapper kills Caro and Andee like I think he will, then you have somebody handy to share the blame.'

'I want that computer.'

'You're not getting it.'

He picks the phone up and sets it on top of the paperwork on the corner of his desk. 'Call your lawyer. I'll arrest you when you're done.'

I don't know the number by heart, not yet, but Smitty's business card is in my wallet, so at least I don't have to call information. As expected, Smitty is in conference with a client, but at least he's not in court. I tell his assistant that this is an emergency, and that I need to speak to him now. She sounds intrigued. I wait three minutes, then hear Smitty's voice on the line. I'm aware that a minor miracle has just occurred.

'What's the big emergency, Joy? And where the hell are

you? I don't know this area code on the caller ID but it says Federal Bureau of Investigation.'

'It's Arkansas.'

'You're in Arkansas? On purpose?'

'I'm here picking up Ruby, Caroline's dog. Evidently, after the break-in and kidnapping, the police dumped her off at the pound.'

'So you drove . . . never mind. And for this you need a lawyer? How did you get tangled up with the local FBI?'

'They're arresting me for obstruction of justice.' I glance at Harris, who is burrowing through the papers in the middle of his desk. He doesn't even look my way.

I hear noises from the other end of the phone line that make me think Smitty Madison's irritation is no longer directed at me.

'For picking up a dog?' Smitty sounds incredulous.

'I went into Caroline's house and crossed the crime scene tape.'

'Why did you do that?'

'I had to pick up Ruby's pills—'

'Who in the hell is Ruby?'

'Ruby is Caroline's dog.'

'Got it. Go on.'

'Anyway, I needed Ruby's food and her bed and her medication. She's old, and has a whole bunch of pills she takes.'

'Don't we all. How'd you get in, and please tell me you already had a key.'

'Well, I did.'

'Good. And I would imagine your daughter-in-law gave it to you, with blanket verbal permission to go in anytime.'

'Yes.'

'Anything else?'

'There was a note from the kidnapper sewn into Ruby's collar.' I do not admit that I destroyed the second page that directed me to the email. The FBI does not need to know that I have met this man before.

'What the *hell*?' Smitty is silent. Then, 'What did it say?'

'Instructions for me to log on to a computer he put in

the attic of Caroline's house. I'm supposed to talk to Caro and
Andee on a web cast three hours from now.'

'Jeez Louise,' Smitty mutters. 'At least we're getting somewhere. He'll probably ask for a ransom. That will be good
news for you, on the legal front.'

'Maybe not. I took the note straight to the local FBI office
and they don't want me doing the web cast. They want one
of their agents handling it. And I think that's a big mistake.
So I've got the computer and I'm not giving it up till they
agree.'

'Oh my God. Is Harris in there with you?'

'He—'

'Yes or no.'

'Yes. He says I have to stay in their interrogation room until
they get a free moment to put me in jail.'

Smitty inhales deeply. 'If it comes to that, which it very
well might at the rate you are going, you sit there and drink
their coffee and don't say a thing. As far as the web cast goes,
listen to me, Joy. You got your opinion and they got theirs,
but this is their job and some of them are pretty good at what
they do. And you're out of time. And God knows you're in
enough trouble. So you suck it up and cooperate. Ask Agent
Harris to put us on speaker phone.'

I cradle the receiver on my shoulder, thinking what
to do.

Harris looks up at me.

'My attorney wants you to put us on speaker phone.'

Harris pushes a button and takes the receiver from my
shoulder.

'You there, Agent Harris?' Smitty's voice is booming.

'Right here.'

'It looks to me like this is a simple matter of miscommunication between you and my client. I personally see no reason
why we can't clear things up without getting into any kind of
accusations of false arrest. My client, who has a key to her
daughter-in-law's home, entered the premises to pick up medication for the family dog, who she drove all the way out to
Arkansas to retrieve from the pound. I'm sure she

misunderstood you. She seems to think you feel this constitutes reason to put her in jail.'

'No, of course not,' Harris says.

I stare at him but he avoids my eyes.

'Mrs Miller is in possession of a computer left by the kidnapper. I'm arresting her for obstruction of justice and withholding evidence because she's refused a direct request to turn it over.'

'I find that hard to believe, Agent Harris, since she went straight to your office as soon as she got the kidnapper's note. In the dog collar, wasn't it? Too bad your own investigators didn't find it themselves, but no doubt you're understaffed.'

'We are not understaffed, Mr Madison. Your client objects to the way we're running the investigation and seems to be convinced she should be running things herself.'

'I think we can all see why she might feel that way. Joy, are you there?'

'Yes, Smitty, I am.'

'Joy, you can't tell the FBI how to do their job. After all, they're the ones who will be accountable for whatever happens to Caroline and Andee, isn't that right, Agent Harris? I think this is another miscommunication. No doubt, Joy, you were confused by the whole thing with the computer. And if you've actually got it, you'll give it back.'

There is a long moment of silence. Harris looks at me and I'm not happy. Maybe Smitty is right, but it isn't his call. Every attorney I've met is a judge in waiting. Part of their training must be arrogance school.

'Look, I need to get back to my conference,' Smitty says. 'And Agent Harris, you are clearly on a very tight schedule, so I'll let you get to it. If you need me, Joy, call me back.'

SIXTEEN

The Arkansas FBI agents make better coffee than the ones in Kentucky. Their furniture evidently comes from the same catalog. I sit alone in an interrogation room and time one hour and forty-seven minutes, more than half of the three hours left before the Dark Man expects to see me on the web.

I have been cycling between despair, rage and stoicism, and am in the stoic part of the cycle when the door finally opens, catching me in a moment of outward calm. The woman who peers in from the hallway wears a slimming pantsuit of navy blue. Her hair is collar length, and dyed blond. She emits energy and the slightest hint of Chanel.

'Mrs Miller? I'm Agent Tina Buckman. I'm going to coach you for the web cast. Will you please come with me?'

I take a breath. Coach me for the web cast?

I like the fine lines of experience in Agent Buckman's face and the intelligence in her eyes. I follow obediently.

People look up when we walk by. Agent Buckman is early forties to mid, and has excellent posture. She smiles and waves at two or three other agents, winks at a man carrying files into a storeroom, and points me into a tiny office. She guides me to a chair before she settles behind the desk.

'I thought we'd be more comfortable in here. I don't want either of us distracted, wondering if somebody's peeping at us through the two-way, just to see how it's going along.' She cocks her head and looks me over carefully. 'You should know that I'm an experienced field agent. I have twenty-three years with the bureau, and I worked the kidnapping detail in St Louis for eight years. I've been on domestic terrorism since Nine Eleven, but they pulled me off for the afternoon to work with you. I'm good.' She winks at me, and I see an actual dimple. 'You seem pretty steady yourself. It's my call to decide whether or not you can pull off the web cam meet with the kidnapper. I'm saying yes. You're still up for it? You'll work with me on it?'

'Absolutely.' I glance at the clock on the wall.

She shakes her head at me. 'Don't do that. Thinking about the time is my job, and I want you to trust me to do it.' She leans forward. 'Our agents are already at Caroline's house, and the techs have the computer system up and running. We'll do the broadcast there, so it'll go out on the right server with the right IP address.'

She taps a fingernail, gathering her thoughts. The desktop surface is clear except for a paperweight, a painted rock that looks like a child's project from school. 'Here's what I think we can be safe in assuming. One, the kidnapper wants *you* to know that Caroline and Andee are alive. Harris seems to think this little bit of theatre will be followed by a ransom demand, but I'm not so sure. My gut says the time for that has come and gone.

'Second, the kidnapper wants to *connect* with you. The only way he feels sure you'll cooperate is by using your granddaughter as bait. He wants your attention, and he dreads any possibility of rejection. That's why I think that not using you on the web cast, as he instructed, would be a fatal mistake.'

The word *fatal* sticks in my mind. My stomach is cramping suddenly and it takes concentration not to double over.

'We have three major goals. One, make contact with the kidnapper, and confirm that both Caroline and Andee are alive. Two, get anything we can on their location. We'll be looking at the visuals from the web cast itself, and tracking down coordinates through the net.'

Agent Buckman leans across the desk. 'No matter how smart this guy is, no matter how careful, we're going to get a lot of information from this web cast. Our tech guys will follow the bounce across the Internet. What you need to do is pay attention to what Caroline *says*. Be sensitive to the possibility that she's trying to lead you.'

I nod my head.

'I want you to ask her questions. Ask her if she knows where she is.'

'But—'

Buckman holds up a hand. 'Ask her if she knows where she is. The kidnapper will expect that. Chances are she *won't* know. Ask her if there are highway noises, diesel fumes. Think sight, sound and smell.'

'But don't you think it could backfire?'

'You're worried about making him mad? Don't be. He's left himself open for this, he'll be expecting it. He'll control his end, don't do it for him. If Caroline gets upset with your questions, then back down. But be prepared to get everything you can.

'Third, and this is more important than you may realize. We want to give Caroline and Andee hope and confidence. We don't want them giving up. If an opportunity to escape comes up, we want them in the frame of mind to get away. It might surprise you, but sometimes people are afraid to try. The mental prison is always more confining than the physical one. On the other hand, we don't want them going to the other extreme and doing something desperate that has no chance of working out.'

'How do I do that?'

'By looking at them the same way you looked at me before you started watching the clock.'

'Sorry.'

She turns sideways in her chair. 'I have an idea I want to run by you. One reason you drove all the way out here was to pick up their dog, right?'

'Right.'

'What kind of dog is it? Is it fairly calm?'

'She's a golden retriever/Irish setter mix. She's old. She's calm.'

'Perfect.' Agent Buckman leans back in her chair with a small smile. 'I want you to get the dog in front of the camera. It will do a world of good for Caroline and Andee's morale, don't you think?'

'Brilliant. Yes.'

She points to the clock. 'We'll talk more on the way – if you have any questions, the drive over is the best time to ask them. But I don't want you scripted and looking over-rehearsed. Remember, we want him to think you're on your own, and that you didn't come to us for help. I'll be there, inside the house, and so will several other agents, but none of us will be in sight during the actual web cast.' She grins. 'It'll be a battle getting the techs out of the room, but I don't want any possibility that someone sneezes, or that you slip and look at me or one of the other agents. So it'll just be you and the web cam.'

'And Ruby the dog.'

'There you go.'

SEVENTEEN

The flutter of nerves hits my stomach as soon as Agent Buckman and I walk up the driveway to Caroline's house. The dogs are barking. If Leo had been here the night Caro and Andee disappeared, either Leo or the Dark Man would be dead.

I check my watch. If all goes well, I'll be seeing Andee and Caroline and hearing their voices in less than an hour. I am starting to feel strangely unreal, as if I've taken a double dose of cold pills.

But I am full of hope. I am not alone anymore.

And however good the Dark Man is with computers, he will be up against the FBI. On the drive over, Buckman gave me an overview of their Cyber Crimes Program, including the well funded Innocent Images National Initiative (IINI), an international, intelligence-driven, multi-agency operation that goes after online child pornography and child sexual exploitation.

The closest Cyber Action Team (CAT) is already inside the house. FBI agents, analysts, computer forensic experts and malicious code experts who travel worldwide at the drop of an e-mail.

Our team leader is Salvatore Pacino, no relation to actor Al Pacino. 'Brilliant, but irritable,' Buckman told me on the drive over.

We ring the bell, then go inside. A short man, robust and white-haired, is walking toward us from the bathroom off the hall and I can hear the rush of water that means the toilet has just been flushed.

'Please close that front door up,' he says. His shoulders are slumped. He looks like he's had a long day already.

Buckman waves me in. 'Sal, this is Joy Miller.'

I shake his hand. I hear noises in the kitchen, and see a man in shirtsleeves move in and out of the dining room.

Pacino takes my hand. His eyes are bright and alert under heavy eyebrows that ought to be trimmed. 'This is a terrible thing, the young mother and the child. They have put up the good fight, good for them. We will get him, this bastard.'

I don't have the courage to admit that it was Leo who knocked over the chairs and mangled the carpet chasing after Ruby when I brought her in.

He points a thick finger at his watch. 'I show you what we got here set up.'

I lied to Agent Harris. I didn't touch the laptop, I left it where it was. It has been unpacked and set up on the dining room table. It is an Apple MacBook, slim and black, the screen thirteen inches square. It is wedged between three open cases that hold interesting electronics.

Three men and one woman are moving from the kitchen to the dining room. The CAT team in action around the coffee pot. No one introduces me.

Buckman shakes her head and starts pointing. 'Sal, we've got to modify this set up. We don't want the kidnapper catching sight of all this stuff.'

Pacino's eyelids droop, lizard-like. 'You think I don't check the line of sight?'

'I want Joy alone when she's on camera. I don't want any chance she'll look at one of us, if something comes up.'

'For this you give me a whole ten minutes' notice?'

Buckman taps his cheek with a long acrylic nail.

'That's why I asked for you, Sal. I wanted someone who can deal.'

One of the CATs, the youngest male, makes a funny noise. Pacino glances my way and his frown eases.

'Do not be looking so worried. This will be OK.' He looks across at the noisemaker and raises an eyebrow. 'Get the move on, Atkins. Where is Bose? All of you, get on it. Everything to go into the kitchen – you have three minutes.'

The team is quick, their fingertips moving over the equipment like a confident caress. I back up to get out of the way.

'New stuff?' Buckman says. There is something edgy in her tone.

The word *stuff* makes Pacino wince. 'Not so new we don't shake out the bugs already.'

A man in his thirties with comb tracks in his hair, Bose, I think, looks at me over the top of an open briefcase. 'Just confirming. You have no e-mail from this guy?'

I have withheld the e-mail. I shake my head. 'No.'

'No metadata, then.'

I don't answer because I don't know what metadata is. Would the Dark Man know if I gave them metadata?

'Too bad for that,' Bose says. 'It brought down the BTK killer.'

Pacino snorts as he moves a case into the kitchen. 'This one is too smart for that, Bose. He gives us the laptop right out of the box.'

Agent Buckman is in the living room talking loudly on her cell phone, making something very clear to someone. The CAT agents buzz back and forth between the dining room and kitchen, moving and adjusting the equipment.

'Mrs Miller, if you please.' Pacino waves me to the dining room and points to a tiny square lens at the top of the computer screen. 'This laptop, now, she has a camera. You see them, *they see you*. You got to—'

Agent Buckman has come up behind him and puts a heavy hand on his shoulder. 'Get on with it, Sal. She's been briefed.'

'Am I stepping on your toes that you need to show me the teeth?' Pacino waves a hand. 'I am helping to catch this kidnapper. And, excuse me, please, but *what* is that scratching noise? It sound to me like mice in the ceiling.' He looks over at me. 'You got mice in the ceiling? Big ones?'

'It's the dogs. They want in.' I head for the kitchen door. Ruby is on the porch, head low, panting hard. Leo crowds her out of the doorway.

Buckman looks over my shoulder. 'The older one. That's Ruby?'

I nod.

She leans across me to let Ruby in. She gives Leo a quick pat, then closes the door, leaving him outside on the steps. I get the feeling she knows who knocked over all the living room chairs.

I fill Ruby's water bowl and she laps loudly, slinging droplets on to my ankles. I should put a bowl out for Leo.

There is a shriek from Pacino. 'I say to you that animals stay outside in the fence. Do you know what the dog hair can do to electronics?'

'You're the computer expert, Sal, not the animal wrangler.' Buckman clucks her tongue at Ruby. 'This old lady isn't going to bother you. I left the scary one outside.'

A tinny alarm sounds and Buckman taps a button on her watch. 'It's time.'

EIGHTEEN

It is the delicate and familiar prettiness of Andee's heart-shaped face that I focus upon. The darkness beneath her eyes, the pale and pasty tone of her skin.

'It's really you,' Caroline says, and she sounds breathless, a little hoarse.

I am struck by how oddly elongated they look, Caroline and Andee, as if they are surreal, ghost portraits, caricatures of their true selves. It startles me, how ill they seem, though it may be due in part to the odd effects and camera angles of computer video.

'Nina is crying,' Andee says. Then, as an aside, 'I told you she would come.' Andee looks straight at the camera. She is perched on her mother's lap, the top of her head tucked under Caroline's chin, and the two of them give the impression of being glued together. 'You're coming to get us, aren't you, Nina?'

Such faith. My throat tightens so that I cannot talk, and Andee puts her face right into the lens, so that her features balloon into a weird monstrosity, illuminating the pores of her skin.

'Andee,' Caroline says gently, pulling her daughter away.

'I'm coming,' I tell them. 'I promise you, I'm coming.' And hearing the words come out of my mouth with such conviction, I believe it too. I will find them. I will bring them home.

I can't stop myself from touching the screen, and I see that Caro is doing the same.

'We've got ten minutes,' she says. She has lost weight – I can see it in her face and her throat. Her hair looks slept on, her clothes crumpled, at least the shirt, which is all I can see.

'Are you alone?'

She nods. 'But he's probably monitoring, don't you think?'

'Are you OK?' *OK* is a silly, inadequate word for all that I want to ask.

But Caro seems to understand. 'We're OK for now.'

I take this to mean that she is as afraid as she ought to be.

'Do you know *where* you are?' I ask her.

'It's dark here. All the time,' Andee says. She is sucking two fingers, which I have not seen her do since she was three.

'We drove a long way,' Caroline says, 'after he took us. All night. Half a day. Then he brought us in blindfolded. Wherever we are, it's cold and quiet. Sort of muffled, if that makes any sense. They've put us in some kind of RV.'

'It's got a baffroom,' Andee says.

'Good thing,' I tell her. She almost smiles.

'We have food and water.' Caro's chest heaves, and she is

more breathless with every word. 'Outside the windows, it's always dark. We can't see anything.'

'What do you hear? Planes? People? Traffic?'

'Nothing. It's always quiet. There are never any noises at all. I don't know what day it is. How long have we been gone?'

'Three days, give or take. This is Thursday. He took you in the middle of the night on Monday.'

Caroline swallows. 'It seems longer. Is anyone looking for us?'

'Everyone is looking for you. And I'm going to find you. Do you believe me?'

Andee nods but Caro keeps swallowing. I can almost see the outline of the scream she keeps shoved in her chest.

'Quickly, Caroline. Details. Anything. Do you know who took you?'

'A man. Tall, and he's got dark, greasy hair and he's very . . . tall . . . I said that.' Caro frowns and shrugs. 'We can't break the windows, they're boarded up. We don't see anything, we don't hear anything. No particular smells, other than a kind of basement feeling. Sort of damp and musty. It's like—' She shrugs suddenly, and wisely she does not speculate. I remember a terrible kidnapping that happened when I was a child, a woman who was put in a coffin and buried alive.

'I'm sure it seems that way because they've boarded up the windows,' I say.

'Yeah.' Caro moves a hand to her throat and even on the distorted visual of the computer camera I can see the crooked-ness of her wrist, how it cants slightly off center, the joint thick and heavy. I remember how delicate and slim her wrist was, before my son broke it in three different places.

'Did you go to the police?' Caro's voice is trembly, and I sense a warning.

'No,' I lie. 'No law enforcement. I'm doing everything just like he said.'

'*You* can't call them,' Caro tells me, though I think she wants me to do exactly that. Is it my imagination, the plea in her eyes?

Caro jumps, and Andee hides her head in her mother's shoulder. 'Footsteps. He's coming.'

I hear a whisper from the kitchen and look up to see Ruby being pushed in my direction. I forgot about the dog. I call Ruby over, and she comes immediately, shoving her nose into my lap.

'Andee, Andee, look who's here.' Ruby snuffles and squirms and I pull her higher to make sure she's in front of the lens. 'Speak, Ruby. Speak.'

'Mommy, look, it's Ruby. Oh, Ruby Ruby *hello.*'

Tears stream down Caro's face. '*Ruby.*'

'Caro, listen to me. I'm going to make sure everything turns out OK.'

'I know. I know you will.' Caro's voice is so tight it is unrecognizable.

'Trust me, Caroline. *Be ready.*'

Caro looks over her shoulder, then glances back at me. I see her nod, mouth the word *OK*.

A shadow looms behind Caro and Andee. The view is hazy, but I get the impression of a man, very tall. He bends over Caro, and I see the ski mask. The screen goes dark.

My stomach is tight and painful, and my throat is so constricted I can no longer speak.

In spite of the mask, I've seen just enough to recognize the man that I know and remember. He is keeping his face covered, so they will not be able to identify him. Does this mean if I do what he says he will let them go?

It is eerily seductive – believing when they tell you what you want to hear.

NINETEEN

I am alone in Caroline's backyard, sitting on her porch swing crying gustily. My cell phone rings, and I see Agent Russell Woods' number on the caller ID.

I swallow hard, and answer. 'Anything?' I ask. The dogs mill nervously around my feet.

'Not yet, I'm afraid. But I'll let you know the minute we get something.'

'You've got something now, you're just not telling me.'

'I wish that were true.' The defeat in his voice seems genuine.

All that equipment, all the hope. I trusted the FBI and I betrayed the Dark Man and now they're gone and I'm second guessing. Buckman and the FBI CATs have taken the laptop and all of the equipment.

'Look, I just got off the phone with Agent Buckman. She said you were really great.'

Buckman gave me a pep talk before she left about results very soon. But Pacino headed out with a worried look that I can't get out of my head.

'She promised you would call me and let me know what was going on.'

'That's what I'm doing, Mrs Miller. You're going to have to hold on for a while. Give us a little time. We'll get your girls home safe. They've survived the first seventy-two hours. According to our statistics, that's a very good thing.'

'Did you make that up?'

'Look it up on the Internet, if you don't believe me. It's probably out there somewhere, everything else seems to be. Now listen. We need to know where you are every minute, and we need to know if he gets back in touch. You understand what I'm saying?'

'I understand. What about Buckman? Can she still work on the case?'

'She's back on her regular detail. Harris will handle the Arkansas end and I'll take it from here. When are you heading back this way?'

'First thing tomorrow morning.'

'Give me a call when you get to town.'

'OK. And *you'll* call *me* if—'

'I will.'

He won't. I'm not stupid. That's not how these things ever work.

That night, I dream of my son. I have not seen him, even in my dreams, for such a long time. And though I am sound asleep on the living room couch, in my dream I sit on the porch swing, Leo and Ruby at my feet.

It begins with footsteps. The gate to the backyard opens, and I can see the figure of a man. It is not until he is through the gate and around the tree that I see it is my son.

'Hello, Mom.'

'*Joey?*'

I start to stand, but he leans over and gives me a hug. He is solid, and he looks so good. So healthy. So handsome and strong. I hear cicadas in the hedges, and smell the scent of the aftershave my son always used to wear.

'Joey, how can you be here?'

'You mean, since I'm dead?' He winks at me. 'It's OK, Mom, I just thought you needed to see me. And I wanted to bring you these.' He hands me a bouquet, three pink roses surrounded by nine white.

The scent of roses is so strong and sweet I can still smell them when I wake.

TWENTY

It is a long way home to Kentucky, a hard and tedious drive. I'm a sponge to the quiet. Leo and Ruby are snoring softly, stretched out together in the back.

Not long after a very late lunch, I cross the state line from Tennessee to Kentucky. An hour later I'm on the Bluegrass Parkway – a lonely stretch of road, no more than a couple of places to gas up your car, and limited, static-filled radio reception.

Another hour and I'm on the outskirts of Versailles. I make a point of cutting my speed. Patrol cars circle like sharks in Woodford County.

I now have my pick of radio stations. News from the BBC will see us home. I am cruising New Circle Road, just a few miles from the house, when the news of the nation gives way to local events. The governor is courting the relocation of a large manufacturing plant with tax incentives, and tuition at state universities is going up again. The Lexington Fire Department is battling a blaze at the south side residence of local evangelist Joy Miller. It is believed, but not confirmed, that Miller has died in the blaze.

I move from the left lane to the right lane and pull to the side of the road. I listen to an obituary-flavored run down on the highlights of my adult life.

Local evangelist Miller, I learn, was the guiding force behind the Joy Miller Ministries, and once had a popular show on cable television, which in its heyday was widely watched over a region of thirteen states. Miller made headlines seven years ago when her son, Joey Miller, her only child, was shot and killed by his estranged wife Caroline, who was five months pregnant at the time. Miller's life had been struck by tragedy seven years before with the death of her husband, Carl, an apparent suicide. Miller testified at the trial of her daughter-in-law, and was considered the pivotal factor in the jury's verdict of not guilty. Immediately afterwards Miller suffered a breakdown, and never appeared in public again.

In other news, the price of oil was going up.

TWENTY-ONE

I smell it before I see it, smoke clouding the air. I brake for the stop sign that is less than a mile from my house. The dusky light of fall is just giving way to a night of darkness and no moon. I turn left from Wilson Downing Road, and left again, to the street where I live.

I have been afraid of fire since the seventies when the Beverly Hills Supper Club burned. I remember photos of bodies on the lawn, newspaper reports of refrigerated grocery trucks used as temporary morgues. The death toll reached one hundred and sixty-five, setting off a domino of lawsuits.

Ruby sits quietly, watching out the back window, but Leo paces from side to side and slams into the partition between the cargo hold and back seats no matter how gently I brake. He lets out a low grumbly growl when he sees the men who mill purposefully around the fire engine and police cruiser in front of what's left of our house.

I park in the street near my favorite neighbor. Leo is barking and Ruby joins him. The police officer is waving a hand at me and yelling but I can't hear a word he says. There is a fire engine in my driveway, and I look, but Marsha's car is not on the street. I feel nearly weightless. Relief. I have been reported dead, but not because Marsha was in the house.

I leave the back windows down two inches, lock the dogs in the car and step out. The police officer who has been shouting at me looks angry.

'Ma'am, unless you have business in this area, we're asking everyone—'

'This is *my* house. *Was* my house.' I lean against the hood of the car and it radiates heat – I've driven over seven hundred miles. I try to take it all in.

My house smokes like a cigarette butt that won't go out, a blackened, gutted shell. Part of the roof is intact, and so are over half the outside walls. Everything is badly scorched, and I can see the glow of burning embers and coals.

'Your name, please, ma'am.' The police officer is young. He has short dark hair, brown, hungry-looking eyes, a look of intelligence in his face.

'Joy Miller. They reported me dead on the radio just a few minutes ago.'

He nods at me. 'Yes, ma'am. Can I see your driver's license, some form of ID?'

My purse is locked in the Jeep with the dogs. It is embarrassing how much trouble I have trying to get the purse out, while leaving the dogs inside. The policeman watches Leo warily, and shoves the door shut quickly when my purse and I are free.

He takes a quick look at my license, gives me a sad smile. 'Glad you're OK, Mrs Miller. And sorry about your house. You got insurance?'

'Yes.'

'That's good.' He tucks my license into his clipboard. 'I better call this in.'

I look at the house again over my shoulder. It is hard to believe, though I can see it and smell it, and I heard it on the news.

Leo is barking again, but I don't hear Ruby. I tell Leo to hush. I trip over the broken concrete of the curb and stumble on to the lawn, which is soggy with run-off from the hoses. The curb was intact when I left for Arkansas. Crushed, no doubt, by one of the fire trucks, maybe the one that left deep ruts in the grass.

What smoke and flames do not destroy, water and axes will. I hear someone call out as I head for my sagging, splintered front door.

They have rigged up high power emergency lights, and portions of the interior are illuminated, as alien now as another planet. My living room has morphed into a blackened garbage dump and vapor rises like a haunting.

A hand on my arm stops me before I go through the door.

'Ma'am? You can't go in there—'

'I'm Joy Miller, and this is my house.'

'Yes ma'am.' The firefighter is grimy with soot and sweat. Age and physique are swallowed by the androgyny of the gear, the helmet, the dirt.

Another man approaches – he wears a uniform and carries a radio, but he's not weighed down by the tools. He is talking low into a radio and has the air of the man in charge.

He stops in his tracks and his smile is radiant with relief. '*Joy?*'

I know him. But my mind is not working properly.

'Joy, it's me. Hal Reinhardt.'

'Hal. Of course, I'm sorry, I'm just so – I didn't recognize you without your dog.'

'Cindy Lou? She's in the truck. You know I never go anywhere without her.'

I smile and tear up. Something about a friendly face at a time like this.

Hal Reinhardt is a captain in the fire department, but he also trains dogs for K-9 and search and rescue – he is the one who gave me Leo. My ministry has donated to his non profit for years.

He takes my elbow gently and turns me away. 'Is that Leo I hear barking in your Jeep?'

'Yes, that's Leo.'

'So you're both safe.' He puts an arm around my shoulders. 'I'm so glad. Even though you and I both know that Leo is a thoroughly bad animal.'

'He's not and you know it. And you can't have him back.' I look back at the house. 'I need to go in, just for a minute, I have to—'

'No, no, Joy, you can't. It's not safe in there, honey.' He looks over his shoulder, craning his neck. 'Looks to me like that second floor could go any minute, and I don't want you or my crew getting hurt.'

I am now officially under the wing of Captain Hal Reinhardt. He is solidly built, with a deeply scarred right cheek, and though he is fit he carries enough excess weight to make him cuddly. His calm self assurance is soothing. He settles me high up in the front seat of the fire engine, a blanket around my shoulders, hot coffee in hand. His dog, Cindy Lou, puts her head in my lap. She is an odd-looking dog – part blue heeler, part corgi, the color of buckskin. A departure from the German shepherds and Labs Hal usually trains.

I stroke Cindy Lou's scoop ears and tell Reinhardt my story – how I've just come home after two days out of town. How I heard the news on the radio, the announcer broadcasting my demise.

'Joy, was there anyone *in* your house when you left? Does someone live with you? Did you have someone house sitting, or picking up your mail, or staying there for a visit?'

'It's just me and Leo.' It occurs to me that there is a reason for these questions. 'Did you find – was there somebody in the house?'

My hands start shaking and I drop my cup of coffee. The Styrofoam splits, the plastic lid falls off. Brown liquid splashes the toe of Reinhardt's boots and the cuff of his soot-stained trousers.

Reinhardt looks over his shoulder. The police officer is

headed our way, holding my license out like it is radioactive. Reinhardt puts himself between us. 'Give us a minute, will you please, Jordy?'

Reinhardt puts a hand on my shoulder. 'We did pull someone out. A woman – we assumed it was you. She was packed into the ambulance before I got a look so—'

'*That's why* – how bad was she hurt? She wasn't dead?'

'She was alive when we got her out, but she was in pretty bad shape. We radioed the hospital a few minutes ago about the mistaken ID. The word is they've moved her from the ER into ICU. Which means they've got her stabilized, so that's something. Do you have any idea who the woman might be?'

'My first guess would be my assistant, Marsha Dewberry, except she wasn't supposed to be working.' I knew better than to say she was fired. 'And I don't see her car. How did it start? Was it wiring or – I don't smoke, and I know I didn't leave the oven on. I don't even own an iron. On the radio, they said something about arson.'

Reinhardt nods his head. 'It's not official, understand, until we file the reports and confirm the details, but it burned hot and fast, and there were obvious signs of accelerant. I had Cindy Lou out earlier and she picked up the scent.'

'Accelerant?'

'Something to make the fire burn. Something like gasoline.'

'Someone did this.' I shiver, and Reinhardt pulls the blanket up around my shoulders.

'What kind of car does your assistant drive?'

'Dark grey. A Ford Taurus.'

Reinhardt touches my forearm. 'I had to send the crew in through the attic, right over the garage – it was the safest approach. We had to tow a car out of the driveway. It was blocking the trucks and equipment.'

'Was it a grey Taurus?'

He nods.

'Oh, God.' I take a breath. 'It's got to be Marsha then. It was her in the house. Look, I have to go now. Go to the hospital, go call the family.' I am so high up in the truck I have to turn around backward to climb back down.

Reinhardt takes my waist as I make the leap from the bottom step. He leans close and lowers his voice. 'Joy, listen to me. There were two FBI agents here earlier. A man and a woman, and they had a lot of questions. They seemed to know you, from the things they said.'

'They know me.'

'Look, if—'

The grind of the police officer's shoes on grit and loose gravel interrupts whatever Reinhardt was going to say.

'Mrs Miller?' the officer says. 'I just got off the phone with Special Agent Russell Woods of the FBI. He said you would know who he is?'

'I know.'

'He asked me to drive you down to his office, so they can get this identity thing sorted. He wants me to take you right now.'

Reinhardt frowns. 'The identity is already sorted. Can't this wait till tomorrow?'

'It's OK, Hal,' I say thickly. 'Give me a minute to see if my neighbor will look after the dogs. I'll follow you in my—'

'I'll take the dogs,' Hal says. 'Jordy, you drive her down there. Joy, you don't need to be driving right now.'

'But—'

'It's OK,' Reinhardt says. He squeezes my hand. Sees me to the patrol car and tucks me into the passenger's seat up front. I am relieved not to be riding in the back, like a prisoner.

I know that Jordy talked to me on the way down. Told me how sorry he was about my house. I didn't answer. My mind was full of images, the smell of gasoline, a vision of Marsha surrounded by fire. And the realization that I had been punished, just like the Dark Man promised. He warned me not to go to the FBI.

TWENTY-TWO

Agent Russell Woods motions me through the doorway. I am swamped by a wave of dread, finding myself, once again, in an interrogation room with the FBI.

It's me and Woods, one on one. He doesn't bother to read me my rights and I'm not asking for a lawyer. He motions me to a chair but I don't sit down.

'No good deed goes unpunished, does it, Mr Woods? He warned me. He told me not to bring you guys in. Now he's mad as hell, he's burned down my house, and God only knows what's happening to Caroline and Andee. And you still don't know anything, do you? Who he is? Where he is?'

'I was hoping maybe you could tell me.' Woods straddles a chair and rubs his thumbs together – one of his many odd habits.

'What is *that* supposed to mean?'

'It means that it seems awfully convenient that you are out of range and on the road when your house gets burned down.'

Now I do sit down. I look down at the table. 'I am dealing with lunatics. You people are just as crazy as the kidnapper.'

Woods opens a file and I slap it shut.

'And you *know* where I was. I was in Arkansas cooperating with your office. I was on the computer with Andee and Caroline, while your CATs were trying to find out where they're being held. Are you people getting *anywhere*? Do you have *anything*?'

Woods hesitates. 'So far we've tracked it to a bounce in Nicaragua. Obviously, we're going from there.'

Every bit of energy and hope drains out of me. 'So that's it, then? The best you can do?'

'The kidnapper did a good job of covering his tracks, but we're on it and we *will* find them, it'll just take a little more time.'

'And meanwhile, your experts have tripped all over his software alarms. Well, he warned me. I can only hope that burning down my house satisfies him so he doesn't kill Caro and Andee in revenge.'

'That's your theory? The kidnapper burned down your house to punish you for bringing in the FBI?'

I settle back in the chair. 'You read the note. Don't bring in the FBI or there will be repercussions. You have a better theory?'

'I'm just wondering here, you know? Why it is that *Marsha* gets victimized in *your* house, right after you supposedly find out she had an affair, back in the day, with your husband?'

'Oh, please. That was years ago. And I already knew he was having an affair, I just didn't know who with.'

'You seemed pretty upset when we confronted you with it the other day.'

'My granddaughter has been kidnapped. How do you expect me to react? You are a complete moron. I have bent over backward to work with you, and to cooperate with that idiot Harris in Arkansas, and my house gets burned down in the process? And there you sit, like a lump on a log, still making accusations?'

'I think it's a leap, that this guy burns down your house twelve hours after you come to us. We were very careful to cover our tracks.'

'So, what, you're telling me it's unrelated? Because I think it's a leap to think he didn't. And the smoke coming out of my house says to me you guys *didn't* cover your tracks. Face it, your computer people klutzed it up, and the kidnapper knows you've tracked his location. He may move the girls by the time you figure it out, and then we'll have a big fat nothing. No location, and a totally pissed off sociopath. Stop rubbing your thumbs.'

It was out of my mouth before I knew I was going to say it. Woods sighed and laid his hands flat on the table.

'We *will* get that address, have a little faith. In the meantime, let's clear the air. Take a lie detector test. Then we won't have to keep having these painful conversations.'

'That's what this is about? You bring me in here right out

of the damn fire truck to pressure me? Because I'm vulnerable?'

'Some of the people on the team think there's a connection between you and this kidnapper. They think you're withholding critical information, which, by the way, is a Class D Felony offense. Now if that's *not* the case, then let me rule it out. Of course, if there *is* some connection, then by all means *don't* take it.'

I stand up and speak softly and slowly. 'I have been up since four a.m. this morning. I have driven twelve hours straight. I have heard my own death announced on the radio and I've come home to find my house burned down. I've lost everything that I own. My cousin Marsha is in the hospital, and instead of going there, which is where I need to be, I came straight here under police escort because you supposedly need my help.' I take a breath. 'And what I get from you is harassment, insults and *ludicrous* accusations. Now, Agent Russell Woods, you will listen to me.'

I open my wallet and take out four snapshots of Andee. I lay them across the table.

'See this picture, right here? It was taken in the pool behind the house in Arkansas. Look, isn't Andee cute? I said *look* at it. She's wearing a little shark hat that makes it look like there's a fin in the pool. Amazing, isn't it, the stuff they make for kids these days? When Andee was three years old, and one night I was cooking dinner, she came in the kitchen and hugged my leg and said "I smell hungry". That's funny, don't you think? Look at this one, it's my favorite, this is Andee with her pet chicken. She was four then. That's the kind of mother Caroline is, the kind who lets her little girl have her own pet chicken. It belonged to a friend of theirs who had a farm and it was little and being picked on, so Andee took it home and took care of it – it lived three years. They buried it under the biggest pine tree in their backyard.'

I push another picture across the table. 'Look at this one. This is Andee in my kitchen with her dog Ruby who, as you can see, is wearing a t-shirt. Andee loves to play dress up and Ruby just goes along.'

Woods holds up a hand. 'You don't need to do this.'

'Why not, Agent Woods? You show *me* pictures. You show me pictures to evoke emotions and confessions, so I'll do the same for you. I want to evoke you to stop wasting your time on me and find my granddaughter. She's a real little girl, different from every other little girl in the world. So, here are some things you might like to know. Andee won't eat cheese or yogurt. She's very quiet around people she doesn't know. She has chapped lips a lot – if you look hard here in this last school picture you can see a ring of pink around her mouth. She sleeps on top of her blanket and sheets, but under the bedspread. She used to color everything pink and yellow, even though I bought her the biggest box of crayons they make. When she was in first grade she had trouble learning how to skip, and she still doesn't know how to whistle, but she works on it all the time. When she stays with me, I cook her a Moon Over Miami for breakfast. Do you even know what that is?'

'You take a piece of bread, tear a hole out of the middle, put it in a frying pan with melted butter and put the egg in the hole.'

'You amaze me, Agent Woods. Is it possible you might be *human*?'

'Look—'

'Andee's afraid of basements. She's afraid of worms. She's afraid to sleep without a nightlight. Wherever she is now – what if she doesn't have a nightlight? It's been four days. What do your statistics tell you about her odds after four days? My only child is dead, and Andee is all that I have left of him. She is the only connection I've got, the only person who makes the pain go away. You *find* her and you leave *me* alone.' I take a step backward, pull my purse strap over my shoulder. 'I'm leaving now to see my cousin Marsha in the hospital.'

'We're not done here.'

But we are done. I hear him in the hallway, Hal Reinhardt, asking for me. I hear objections and Hal apologizing and all kinds of noise and the door to the room bursts open. Leo comes running in, followed by Cindy Lou, Ruby and a sheepish-looking Hal Reinhardt. I bury my head in Leo's neck and he pants and licks me and knocks over the trash can with the wag of his tail.

'I'm so sorry,' Hal says to Woods, then looks over at me. 'The hospital is trying to reach you. Marsha is conscious and she's been asking for you.'

Woods waves a hand at us. '*Go*. And take those dogs.'

'It's OK, sir,' Hal says. 'They're specially trained service dogs.'

Ruby puts her paws up on the table and noses an old cup of coffee. The Styrofoam cup tips and spills. She takes a tentative lick, loses interest and heads my way.

'Sorry about that,' Hal says.

Woods slumps in his chair, shrugs. 'It's bad coffee. I don't drink it myself.'

TWENTY-THREE

The hospital ICU has its own waiting room, cozier than the one off the main lobby downstairs. The floor has aqua carpet. There are six recliners, two couches and eight chairs. Also two televisions, a coffee pot and a phone with an outside line. A third of the chairs and couches are full and I see Marsha's parents, Aunt Cee and Uncle Don. Marsha's Aunt Chloris is probably on her way in from Detroit.

I am plotting, planning, coping. Marsha will take whatever time off she needs to heal, and once she is well I will give her the job back if she wants it. She's going to need careful nursing once the worst is over, and my mind jumps between home care nurses, skin grafts and rehabilitation. Our insurance coverage at Miller Ministries is no better than average, but the board has been known to make special dispensations for times like these. If I have to, I'll put her down as one of our charities, and funnel a reasonable portion of funds her way. I have the final say, though I rarely exercise it.

'Joy?' Aunt Cee has spotted me from one of the recliners in the waiting room. A stranger would see an aging woman, grossly overweight, with heavy glasses and coarse red hair trimmed unattractively close to her head. I see the woman who came to my dorm room the night my parents died. In my mind's eye I hold the image of the stunning beauty with the radiant smile who graduated with a degree in elementary education from EKU.

I go straight to her and she stands up and gives me a hug. She is crying and so am I.

Uncle Don nods at me and pats Cee's back. Over and over. Pat pat pat. He always reminds me fondly of a giant penguin, the way he hunches over us, the way he moves. His face sags like the jowls of a bloodhound. His signature eyebrows are thinning, and his hair is a mix of brown and grey.

Cee holds a crumpled tissue in her fist. 'You need to go in there, honey. She's been asking for you.'

I try not to think about my last conversation with Marsha. I wonder if Cee knows I fired her daughter the last time we talked.

Uncle Don looks at Hal. 'Are you one of the firemen who pulled my daughter out?'

'Hal Reinhardt, sir.' He shakes hands with my uncle. 'Why don't you head on in, Joy? I'll sit with your aunt and uncle and answer any questions they might have. I'll be here to drive you home.'

'Oh, honey.' Aunt Cee breaks into ready tears. 'I just can't take it in. Your house burning down like that. But you come and stay with us. We're your family. We're your home.'

'I'll keep it in mind, Aunt Cee, thank you.'

'Why don't I make a fresh pot of coffee?' Hal says.

'Sounds like a fine idea.' Uncle Don is still patting my aunt's back.

I push through the swing doors that lead into ICU, ignoring the posted set of rules and warnings. A muscular man in scrubs sits behind a horseshoe desk making notations in a stack of charts, and he frowns and flushes red when he sees me.

'Excuse me, but you—'

'I know. I'm sorry. My name is Joy Miller, and I'm here for Marsha Dewberry, the burn victim brought in late this afternoon.'

'*Joy Miller?* Good. She's been asking for you. We were afraid you weren't going to make it in.'

I close my eyes, thinking of the time I have wasted with the FBI.

'Is this her?'

The voice is female and I see the nurse nodding at someone behind me. I turn to see a trim woman, looking fresh and focused in her scrubs.

'Joy Miller?'

'That's right.'

'I'm Dr Samuels, Marsha's physician. I thought I was *your* physician. When they brought her in, they identified her as you.'

Dr Samuels has a narrow, cat-like face, and she wears black-framed glasses with small, rectangular lenses, like the reading glasses you buy at the drugstore. A surgical mask hangs by a string around her neck. For all that it is three a.m. in the rest of the city, it might as well be high noon, here in ICU.

'Yes, I heard. How's Marsha doing?'

'Well enough that she's been asking for you since we got her stable,' Dr Samuels says.

She gives my shoulder a quick squeeze. Her energy is reassuring. I feel like a zombie beside her.

'As to how she is?' Dr Samuels' tone is low and she looks me straight in the eye. 'We're making her as comfortable as we can.'

I have seen this before, while counseling families in the small private niches a hospital offers when the people you love face death. Some patients survive against the tide, others go under the smallest wave, but there's no doubt that Dr Samuels is hanging the crape.

'Her burns are severe, third and fourth degree, which means careful management and a long recovery period on down the road. The immediate concern is lung trauma, inhalation injuries. It appears that only one lung sustained significant trauma—'

'That's good, anyway.'

'Yes and no. Hyperemia is mediated by a neural

inflammatory response. Which means that even though the other lung wasn't initially affected, there's a strong chance we'll see edema and tissue damage there too. We're treating the airways aggressively. If we're lucky we can head off complications in the gas exchange.'

I am trying to follow all of this and look intelligent but all I understand is that Marsha is in trouble.

'She has second degree burns to the chest wall, which is a problem with the inhalation injuries. We're monitoring respiratory deterioration – her breathing is labored, you'll see that when you go in. We may have to put her on a ventilator, but that can complicate things, so we'll avoid it if we can. So far we don't think we'll have to get a surgeon in for an escharotomy, which is surgery to the chest to mitigate the tightness and pressure. At this point, she's hit the peak of edema formation, and I'm optimistic we won't have to go there. If we do, then we'll definitely have to ventilate.'

She raises an eyebrow at me and I wonder if she knows how little I understand. 'So. Go in. Be calm. Don't stay more than five or six minutes. And you're going to need to wear a mask and gown. Janet?'

A woman in blue scrubs stops in her tracks. 'Yes, doctor?'

'Help Mrs Miller get suited up. She's here for the patient in three.'

Janet, clearly on her way to do something else, takes us all in and regroups. She is a large woman, big-boned and heavy, with dark roots and a blond ponytail. I follow Janet to an anteroom off a supply area, and she guides me into a mask, a gown and antiseptic booties that go right over my shoes. Janet is talkative and brisk, and I don't register a word that she says.

Three is one of eight cubicles arranged like spokes on a wheel. I see machines, monitors, a complex bed and Special Agent Mavis Jones, masked and gowned, leaning over a horrifically bandaged patient who I can only assume is my cousin Marsha. The name over her bed says MILLER, JOY.

Janet looks at Mavis Jones in a way that is almost predatory. 'You have been told to leave twice already. If you don't go *right now*, I'm calling security.'

Jones gives Nurse Janet a long look, and I wonder if she is going to point out the irony of calling a security guard to deal with an agent of the FBI. Instead, she puts a hand up like she is stopping traffic, and slips a small tape recorder into the pocket of her trousers.

Janet seems to have a multitude of personalities and the tough woman disappears the minute Agent Jones leaves the room.

'Hello, Miss Marsha. Just checking your morphine drip.' Janet is upbeat and friendly. She bends over a beeping blue machine on a pole near the bed, and checks a tube in Marsha's arm. 'Are you in any pain?'

The bundle on the bed moves a fraction of an inch.

'That's good, sweetie. You don't worry about a thing, OK, Miss Marsha? Janet's going to keep you happy. Now, Marsha? Honey? I got that Joy you were talking about here to see you. She's standing at the foot of the bed. No, no, you stay still. Come on over, Joy. Come say hi.' Janet pulls a chair in close.

There is a sudden swoosh of sensation in my ears, as if the room is a vacuum – no noise, no air pressure, just a deep and abiding silence. One half of Marsha's face is perfect, the other half a nightmare of flesh that looks like scorched, raw meat. She must have been on her side when they found her, the good half of her face resting on the floor. There is a wad of heavy bandaging over what used to be an ear. The hair that survived is still curly. The part of her neck that is exposed makes her look as if she has been flayed alive, and all else is a bundle of gauze, bandages, a mummy-wrap from hell.

My last conversation with Marsha rings in my ears, and a sob rises in my chest.

'What took you so long?' Her voice is raspy. 'Shouldn't keep hurt people waiting.'

She makes little gasping noises every few words, but what she says is pure Marsha, and my sob turns into a choked laugh.

'The FBI had me pinned down in their interrogation room. I only just now got free.' I pause for a moment, thinking how to word things. 'You have nothing to be afraid of, you know that, don't you?'

'Joy, sweetie.' A moment to breathe. 'Don't have to go through that evangelist thing.'

'I saw your mom and dad, out in the waiting room.'

'Yeah. They. Were just here.' Marsha moves a bandaged hand in my direction. 'I need to know. Forgive me, Joy?' Her voice arcs higher, and I scoot my chair close. 'Know you understand. I'm Carl victim too.'

'An ass like Carl can't come between the likes of you and me. We're family, right? Like you told me.'

'Family.' She sighs and closes that one healthy eye, and a tear leaks under the lid.

'Marsha, I'm so sorry about all this. It should have been me, not you. But what were you doing there? How did it even happen?'

The good eye opens, but she seems to be focused on something across the room.

'Called board.'

'The board?'

'Ministries. Called Brice, other day. For your lawyer. Smitty thinks going to arrest.'

She fades. My stomach drops.

'Board going pay legal fees.' Marsha moves restlessly. 'Brice says have meet to make official, but don't worry, cause be OK.' She breathes, a frantic sucking noise.

'Listen,' she says suddenly. 'To me.'

'I'm listening.'

'Saw him. The one who did. Didn't expect me. Hit me, tie me up.'

'Marsha—'

'*Listen.* Thought unconscious. Had eyes closed, playing possum. He talking cell phone. Somebody . . . what to do. With me. He said I see him, so I had to go.'

'What did he look like, can you remember?'

'Mean. Grease black hair. Tall.' She pauses. 'That woman, FBI woman.'

'Special Agent Jones?'

'Showed me his picture. FBI knows who he is.'

'*They know?* Then—'

'*Listen.* On phone. Him talking, say "take them food". *Them.* Got to be Andee and Caroline. Drive from house, to there, is hour and half. Heard him say it. One hour and half. Told FBI woman. Thought she understand prove you innocent. *Proves* it.' Marsha turns slightly on the bed. 'But didn't.'

'Didn't what, Marsha?'

'She ask if he talking to man or woman. When on phone. She say voices change when you talk to opposite sex. *Warn you.* She thinks he talking . . . talking you.'

'Ah, hell.' I close my eyes for a moment. 'Good work, Marsha. You may have saved my neck.'

She makes a grimace that I take as a smile. 'Not fired?'

'I missed you the second you were out the door, just like you told me I would.'

There is a feeling in the room, very strong, something I have felt many times before – it is energy and a sort of glow and shift in air pressure.

Marsha, a woman distracted, still trains that good eye back on me. 'Told you so.'

She drifts with the morphine. I wait until she seems peaceful, then ease quietly out the door.

TWENTY-FOUR

Hal walks the dogs in the hospital parking lot. I sit in a wood and vinyl chair that is an offensive shade of aqua, making arrangements for the ministry to cover Marsha's medical bills. Hal is pacing the waiting room outside the ER when I'm done. He puts a hand on the small of my back to direct me to a dark blue Toyota 4Runner.

He opens the door for me and points a finger when Leo makes a move to bound up from the cargo area in the back section. Leo obeys immediately.

'Someday I'm going to have to learn to do that.'

He smiles at me. 'You will. He's already better than when I left him with you. He's making progress.'

I lean back into the seat and close my eyes.

'Hungry?' he asks.

'I'm too tired to eat.'

'You need food.' Hal checks his watch. 'Let's try Ramsey's. We should just make it.'

The restaurant is right around the corner at Tates Creek Center, and it is empty enough that we're seated immediately. There are a few late diners finishing up and every other bar stool is filled. We take a seat in the back, at a wood table spattered with paint, surrounded by four mismatched chairs. Black and white photos of city scenes from the past are hung in random places on the wall. I order the meat and three – pot roast, creamed corn, fried green tomatoes and mashed potatoes. Hal has pork chops. I have a wheat beer and he has a Guinness, and Hal asks for an appetizer of fried banana peppers.

'I love fried banana peppers.' I am feeling starved.

The beers come fast and they come cold, and I take a long sip and melt into my chair.

Hal grins at me. 'Better get some food into you, while you can still hold your head up.'

My cheeks are pink. 'One sip of beer shouldn't hit me that hard.'

'It's relief, Joy. Reaction. Don't fight it, I'll make sure you and the dogs get home safe.'

'Yeah, but we still have to pick up my car—'

'I took care of that already. Your best place to stay with Leo and Ruby is the Residence Inn. I hope you don't mind, but I had a couple of the guys drop your Jeep off there. I've set up reservations for the next three nights with Red Cross vouchers. You need Leo with you right now. He'll keep you safe.'

I take a deep breath and let it out slowly. 'I don't even know how to thank you, Hal.'

He grins at me. 'You know what they say about you, the board and all?'

'That I need a keeper?'

I take another long sip of beer. It is cold and sweet, and

bites just a little. The waitress arrives with banana peppers draped in batter, and cocktail sauce on the side.

'Dig in,' Hal says.

I chew slowly. Close my eyes. It's the little things that make you happy, I think.

'Close calls and catastrophe,' Hal says. He raises his glass.

'To close calls and catastrophe,' I echo.

When the food arrives, Hal orders two more beers.

'I won't be able to hold my head up,' I warn him.

'I'll factor it in.'

Hal manages pie, but even though they have my favorite, which is butterscotch, I can't do dessert. And once in the car I slide sideways. Hal has to wake me when we get to the hotel.

I know that I should straighten up and deal with things, but I am floating on beer and fatigue. Somehow I get checked in, and I'm aware that all the studio rooms are full and Hal and the desk clerk are arranging an upgrade. The hallways are a blur, though I am aware of Hal's hand on my elbow, and the dogs milling excitedly in the hall.

I find myself sitting on a couch in a two bedroom suite, with the bags I packed for Arkansas lined neatly at the edge of the kitchen.

'I hate to leave you,' Hal says. 'You going to be OK?'

He is standing over me and I reach up and touch his face.

'Such a nice chin,' I say.

'One too many beers, I think.' But he leans down and kisses me. A soft sweet pressure, over very quickly. 'I'm going now. The room key is on the kitchen table.'

I smile at him. Hiccup once or twice. He shakes his head, laughs a little, and then he's gone.

I am deeply asleep on the hotel-ugly couch several hours later when the call comes in. Marsha has succumbed to an infection that flared into virulent sepsis. Her kidneys tried and failed. The rest of her organs followed like a trail of dominos, shutting down one by one.

Marsha has given up the fight.

TWENTY-FIVE

The Residence Inn is dog friendly. I have a magnetic placard that says PETS INSIDE which goes outside my door. It is people friendly too. There is breakfast every morning, happy hour in the afternoon. Washers and dryers are available and, most amazing, there are staff members who will take the dogs for short walks on request. If I fill out the shopping list in the kitchen, groceries will be magically delivered. Maid service is a daily possibility.

I take a hot shower to wash the smell of smoke from my hair, and the dogs curl up in the bedroom where I have put my things. Neither of them shows any interest in staking out territory in the other bedroom across the living room. The three of us are now a pack, and they are happiest staying close. Ruby stretches out full length on the floor by the bed and Leo sleeps lightly, ever on guard, between me, Ruby and the door.

There are no relatives I need to call with the joyful news that I am still alive, and I don't think my insurance agent was all that glad to hear from me. He is confident that my homeowner's company will swiftly pay the claim, as soon as it is officially established that I had nothing to do with the act of arson that started the fire.

I make a quick foray down the road for dog food and a few treats and toys. Ruby and Leo are mulling their choices: a rope attached to a Frisbee, a stuffed quail, three brown tennis balls that smell like peanut butter and two squeaky toys – a stuffed hedgehog and a green plastic porcupine. Ruby settles with the quail, squeaking it gently and methodically in her jaws. Leo hides a rawhide bone behind the couch, and fits one tennis ball and the squeaky porcupine in his mouth. He deposits them hopefully in my lap.

The phone rings. Nobody knows I'm here but Aunt Cee. She will be calling to make plans about Marsha, funeral arrangements and such.

'Joy? Brice Barksdale. I just got off the phone with Cee.'

Brice and Abby Barksdale are on the Joy Miller Ministries' Board. Brice is seventy years old. He and Abby have retired from building their empire of automotive supply stores, and both have been with me from the beginning.

'We saw the fire report on the news last night. Abby called Cee to find out if she knew where you were. They said on the morning show you weren't dead after all.'

Leo starts squeaking his porcupine.

'You got the news about Marsha, I guess?'

'Cee let us know. Terrible thing,' Brice says.

Abby chimes in from another extension. 'But we're holding up, hon. We're holding up. And thinking about you.'

'I can't begin to understand this business with the FBI,' Brice says. 'Now the sooner they stop bothering you, the better off you'll be. We've faxed an authorization to Mr Madison regarding any legal fees. I just want to know if he's getting anywhere at all, or if you want me to make some calls. You've done a lot for this community, Joy. Time people showed you some appreciation.'

I don't hesitate to take advantage. 'I'm not happy with the way Agents Woods and Jones are running their investigation. They're making a mess and they're spending too much time coming after me. If there's anything you can do to help, please do it.'

'I'm on it,' Brice says.

'Brice, honey, you need to call Kent,' Abby says. I wonder who Kent is. 'And Joy, Cee is worrying about Marsha's funeral. She wants you to do it, of course. If you feel like you can.'

'Of course I'll do it.'

Brice clears his throat. 'Now, look here, honey. We all know you're strong, but that doesn't stop us from being worried about you.'

No doubt they are remembering the aftermath of Caroline's trial. The board had to cancel the television show and a year of speaking engagements. It took another year before they finally gave up and accepted that I was not going back. No cable show, no revivals, no counseling, preaching or newsletters. As expected, the donations dwindled and dipped, but a website and mailing updates from the Board of Directors encouraged the flow, and we've had a slow but steady stream ever since.

Brice clears his throat. 'I've got a little problem come up, and I need you to tell me what you want me to do.'

I picture him in the office of their perfect monster house – the leather, the giant desk, the custom made valances and blinds.

Leo noses the hedgehog in my lap, hinting. It occurs to me it might have been a mistake to give the dogs all the toys at once.

Brice clears his throat yet again. 'I got a call from those people doing the Sanctuary Event, where you were going to give a talk over at Spindletop?'

Marsha had reminded me just last week. I put a hand to my forehead and groan. 'I'm sorry, Brice, I forgot all about it. When was it? Have I missed it already?' I take the porcupine away from Leo.

'It's tomorrow evening at six o'clock. Now, I'll cancel it, if you want. But the thing is, the Sanctuary people have been putting this event together for over a year, and it's your name that's been filling the seats. They sent us a pretty big check – more than triple the usual speaking fee.'

'Brice, I think you're going to have to cancel. I've got so much on me right now, I don't think I can pull this off.'

'If that's what you want, Joy, it's no problem. But it's kind of complicated, because when they heard it on the radio news report that you had died in the fire, they decided to turn it into a tribute instead of getting a replacement guest speaker. But now, we can refund their money if you don't want to do this. No one will blame you if you don't go.'

Am I really going to have to do this, I think? I'm tired. I'm worried. I don't care about this stuff.

'It's not just the money, Joy,' Brice says.

'It's public opinion,' Abby adds. 'Brice can pull his strings, but the best thing all around will be for you to go and just get people all stirred up and on your side. That'll get the donations pouring back in. And the FBI will look really bad if they come and arrest you after your house burned down and everybody thought you were dead.'

I think back to my dinner with Hal. Two beers, falling asleep in his car. Oasis.

'I better do it,' I tell Brice. 'But call them for me, will you, and check the arrangements? Make sure they'll be sending a car out and tell them to pick me up here at my hotel, since obviously they can't pick me up at the house.'

It takes a while to get off the phone. Brice and Abby have questions about Andee and Caroline. I have to turn down an offer of hospitality, but my mind is wandering. I am happy that I took my favorite jeans with me to Arkansas, but they aren't going to fly at Spindletop. I'm going to have to shop.

TWENTY-SIX

The knock on the door of my hotel room is soft and barely registers at the fringe of my sleeping subconscious. I have dozed off on the couch, dogs piled around my feet. Leo is the first to react, and he comes awake with a startled yelp that morphs into his grumbly growl. The knock comes again, and Leo stays one step ahead of me on the way to the door. Ruby follows, but veers into the kitchen toward her water bowl. I remember that I need to give her the pills.

I shove my hair out of my eyes and look through the peephole. I have no idea who the man is, but he knocks again, and though my keyhole view is limited I don't see anything that makes me nervous. I leave the chain lock on and open the door a couple of inches – just enough for Leo to get his nose in the crack.

'Good morning. I'm sorry to disturb you, but I'm looking for Joy Miller.'

The man is at least six feet tall and seriously overweight. His hair is a dark reddish blond, wavy, and he has large jowls, a thick neck and rather riveting blue eyes. There is a box tucked under his left arm, and he is holding a white bag.

'Who are you?'

He shakes his head and gives me a sideways smile. 'Sorry. My name is Goodwin, Dr Johnny Goodwin. I'm a forensic consultant to the FBI.' He reaches into his back pocket and pulls out a leather flip case. 'Sorry, I don't do this sort of thing very often. I spend most of my time tied to a desk.'

He passes the identification through the crack in the door, though it is awkward, his hands are full. The picture is recent, the print a little small, but it tells me that this man is Dr Jonathan Goodwin, a resident of Chicago, Illinois, and Special Forensic Consultant to the Federal Bureau of Investigation.

'I drove down late last night, after Russ called and told me about your house getting torched.'

'Getting torched' sounds odd when it's not on television. I hand the ID back through the door. 'Agent Woods hasn't mentioned you.'

'By all means, give him a call. And look, if you want me to come back later, that's fine. I know you must be over-whelmed, and I don't want to intrude. But it would be helpful if you and I could have a conversation as soon as you feel up to it.'

His voice is attractive and I find it oddly comforting. There is something understanding about it. Something kind.

'I can only imagine how you must feel,' he is saying. 'You're probably just blown away and numb.'

'Is that an official state of mind? Blown away?'

'You'll find it on page two hundred and eighty-seven of the *Diagnostic and Statistical Manual of Mental States* – third edition of the *DSM According to Goodwin*.'

I am smiling, which surprises me. 'Come in, Dr Goodwin.'

I have to close the door before I can unlatch it, which feels awkward, particularly as it takes me a little while to fumble my way through the locks. Jonathan Goodwin, Special Forensic Consultant to the FBI, seems at ease and unperturbed when I finally get the door open to let him inside.

Goodwin watches to see that I lock the door behind him. This is one person who understands the danger of the Dark Man.

'I just heard about your cousin Marsha. I'm so sorry.' He

heads straight to the little kitchen and puts a briefcase, a box of doughnuts and the paper bag down on the little table. 'I know it must seem like the world is falling down around your ears right now, Mrs Miller. I know you probably don't feel like talking to me. But I also know you want to bring your girls home. Having this talk may help.' He unpacks two cups of coffee and two bottles of orange juice from the bag. He is a graceful man, with the physical confidence of someone who is automatically good at sports.

'Behind this curtain we have chocolate-glazed doughnuts, still hot, from Krispy Kreme.' He raises an eyebrow and nods his head toward my dog. 'Uh oh.'

I turn and see that Leo has had an accident on the kitchen floor.

'*Hey.*'

Leo hangs his head and backs away, and I shoo Ruby off when she decides to have a sniff. I grab paper towels and begin to clean up the spatters of dark yellow.

'Sorry,' I say to Goodwin. 'It's been a weird few days.' I throw the first batch of soiled paper towels away and gather up another handful. From the corner of my eye I see Ruby wander into my bedroom and heave herself with great effort into the middle of the bed. She groans and stretches out. It's embarrassing how, the minute a stranger shows up, Ruby and Leo morph into candidates for an episode of *When Good Dogs Go Bad*.

Goodwin heads to the living room coffee table with the doughnuts, the coffee and juice. 'OK if I set things up over here?'

'That's fine.' I wash my hands. Goodwin claims the easy chair, and I settle on the couch, Leo at my feet. He lies with his head between his paws, watching.

'Is there any chance you've got some good news for me, Dr Goodwin? Has the Cyber Squad, or whatever you call it, nailed down the location from the web cast? Agent Woods doesn't tell me much, you know.'

'I don't have news for you there. They're probably still working backward from the last bounce.'

'Nicaragua.'

'All the bad guys bounce there. Think of it as a way station along the route.'

'Too bad they tripped this guy's alarm system.'

'I'd say it was inevitable. Collateral damage, I guess.'

'Is that how you guys look at my house burning down and my cousin getting killed – collateral damage?'

'Sorry for sounding like a hard ass. But I may as well be honest with you here. The kidnapper told you not to bring the Feds in, which is exactly what you did.'

'So my house and Marsha were the repercussions.'

'I think so, yes.'

'And you don't agree with Woods? You don't think I burned my own house down to kill my cousin Marsha for having an affair with my husband fourteen years ago?'

Goodwin's eyebrows go up. 'Completely ridiculous.'

'I saw my cousin in the hospital last night. She talked to me before she died. She told me you guys have a picture of the kidnapper. You know who he is.'

He seems startled, then nods his head slowly. 'We do, actually.'

'You admit that?'

'Yes. I think they should have let you know immediately, but it wasn't my call. Woods is still pretty wound up about that lie detector test you won't take.'

'You guys are doing a really bad job.'

'I understand why you feel that way. Here, Mrs Miller. Have a doughnut. Ladies first.'

'Under the circumstances, I can't believe you're offering me doughnuts.'

'What ticks you off the most – that I brought them or that you want one?'

I fiddle with Leo's collar. 'Both, I guess.'

He grins at me. 'Carbohydrates and chocolate stir up endorphins and are listed in the literature as reliable mood enhancers – something all women know by instinct.'

There is no point fighting it. I skipped the breakfast buffet earlier, and I'm hungry. The doughnuts are so fresh they're crisp, the chocolate coating fudgy and rich. I feel my blood sugar rising. No doubt the endorphins will flow. I wonder if

Andee and Caroline have had breakfast. I wonder if they're still alive.

'This was nice of you, I guess.' I wipe icing off my chin.

'I figured you could use a little bit of nice.' Goodwin finishes off a doughnut and drains half a bottle of juice. He brushes crumbs off his lap.

'I consult in a lot of cases like this, Mrs Miller, but usually not hands on. They overnight me a file, we talk on the phone. Send e-mails. But this situation is unusual for two reasons. One, we've got your granddaughter and daughter-in-law *out there* somewhere, in the power of this man. And two, I have history with the kidnapper. Like you said, we know who he is.'

I lean forward. 'So you know him, then? How did that happen?'

'He read an article I wrote a few years ago on apex predators. He was intrigued and he got in touch.'

'What is an apex predator?'

'Top of the food chain. You know – like great white sharks, the man-eating lions of Tsavo, Romanian brown bears. My theory was that serial killers are apex predators, functioning as a form of natural selection, culling the human herd. Which is how an apex predator functions in nature. Our kidnapper was interested in the premise that it's a matter of fate or nature; that serial killers are meant to be. He was particularly interested in the possibility that without serial killers the human race would not survive, in the same way that if we kill off all the sharks in the oceans, then the ripple effect will kill off all other forms of ocean life.'

'He has an ego, doesn't he?'

'Goes with the territory. But I also get the sense this guy is finding his way. For what it's worth, I think it's genuine. That he's trying to understand why he is who he is.'

I rub my forehead. 'And what do *you* think, Dr Goodwin? Do you believe the kidnapper is looking to me to show him the way to redemption? Do you think I'm the reason for his epiphany? You said you thought he was genuinely looking. You don't think he's just playing games?'

'I think it's a complex mixture of both. But he was serious about what he said in the note. *You're the one.* You, Joy Miller. I think he's looking for a way out of who he is, but at the same time the possibilities make him feel extremely vulnerable. Do I think he has hopes? Yes. That's what he's looking to you for. Hope. But I don't think he actually believes it's possible, there at the bottom of his heart. Provided, of course, he has one.'

'Oh, he has a heart. It's a question of whether he's got access.'

'I wonder if you'd still think so if you were aware of all the things he's done.'

'No one is beyond redemption.' I pull my hair up off my neck. It's cool in the hotel room but I'm sweaty. 'Evil can be a habit. A way of thinking. Kind of like an infection of the thought processes. This guy has spent years swept up in a love affair with being bad. But he can put a stop to it. He can redirect his thought processes.'

Goodwin stares at me. 'So you're still a believer. You haven't been active, in the ministry, for so long now. I guess I was wondering.'

'I work behind the scenes now. It was time for a change.'

Goodwin waits for me to continue, but I have nothing left to say. He shrugs and slaps his knees with the palms of his hands. 'This will be easier than I thought, then. You can answer his e-mail. Give him the answer he wants to hear. Tell him he is capable of changing his nature, and how.'

'You know about the e-mail?'

'Yes. It didn't look good, you hiding that. It's another reason Russ doesn't trust you.'

'I don't care about Russell Woods.' I chew my bottom lip. 'But my answer to the e-mail worries me. You're saying just tell him what he wants to hear?'

'Well, now, that's tricky, Mrs Miller. If you really believe it, tell him. But he isn't going to be convinced just because you play nice, right? We've got three gutted evangelists to prove that method wrong. Whatever you tell him, you're going to have to back it up with conviction supported by some kind of cogent logic.'

'Even if I do that, I don't think he's going to like what I've got to say.'

'Really? Don't you want your granddaughter back alive?'

TWENTY-SEVEN

Goodwin opens his briefcase, an old-fashioned mail carrier's leather bag, scratched and worn. He puts a picture out on the coffee table just inches from the remains of my doughnut and a few drops of spilled juice. 'Is that him?'

I feel the life draining out of me, as if my wrists have been slit. Leo lifts his head and puts his nose on my knee.

'How would I know?'

Goodwin waits patiently, not saying a word. Leo presses his head into my lap. If Goodwin is trying to wait me out, we're going to be sitting a while.

He cocks his head sideways, and his voice is gentle. 'It's obvious that you recognize the man in this picture.'

'Mr Goodwin, I've had a hell of a week. If you're here to play games with me, then leave, and take your doughnuts with you.'

He sighs deeply. 'Mrs Miller, you *know* this man, and we both know that you do. Even if you hadn't recognized the picture, which clearly you have, it's obvious that there's some kind of history between you.'

I stroke Leo's ears. Normally he'd tuck his head in my lap, but for now he is keeping watch.

'You must know that Woods keeps you under loose surveillance, right? They don't have a detail on you every minute but they check up on you regularly, intercept your mail, keep track of your cell phone and e-mail.'

Goodwin leans toward me and I sit further back on the couch. Leo growls very faintly, something I feel more than hear, a vibration deep in his chest.

'There are two possibilities here. One. You and the

kidnapper are working together. You've brooded for years and gone over the edge and you're exacting your revenge at last. That's the working theory for Russ and Mavis, and they're not in love with it, but it is what makes the most sense, when they factor everything in.' He shrugs. 'Start coloring outside the lines, and the FBI has no idea what to do. There hasn't been a ransom note. They don't understand why, and when they don't understand something, they don't like it.'

'And is that what you think?' I ask him. 'That I'm the mastermind behind some convoluted plot? That I burned down my own house? Wait, don't tell me. That's revenge too, against Marsha for cheating with my husband way the hell back when.'

'Me? No, Mrs Miller, I think the whole idea is ludicrous.' He waves a hand. 'That means we go to option two. That you know this guy, somehow, some way, something in your past, but there's a reason you're afraid to give us the connection. A good reason. That's the one I like.'

He's right, of course. I give him credit for that.

'That's why I'm here, Mrs Miller. To ask you to give me the back story. Whatever it is that you're afraid to tell, I promise you – I give you my word – it isn't going to come back on you in any way. We don't care what happened between the two of you, except as it pertains to *this* case. And I'm convinced that whatever the connection is, that's going to be the key that unravels this mess.' He leans toward me. 'Right now we've got two teams working your granddaughter's disappearance, and they're all off track. They're looking at *you* and by the time they get their heads out of their asses, it might just be too late for an *optimal conclusion*. Which is how Woods will word it in the final report.'

Goodwin holds a hand up to stop me, though I haven't said a word. 'Here's what I'm going to do. I'm going to start by telling you what *I* know. What I've put together about this man in the years I've been following his trail. And it's a nasty trail, Mrs Miller, a bloody one. Don't kid yourself. A guy like this – no way someone like you can handle him. You put together all the resources they've got in law enforcement these days, and he still may just beat them at the game. And while I talk you'll have time to think. If it's a risk for you, I'm sorry. But if you love your granddaughter – and I have no doubt you do – it's a risk you're going to have to take.'

Then Goodwin laces his fingers over his large loose stomach and tells me what he wants me to know.

'His name is Cletus Purcell and he was born in Jackson, Kentucky.' Goodwin rubs his forehead. He is frowning, like he is somewhere else in his head. I suppose, in a way, he is.

Like any good psychiatrist, Goodwin focuses his initial attention on Purcell's childhood. 'If you want a sure fire recipe for creating a sociopath, place them in seven different foster homes before the age of three.'

'Seven?'

Goodwin nods. 'Before the age of three. He stayed with number seven until he was fifteen, then he ran away and after that he was out of the system. It was a bad placement. The Hermans. They kept an average of five foster children, all coming and going constantly, all considered "at risk".

'The Hermans were fundamentalist Christians whose motto was "spare the rod, spoil the child". The father was a skinny guy with bad asthma, Benedict Herman. He actually started his own little church. Lana Herman was a mountain girl, and she was the disciplinarian. Every child I've interviewed who was placed in that home talks about her with a air of what you might misunderstand to be respect, but is actually terror. They look at her the way small animals look at predators.

'Two years after Cletus Purcell ran away, the Hermans were investigated by social services and shut down. All their placements were removed, and in a few months' time the couple were put under indictment. None of the charges went anywhere in court, even though they were abusing and neglecting their kids. They were also suspected of trading children back and forth with other foster parents who were involved with their church. The children received no medical care, the Hermans didn't bother to use benefits that wouldn't have cost them a cent. The kids wore hand-me-down charity clothes and got precious little food. As far as the investigators could tell, the Hermans didn't spend money on themselves either. Their social service checks were growing in a savings account at their bank that had an interest rate of one percent.

'Four months to the day after all charges against the Hermans were dropped, they were found dead in their living room, both of them shot in the throat.'

I pick up the picture of Cletus Purcell. He looks about twelve, skinny and tall, stooping slightly at the shoulders, head canted to one side, a matchstick in the side of his mouth. Even then his eyes are black and malevolent. Impossible to stare down. The next is a regulation mug shot, and this is the man who lurks in my subconscious. He stares straight into the lens of the camera with a look of deadness and menace that I have seen up close.

'Do you know what the statistics are, for sociopaths in the general population?' Goodwin asks.

I nod. 'One in a hundred, roughly one percent. Fairly accurate, I think, though there are some who think that statistic is overly conservative, and put it higher.'

He nods, and I see a glint of surprise. People never seem to realize that in my line of work the good is always balanced with the bad.

Goodwin runs a hand through his hair. 'Now we take our second ingredient, a simple one but a standard. Take one budding young sociopath and add some variation of the following three ingredients – abuse, brain damage and mental illness.

'We know Purcell was abused by the Hermans. There's no telling what happened to him in the initial series of early foster homes. But we know that he was riding on the back of a friend's ATV at the age of fourteen and that they crashed it into a tree. The hospital records mention a broken rib and a head injury, to the prefrontal lobe of his brain, resulting in unconsciousness and severe concussion. Mental illness? That's anyone's guess. His foster care records describe a colicky infant who cried continuously and could not be comforted. By the time he was eighteen months old he had frequent temper tantrums, and by age nine was labeled sullen and withdrawn.

'End result? A boy grows into a man looking for empowerment and ways to get even. All that's needed is a trigger, and a serial killer is born.'

'And the trigger?' I ask. 'Do you have that in your files and records?'

'I imagine his years with the Hermans gave him all the triggers he'd need. And even under their care he didn't become any kind of a discipline problem until he was twelve. At that point it was only minor stuff – small time episodes, immature, juvenile delinquent kinds of things, nothing hardcore. According to early foster care records he was attached to and loving with animals. In fact, in one of his early placements, the couple reported that the only thing that would calm him down, when he was upset, was curling up with the family cat.'

'Too bad that one didn't keep him.'

'The wife died suddenly, and the husband couldn't take care of a toddler and work his job.'

Purcell's childhood history twists like a bad bedtime story. Is it a good sign that Purcell didn't hurt Caro's dog, Ruby? It was to Purcell's advantage to leave Ruby alive, but there were other ways to get his message across.

I notice that Goodwin stares off in the distance as if he is watching a movie only he can see. His eyes seem different, then he seems to come back to himself, and the moment reminds me of something – the nictitating membrane in the eyes of a snake. I see it in Dr Jonathan Goodwin, the same thing I see in people I've counseled and what I see, just a little, in myself. The dark side of the world infects you. Takes your innocence and files it away.

'Purcell's first conviction was for felony assault. Somebody rear-ended his van at a stop sign. It was nothing more than a fender bender, but he nearly beat the man to death. After that, he went into the business of murder for hire. Nothing personal – just a sociopath making a living doing a job he enjoys.' Goodwin purses his lips. 'I can't say definitively that he's been inactive, but he's either slowed way down over the last few years or has been flying under the radar. Some of them do wind down as they age, some stop killing altogether.'

'Why do you think that is?'

'Less testosterone.'

'Testosterone seems like a hell of a burden, the more I understand about men.'

Goodwin narrows his eyes at me in a way that makes me feel like a particularly bright student. 'Let's say it's powerful, and like anything powerful it's got its good and bad sides. Evidently, Purcell *isn't* suffering from a loss of testosterone. In the last eighteen months he's been active again, but he's gone from murder for hire to this new religious quest. Which makes him unpredictable and even more dangerous. And it's also where you come in.'

'Those evangelists who died, and all the pictures I got in the mail. Has the FBI confirmed the killings were done by Purcell?'

'They knew it all along, they've got DNA evidence. What they had to confirm was if it was actually Purcell who kidnapped your granddaughter and daughter-in-law. One of the many theories about you was the possibility you were using the deaths of the evangelists as a cover for your revenge. Can't you see, Mrs Miller, how everything always comes down to you? Purcell has killed three evangelists who were classmates of yours in seminary, and there's no coincidence there. Now he's kidnapped two members of your family. There's been no ransom note, though he's gone to great pains to establish that both Caroline and Andee are still alive. He wants *something*. Something only you can give him. We can't solve this case unless you tell us why he is fixated on you.'

I take a deep breath, then let it out slowly. 'Let's say for argument's sake you're right. Consider the following scenario. I tell you everything, Agent Woods gets the connection he needs to have me arrested. Once in custody, I'm not in a position to give Purcell what he wants, and Andee and Caro get killed.'

'So that's it.' Goodwin stands up and paces to the kitchen and back. He stops abruptly, puts his hands in his pockets and bounces up and down on the balls of his feet. 'Why would you assume that Woods would arrest you?'

'Because Woods has wanted to put me under arrest since the first time I was questioned. He's convinced I hired Purcell to take revenge on my daughter-in-law.'

'That theory doesn't hold. Even Woods should be able to see that. Purcell doesn't just have Caroline, he's got Andee. And why would you have them kidnapped? Why not just have your daughter-in-law killed? And what about those pictures you got in the mail? The other evangelists? How does that connect?'

'You're asking me?'

'The only reason Woods won't let go of that theory is he knows you're not telling him everything. And he can't think of any other reason for your refusal to tell him the truth. I don't see a choice for you here. You want this guy caught, don't you, Joy? You want your family back safe? Do you honestly believe you can pull that off by yourself?'

'I might think exactly that.'

'You'd be wrong. And it's not like Purcell doesn't know you've gone to the Feds,' Goodwin says dryly. 'You might as well make use of us.'

He walks close to me and Leo springs to his feet. There is an invisible line that only Leo sees but it's one he won't allow Goodwin to cross.

'What's it going to be, Mrs Miller? You going to talk, or let your dog snack on me for lunch? Keep in mind, please, that Caroline and Andee have been gone for five days already, and the trail is going cold. But by all means take whatever time you need to think.'

'I need a bathroom break.'

Goodwin opens his mouth, then closes it. He shrugs. 'Truthfully, I could use one myself.'

TWENTY-EIGHT

J ohnny Goodwin sits quietly, both hands in his lap. He watches me as if I'm a wild animal and can easily be scared away.

I take myself back fourteen years, almost to the day.

'I've always called him the Dark Man.' I give Goodwin a sideways smile. 'The first time I saw him was in the produce section at Wal-Mart, fourteen years ago. I was picking out strawberries. I couldn't find any I liked the looks of, so I moved on and found a box of clementines. Joey and I had discovered clementines the year before and we were crazy about them.'

'I don't even know what they are,' Goodwin says.

'Small, sweet, like tangerines but seedless. They're grown in Spain.' I close my eyes, thinking. Finding my way back. 'So there I was in my own little world, completely occupied with the grocery budget, the cost of fruit and how much produce I can buy. I wasn't even aware of the Dark Man standing beside me until he tapped me on the shoulder and asked me if clementines were the same as tangerines.

'It startled me. And I didn't like it that he touched me, even if it was just a tap on the shoulder. There was something repellent about him, something hard. He was a tall man, really skinny and greasy. His face looked mean. His eyes were black and the way he looked at you . . . it was kind of flat, but creepy. He had black eyebrows and oily black hair, long and combed back. He was dressed kind of rough. An old flannel shirt, cheap trousers. Scuffed up work shoes, a dirty painter's cap. There were smudges of different paint colors all over his pants.

'"Clementines are sweeter," I told him. "And they don't have seeds. They're better than tangerines, when you can find them."

'I remember how he just stared at me, like he was watching

my lips move but not paying attention to the words. And he didn't buy any clementines. That's when I noticed that he didn't have any groceries, or a basket.

'At this point my internal creep-o-meter hits the high red end of panic. I couldn't tell if he was hitting on me or just weird, but it didn't really matter. It was one of those times where the ingrained habit of being polite is a serious handicap. That's something I had to learn when the cable show started up. I shoved my basket in the other direction and headed to go check out.

'He followed me and it was blatant. I picked up speed, kind of walk-running, and he stayed right behind me. I could just picture him breathing down my neck in the checkout line, and following me to the parking lot and my car. So I turned around and faced him.

'"*Go away*," I told him. "*Stop* following me. Leave right this minute or I will go straight to that counter over there and ask them to call store security."'

'No doubt he was terrorized,' Goodwin said dryly.

'The *look* he gave me – I can't even describe it. The way it was so intent, the way he lowered his head. And then he grabbed on to my basket.'

'That must have scared you.'

'Oh, believe me. I was shaking. But it's not like I was attached to the fruit. I took off, and I was spooked enough that I was going to make sure the store manager called the police. But right when I was turning, I could see that he was reaching into the pocket of his shirt and unfolding a piece of paper. And he gets something else out of his pocket – a photograph.

'"This is your schedule for the next four days," he says. "I can read it to you if you want."

'I just stood there, so he kind of squints at the paper and starts reading.

'"Tonight you're a guest speaker at New Hope Chapel. Tomorrow night you have the revival in Berea. Sunday you're the guest preacher at a church in Midway." Then he stops reading and looks at me. "You work hard at this, don't you? Here, take a look at these pictures I got. This is you, and this is your son."

'And sure enough, he's got a copy of my week's itinerary exactly like the copy in my briefcase. Only mine is still crisp and neat, and his is brown-stained with coffee and smells like cigarettes. And the pictures are wrinkled and dirty, like he's pulled them out and looked at them a lot. All of his stuff has paper clip marks in the upper left hand corner, like somebody put it together for him.

'"Where did you get these?" I honestly didn't think he'd tell me. I remember my heart beating so hard and I was panicky because of the picture he had of my son.

'"Your husband gave them to me, Mrs Miller."

'I stood there and stared at him. And he points to the McDonald's in the front of the store.

'"Let's go over there and get us a cup of coffee. It's full of people, I can't do nothing to you there. You're going to want to listen to what I got to say."

'He had Joey's picture, so I couldn't just let it go. We got coffee and sat down. The table was sticky. Catsup smears.

'"Your husband's name is Carl," he says. "Two months ago he hired me to kill you."'

Goodwin cocks his head to one side. 'Did you believe him?'

I shake my head. 'No. Not at first. I thought he was some pervert trying to extort money. There were some pretty hard-core people who crawled out from under the rocks when I started the cable show. It was early days, but I was starting to get wary.

'I decided the best thing to do was to play him. Listen to everything he had to say, then call the police. This would be a new one for the stalker file. I knew if he actually made a threat there would be a better chance of prosecuting him, and this one I wanted locked away.

'"You don't believe me?" he says. I guess my attitude was pretty clear. So he pulls a pack of Camel cigarettes out of his shirt pocket. He's pretty casual, in no kind of hurry. Takes his time lighting the cigarette and starts to smoke. "Your husband paid me eight thousand seven hundred dollars as a cash down payment. That sum of money ring a bell with you?"

'He starts drinking his coffee then, completely relaxed. I

can still see it. The steam rising up from the Styrofoam cup and me wondering how he could drink it so hot.

'I remember closing my eyes, kind of deflating. Eight thousand seven hundred dollars was the exact figure missing from the ministry accounts. Marsha had been trying to track it down all week.

'He finishes about a third of his coffee and then he starts flicking cigarette ashes into his cup.

'"I get another eleven thousand three hundred when you're dead," he tells me. "Which is supposed to happen tonight, by the way, after you preach. You'll be driving a black Trans Am."

'"That's my husband's car."

'"He's going to switch before you go. He'll take the Jeep Cherokee and leave you the Trans Am. I'm supposed to make it look like a car jacking. Tomorrow he and I are meeting at Natural Bridge State Park, on the bridge itself, at seven p.m. That's where he'll give me the rest of the money."

'"And what about Joey? He's supposed to be with me tonight. Am I supposed to believe that Carl paid you to kill our son?"

'"The way your husband put it to me, Mrs Miller, was he *preferred* me not to hurt your son. Joey, right? Saw him score that goal at the soccer game Saturday. He's a pretty good player, goes all out." He lights up another cigarette. "I told your husband I don't leave witnesses. He said he'd try to make some excuse to keep the boy home. Either way, though, I'm supposed to go on and do the job."

'"Why are you telling me this? You want money from me? You want me to pay you? Because I'm not going to give you a cent."

'He nodded at me, like I was saying just what he thought I'd say, like I was repeating the dialog he'd already written and rehearsed in his mind.

'"Thing is," he says, "I've been going to a lot of your shows. You know. Where you preach. I was there just to get a bead on you, but I admit you got me thinking."

'"Thinking about what?"

'"About good and evil. I've got a lot of bad inside me."

'*The way he said that.* Like it was everyday chit chat. Even now it gives me a chill. And I knew I should say something encouraging, something about how he had good in him too. But I just didn't see any good in those flat, black eyes.

'"I'm not telling you everything I done in my life," he said. "You don't want to know. Most of it's stuff you'd have a hard time even thinking about, much less knowing in detail. But since I started really listening to you, I can't sleep anymore. I'm trained as a house painter, it's what I do when I'm short of cash. I'm thinking I'll try and stick to that. I just wanted you to know that you're the one started the ball rolling. The rest is up to me."

'"And that's all?"

'He gave me a little sideways glance. "Thought you might want to keep an eye on that husband of yours."'

TWENTY-NINE

'What happened next?' Goodwin asks.

'That's it. That's the last time I saw Purcell. That's my big connection to this case.'

'It puts an interesting light on things.' Goodwin rubs his chin. 'Do you think it was sincere? This big religious epiphany?'

'These guys are beyond manipulative, you know that. But still. I can't get my head around it. Why did he call it off? Why did he warn me?'

'So he kept his word.'

'I'm sitting here, aren't I?'

Goodwin reaches for a doughnut. 'For what it's worth, Mrs Miller, I'm convinced. I think he's serious about looking for a way out of *who he is*, to *who he can be*.' He takes a napkin and wipes chocolate off his mouth. 'According to the police report that Woods dug up, your husband, Carl Miller, committed suicide by jumping off Natural Bridge. You think Purcell had anything to do with that?'

'I don't know.'

'Why didn't you go to the police? I take it you didn't?'

'No. I didn't. When I got home it all happened like Purcell said it would. Carl tried to switch cars with me. He tried to keep Joey home. So I took my son and stayed with a friend, trying to think what to do. The next thing I know the police are on the doorstep telling me Carl is dead.

'Maybe if I'd gone right to the police, Carl would still be alive. But I needed to think. I wasn't sure they'd believe me. And there was that money missing from the business accounts. It was going to turn into a big fat mess. I was worried about what would happen with the ministry. How it would affect Joey, if it all came out.

'And then Carl was dead. So I kept quiet and went on with my life.' I look up at Goodwin. 'So there you go. That's my deep dark secret.'

Goodwin gives me a sad little smile. 'So Purcell saves your life really. Maybe your son's as well. That's how he sees it. And now he wants the favor returned. The answer to the big question. Can he be redeemed?' Goodwin scratches the back of his neck. 'It shouldn't be too hard for you to put something together to make him happy.'

'Something like the truth, or something like what he wants to hear?'

Goodwin just smiles at me. 'I guess that's your call.'

'Do you think he'll let the girls go, once he gets his questions answered?'

'Not really. But it'll do to flush him out.'

THIRTY

t is a sadly small gathering in the sanctuary for Marsha's funeral, though Cee's half sister, Chloris, does make it in from Detroit. The number of mourners is swelled by a sturdy turnout of law enforcement.

I scan the faces, looking for the Dark Man, but it is Goodwin that I find. He is sitting on the right side of the sanctuary, maybe ten rows in. His suit looks new, a navy blue that is almost black. He wears a stiff white shirt that looks like he took it out of a plastic package this morning. His tie is powder blue. He's either had a haircut or discovered gel. Either way, he is crisply dressed, properly somber, and although he is far from obvious I can see him watching, sizing people up as they come in. He sees me and nods, and I appreciate his presence even though I know it's all about the business at hand.

I recognize Agents Jones and Woods and tag the drawn, watchful faces of two men and a woman I don't know. They are looking for the Dark Man as well. We all watch television. We all know he'll be drawn to attend.

Yesterday afternoon the local media discovered my hiding place. I have been off the circuit and I'm rusty. It did not occur to me to register in my hotel under an assumed name. One advantage of having the FBI at Marsha's funeral is their hard-line ability to keep the media chained. Their professional stiff-armed toughness is a blessing when they're on your team.

I sit in an anteroom that looks on to the sanctuary of Second Presbyterian Church where Marsha, a vague Presbyterian, kept a connection that was tenuous at best. The service is set for ten a.m., and it is already ten fifteen. Were it not for the presence of the FBI we could all fit into the cozy second floor library, which would be more comfortable, and comforting to the soul.

I look to my Aunt Cee for the signal to begin. I check my watch. I am unable to catch her eye. She wears a chunky brooch pinned to the shoulder of her dress – the jewelry of generations past. She leans against my Uncle Don, and the two of them form a human teepee of grief. They seem so much older than I remember, and it isn't just grief. My relatives have aged and grown tired while I've hidden away the last seven years.

Marsha would be gratified to know that I have been shopping. As of yesterday my wardrobe consisted of a khaki skirt, some well worn Levis, a white silk blouse, two plain black tee shirts and a worn and well washed pair of Keds. I had various items of socks and underwear, but even for me the wardrobe was on the skimpy side.

In a whirl of expense that Marsha would have enjoyed, I doubled the tally with the addition of slingback heels, a black sheath dress, stockings, a matching set of bra and panties and a simple pair of real pearl earrings that I have always wished for but never owned. It occurred to me to hide the earrings as soon as I bought them, but then I remembered that Marsha would not be 'borrowing' from my wardrobe anymore.

My bank account is dwindling. Living in a hotel and owning almost nothing means a myriad of unplanned for expense. And I still have the continuum of before-crisis bills. I still have to pay the mortgage, though the house itself is gone. I wonder if I'll have to sue my insurance company, and how many years we'll be tied up in court. It's aggravating the way so much in life seems to boil down to shopping and paying the bills.

Photographs of Marsha are displayed on the table by the casket, which will remain closed. There are four baskets of flowers lined up by the podium. I imagine that I catch a whiff of fragrance. I imagine how Marsha looks right now, beneath the coffin's tightly shut lid. She'll be wearing the lavender dress she mentioned in the instructions in her will. Her hands, though they look like cooked meat, will clasp a spray of white cymbidiums, fragrant, and soft to the touch. She will rest on a liner of satin, in her favorite color of pink.

Someone taps my shoulder and I look up to see Uncle Don.

'Cee says it's time to begin now, honey.' He pats my shoulder and shuffles away, with the usual sideways sway.

As soon as I walk to the pulpit, the drone of soft conversation fades. The microphone, as always, is set up to accommodate a tallish man. I make adjustments and my voice echoes into the cavernous sanctuary.

I have stood before mourners countless times, and have no need of my notes. I am relieved to find my voice remains steady and calm. It wavers only slightly when I scan the congregation and focus on Uncle Don and Aunt Cee, watching me from the dark place of their pain.

I am good at funerals and I give them the best that I've got, then step aside with a certain relief. Someone's teenage daughter is scheduled to sing. I am trapped up front in the public eye, sitting in one of those throne-like chairs. The singer goes with 'Jesus Is Calling'. Her voice is young and soft, almost unbearably sweet. The organist plays carefully so the music does not overpower the purity and tone. Something in my mind clicks and I look back at the table by the coffin. I squint, trying not to be obvious, but there is a brown envelope next to the display of pictures. An envelope that wasn't there before.

I leave my seat, taking care to avoid eye contact with anyone – particularly relatives of the girl who is singing and agents of the FBI. I'm aware that people are staring, and the organist, well into the second refrain of the hymn, looks up at me, a question in her eyes. She is in her forties, vaguely familiar, and her dress is that annoying color called royal that can't decide if it is purple or blue. I smile and nod. Whisper 'Good to see you again'. She looks perplexed, but my air of being in charge carries me through, and she continues on with the music.

Once I am close I can see I was right: there's an envelope on the table that wasn't there before. I suppose a wiser woman would have left it for handling by the FBI, but I know the Dark Man well enough that if he *has* left this envelope, it is something I do not want my aunt and uncle to see.

In a few quick steps I am back on the second level and out of general view. I pause in the small anteroom where the choir

congregates before the service and tear the tightly gummed
seal of the envelope. There is a single photograph inside and
my hands shake when I hold it up to the light.

Marsha is tied, hand and foot, and her eyes are closed,
though she seems aware and awake. The fire hasn't reached
her yet, but it is close. The picture is blurred by smoke, and
dear Marsha could be an advertisement for whatever product
she has used to hold her hair in place. I want to laugh and
cry when I see that she is wearing the delicate silver bracelet
I bought years ago on a trip to New Mexico. She is also
wearing the turquoise sweater I gave her last Christmas and
her usual pair of khakis, and she has somehow lost her left
shoe.

The handwriting on the back of the photo is familiar to me
now, written in the usual green ink.

YOU DIDN'T TRUST ME.
I TOLD YOU NOT TO BRING IN THE FBI.

FRESH START. AWAITING YOUR ANSWERS.
YOUR GIRLS WANT TO COME HOME.

ONE WAY OR ANOTHER, THEY WILL.

Suddenly I have to sit. My aunt and uncle can just barely see
me from their vantage, and the people in the side pews are
watching as well. Russell Woods is heading my way.

Aunt Cee blows me a kiss, graceful acknowledgement. I
know that she is tortured by the last sight of her daughter as
she died in the ICU. Her thoughts are held by the vision of
flayed pink flesh, and the ravages of burns. She asks for so
little in the face of events – only to remember Marsha in
happier times, before she was devoured by fire and pain.

I would burn this picture if I could, but Russell Woods is
already prying it from my hands.

THIRTY-ONE

I am sound asleep in the overstuffed plaid chair in the living room of my suite when Leo puts his head in my lap. I wake suddenly, and my pen and notepad slide to the floor. According to the digital readout on the cable box, it's seventeen minutes past seven a.m. I spent the night watching the Disney Channel with Leo and Ruby, working on my reply to the Dark Man.

Purcell, I tell myself. His name is Cletus Purcell.

I flip the page on the legal pad, and read over what I have written.

Dear Mr Purcell,

Referencing your request for salvation:

No one can know the heart of another. You have gone to enormous effort to put my back to the wall, as if it were my insight, and mine alone, that might set you on the pathway to God.

Clearly you are intelligent and self aware.

For those of us who agonize over nature versus nurture, you present the ultimate dilemma. Yet justice systems the world over take the stand that you know right from wrong, and this awareness combined with your actions would rate you very high on any scale of evil.

Are you an apex predator, created through the inevitable process of evolution to play the part of a keystone sub-species of man, your function that of controlling the human population? Are you a victim of faulty neurological function, no more able to control your actions than a man without legs can walk?

My guess is you want the world to feel your pain, and you take pleasure in hunting, having made the decision to be a predator instead of prey.

On the assumption that your questions are based on

genuine interest and not another of your manipulative tools, I can tell you only this:

Taking the path to salvation will be just as dangerous for you as you fear. Every essence of your being has gone into the creation of who you are today – your subconscious made this decision and sees it as necessary to your survival. It is your armor, and it keeps you safe. Drop it and you risk annihilation. You will be defenseless from the danger of your past.

So the good news is of course you can find salvation. The bad news is that it's up to you. It was your choice, and only your choice, to veer so far off your path. God is the one who will love you. The one who will judge you is you.

Regards,
Joy Miller
Evangelist (retired)

I harness the dogs in collars and leashes and take them out for their Walkies. Leo is exuberant, and crow-hops at the door while he waits for me to slip my keycard in my pocket. One thing I forgot to buy on my shopping trip was a jacket. I've already started keeping a list. I think of at least three more things every day.

The dogs and I head toward the staircase at the end of the hall. The housekeepers are already in force, and there is a bin of dirty laundry four doors down. A door across the hallway opens and a man in a suit, attaché laptop in hand, eyes Leo warily on his way to the elevator.

Dr Goodwin is supposed to come by today, I'm just not sure when he'll appear. I picture the two of us pacing my hotel room, wads of rejected paper littering the floor.

I know that what I have written is risky. But I have no doubt that Darrin, Jimmy and Gloria told the Dark Man everything they thought he wanted to hear. He's heard the platitudes, he's heard the promises, maybe what he needs now is the truth.

I have no intention of getting tangled up in what truth is either. He'll get the gospel according to me.

THIRTY-TWO

I am in the dining room off the hotel lobby having my complimentary breakfast and watching outside as the leaves come off the trees. I catch sight of a man who looks familiar, and realize it is Dr Goodwin when he walks through the lobby doors. He is casual today – jeans, instead of khakis, and a powder blue sweater and dark navy windbreaker. I put my biscuit down and wave at him.

'Dr Goodwin? Johnny?'

Everyone within hearing distance stares at me except, of course, Goodwin himself. I go after him, catching up just as he opens the doorway to the stairs.

'Hey. I'm down here.'

'Joy? How are you? Look, I'm sorry just to drop in like this. I should have called before I drove over. But Woods showed me the note you found yesterday. And that terrible picture.' He touches my shoulder. 'We agreed that we need to get things moving, and get that e-mail out to Purcell.'

I brush crumbs off my shirt. 'That's OK. I told Woods yesterday I'd get right on it, and I spent most of last night working it up. Look, I'm over in the dining room having breakfast. Why don't you come and get something to eat?'

He rubs his chin, thoughts elsewhere. 'Sure, OK. You've got it written up? Your answer?'

'I finished it late last night. I'd like you to take a look, if you would. Tell me what you think. I may have erred on the side of honesty. Why don't you go on in to the buffet, and I'll run upstairs and get my notes? My table's at the back, right next to the coffee machine.'

He follows me dutifully to the dining room, and I point to the table where my coffee is growing cold.

By the time I return from my room upstairs, Goodwin has settled with coffee, pineapple juice and oatmeal. He takes a pair of reading glasses from the inside jacket of his wind-breaker. He is intent and absorbed, while his oatmeal grows gelatinous and cold.

Eventually he sets the notepad aside. He sits quietly, staring straight ahead.

'What do you think?' I ask him.

He narrows his eyes. 'It's . . . unexpected. Not what I thought you'd say. It will give him something to think about.'

'Do you think it's too harsh?'

Goodwin looks at me curiously. 'It has a certain integrity. Look, Joy, if telling him what he wants to hear was a good idea, I don't think all those other evangelists would be dead.'

'Maybe I should damp it down a little.'

'Leave it, for now, anyway. I still have to run it by Russell. He's not very happy with you right now.'

'He's never happy with me.'

Goodwin places his spoon neatly against the plate. 'I'm sorry, by the way. That picture can't have been fun for you.'

'It was horrible. For a man who says he's trying to find redemption, Purcell seems to get a lot of pleasure from my pain.'

Goodwin gives me a second look. 'There's another way to consider it – that it gets you off the hook with Russell and Mavis Jones. I think he takes a certain care with you, Mrs Miller.'

'You define kidnapping my daughter-in-law and grand-daughter as taking care? Thank you, by the way, for being there. At the funeral.'

He leans toward me just a little. 'I was glad to be there for you, Joy. But you know I was working as well.'

'Yes, I do know that.'

'And just so you know – even though that place was crawling with agents, nobody saw a thing with the envelope until they caught sight of you picking it up.' He grins, just a little one. 'You kind of took them by surprise. You seemed so sure of yourself, going down there to get it, it took them longer than it should have to react.'

'At least my aunt and uncle didn't see it.'

He stands. 'I'm going to head out and run this by Russ. If he likes it, we'll send it out. It's certainly going to stir things up.'

'You don't think—'

'That it will put your girls in danger? I'm sorry, Joy, I think they're in even more danger if you don't. I'll get back to you, later today, and let you know how things stand.'

'Please do, anything at all, any details. I'm going to be a nervous wreck all day. And I don't know if Russell Woods has told you, but I have a speaking engagement at Spindletop, the car will pick me up around five tonight. You'll get to me before then, won't you?'

He tears the sheets of writing off the legal pad and folds them into his jacket pocket with his reading glasses. 'I'll do my best.'

THIRTY-THREE

I am at the halfway point with my makeup when I hear the knock at the door. I frown at the clock. I am expecting the driver from the Sanctuary group, though he's not due for another twenty minutes at least. He or she has committed an escort faux pas – one calls the room, or asks the front desk to do so. You don't just show up at the door.

I am at a critical point with my mascara. Both Leo and Ruby are barking, which agitates me and makes my hand unsteady, and the sooty black color not only coats my lashes now, but the bridge of my nose as well. I wipe the smears away with a Q-Tip, and look at the scatter of tiny black boxes. They're ripped wide open and spread across the bathroom counter, sporting the silver white stamp of Chanel. I'm out about half the amount of my mortgage payment, if you add the cost of the makeup and new clothes.

I'm wearing the same dress I bought for Marsha's funeral. Black, with three quarter length sleeves, and a straight silhouette. I like this dress, which is a good thing – it's the only one that I've got. Life is amazingly simple when you don't have any stuff.

More knocking at the door, which sets Leo off worse than before. I cross in stocking feet to look through the peephole. Johnny Goodwin stares back. My fingers tremble as I undo the lock.

'Dr Goodwin? What's going on?'

Goodwin has an air of frenetic energy. His hair is windblown, and the shoulder seam of his windbreaker has a new tear. He glances over his shoulder to the hallway, then exhales deeply, catching his breath. 'Can I come in?'

'Of course.' I step aside.

'It's happening, Joy. It's going down tonight.'

'Purcell? They've found him?'

'Woods sent your e-mail. They tracked Purcell when he picked it up. We're pretty sure we've nailed the location where he's holding the girls. There's a SWAT team on the way as we speak.' Goodwin puts a hand on my shoulder, as if I need steadying. 'It was a risk, Joy, those things you wrote. We knew it when we sent the e-mail out, but no matter what you do, it's *always* a crapshoot with this kind of guy.'

'What are you trying to tell me?' My mouth is very dry and I feel numb all over.

'He's not happy, OK? It wasn't what he wanted to hear and it set him off. We think he's on his way to kill them, which is why Russ is sending SWAT straight in. It escalates the situation, and it's a hostage risk, but it looks like we're going for broke.'

I back up two steps and prop myself against the wall so that I can stay on my feet. 'Straight in *where*? Where are they?'

'He's got them in a *cave*.' Goodwin shakes his head and tightens his lips. 'Makes perfect sense when you think about it, doesn't it? The cave is outside a place called Wilmore—'

I close my eyes. A cave. I should have thought of that.

'Russ says it's little over an hour's drive away.' Goodwin scratches his head and looks down the hallway. 'Look, Joy, things are happening fast. Russ sent me out to get you, he wants you on hand when everything goes down. You should know I strongly advised him against it. I think if Purcell sees you, it could make things worse. He might be prone to killing Andee and Caroline in front of you, and I told Russ that. He said he'd keep you out of sight, but he still wants you there.'

'No, no, I'm with him on that. I think I should be on hand, just in case. There's no telling, anything could happen.'

'Keep in mind, Joy, if you do get involved, Purcell is fixated on you. It's risky as hell if Russ takes you off the sidelines.'

'Do you think I care? I want my girls. I'll do anything to get them back safe.'

'OK then. Don't say you weren't warned.' He looks at his watch. 'Grab what you need and come now. We're already on the clock.'

I snatch up my Keds. The socks I had on yesterday are still stuffed inside. Goodwin is out the door ahead of me, and I follow, letting it swing closed behind. I hear the latch click into place. Goodwin is already halfway down the side staircase, and I have to run to catch up. I think I hear the phone in my room. No doubt the driver for the Sanctuary Group is waiting for me downstairs.

THIRTY-FOUR

Goodwin's rental is a white Ford Contour. He drives with cool, expert steadiness – aggressive, but by the letter of the law. It is awkward, putting my socks and Keds on. It is cold and I don't have a jacket. I'm wishing I had not bothered to wrestle these pantyhose on.

My stomach flutters with nerves. I sit forward in my seat, mentally cursing every other car on the road. It is not quite six p.m. and we're catching the final brunt of the after-work traffic. I want to go faster. I dig my fingernails into my palms. I feel the tedious passing of each and every second, lagging behind the thud of my heart.

'Where is this cave again?' I sound out of breath. 'Somewhere in Wilmore, is that what you said?'

'You've heard of Highbridge Springs Water?' he asks. 'They're being held in the cave at High Bridge.'

I clench my fists. I am remembering what Caro said on the web cam. How quiet everything was. How it seemed oddly muffled. How it smelled like a basement.

'It seems obvious, now, doesn't it? Now that we know for sure. What do you know about this place, Joy, have you ever been out there?'

'I drink their water, that's about all. And I went up there once or twice, to High Bridge itself, when I was in my teens. It's a local rite of passage.'

'Is there even a bridge up there?'

'Yeah, a railroad bridge. On the top of the mountain, over-looking the river. I don't know about now, but it used to be the highest railroad bridge in the world, somewhere around two hundred eighty to three hundred feet. It was built over a deep gorge between Jessamine and Mercer County. People get killed up there every year. It's a big deal to go out on the bridge.'

He gives me a quick sideways look. 'And did you?'

'I'm afraid of heights. I never knew there was a cave.'

'Russ says it's huge. The spring is actually inside the cave, and the company bottles the water right there. The manufac-turing operation and the business offices are all inside the cave. That's how Purcell did the broadcast on the web cam. He piggybacked on to their high speed wireless.'

'But where in the cave does he have them? Andee said they have a bathroom and—'

'Caroline said on the web cast that they were in some kind of RV.'

'How is that possible? Are you saying Purcell just drove one into the cave and parked it and nobody who works there noticed it?'

Goodwin gives me a little half smile. 'The cave is a *monster*. Thirty acres, one million square feet of *usable* space, not counting God knows how many miles of passageways, and five miles of road. The owner blasted it out and shored it up, and one thing he's got is space. They actually run two businesses out there – the water operation and Kentucky Underground Storage.'

'Are you telling me they store RVs?'

'RVs, cars, boats, library records, legal files. The University of Kentucky is one of their biggest customers. They're even storing the governor's furniture.'

I chew the tip of my finger. I'm thinking of miles and miles of pitch dark and crisscrossing passageways.

'So even if Caro and Andee got out of the RV, they'd never find their way out of the cave.'

'There is method to the madness,' Goodwin says.

'Just when you think it can't get any worse,' I mutter.

Goodwin flicks on the blinker. 'Sorry, but we're going to need to stop.'

He pulls into a left turn lane across from a Pilot station. We've made our way through the Lexington traffic and gotten tangled up in the slow-moving treacle on the outskirts of Nicholasville.

'Out of gas?'

'No, but we could be later. We'll be hitting the back roads in a few miles and I'm not so sure of the way. I don't want to take a risk.'

I rub my forehead, but he's right. Once we get into the countryside, there won't be many places to stop.

'I have a sweater in the trunk of the car, you want it? I didn't give you time to grab a jacket, and it's already starting to get cool.'

'Yeah, thanks, I do.'

The Pilot station is slammed this time of the day and it takes some maneuvering to find an available pump. Goodwin pops the trunk open with a button under the dash, and I get out and head around back. He goes around on the other side, and gets there ahead of me. I see him freeze, then grab a bundle of yellow and slam down the lid.

My body is alive with adrenalin and my senses have expanded. My glimpse of the trunk interior was nothing more than a momentary flash. One oversized suitcase of some nubby brown material, two black leather cases, a navy blue overnight bag and a bright red gasoline can, shiny and new.

I focus on acting nonchalant as I slip the sweater over my head. It is a soft knit, butter yellow, and warm. I can't look any weirder, in an oversized man's yellow sweater, a black silk dress, my socks and my Keds. People are staring, but that's good. I want them to notice me and remember I was there. I want them to be able to describe me and Goodwin in detail.

'Going to hit the ladies' room,' I say.

I am aware of each step I take, and each breath as it goes in and out. The world is louder and brighter, and I am alive to every smell and noise. It takes discipline not to look over my shoulder at Goodwin. I feel a compulsion to know if he is watching me. It is best to assume he is. I step up on the curb at the doorway, feeling a certain relief. Even more when the door shuts behind me and I'm inside.

I glance at the cashier behind the counter. Young, skinny, overwhelmed with customers. The women's restroom is occupied and I wait, thinking furiously, shifting my weight from foot to foot. The bathroom knob turns at last, and a woman and a small boy ease their agonizingly slow way out. I slip in and flip the lock.

I stand with my back to the door. Goodwin is packed and ready to leave, that much is clear. And the rental car license plate says Kentucky, which makes no sense if he drove in from Chicago like he said, and why didn't he drive his own car? Then there's the gas can, brand new, tucked in with all that nice luggage – and why so *much* luggage for a quick few days out of town to consult? And why the gas can, unless he burned down my house?

I fumble through my purse for my cell phone and sit on the toilet to make my call. The phone battery is charged and there are four bars of service. I rummage in my purse for a pen and an old receipt, tap my foot while the four-one-one information operator gives me the number I need, then dial.

'Abbey of Gethsemani.'

It is an emergency, I say, and tell them my name. I assure them that Father Panatel knows me. I tell them I must speak to him immediately on a matter of life and death. I wait for my words to sink in.

The man on the other end finally speaks. 'Your name is somewhat familiar.'

'I had an appointment with Father Panatel Tuesday of last week.'

'Right. I remember that.' I can hear a change in his voice. 'Will you wait just a few moments while I find him?'

'Yes, but hurry.' I try not to think while I'm waiting, till I hear the voice on the other end. But I don't have the kind of mind that turns off.

'Joy Miller, I have Father Panatel for you.'

There is a click as I thank him. Then a man says hello.

'Father Panatel. It *is* you, Father?'

'But yes, dear lady, this is me.'

'I need to ask you – I need you to think. This man we talked about, when I was there the other day?'

'Yes, missus, this one you call dark.'

'Can you remember what he looked like? Can you describe him to me?'

There is a silence. 'It's been so long with the years that have passed.'

I prop my elbow on my knees with my head in my hand, palm plastered across my forehead. 'Think, please think. Anything at all you remember.'

'He is a large man, this I do recall, maybe sixty pounds of extra weight. Still, there is a physical grace. Also that I am first confused when you would call him this dark man. His hair was a red sort of blond, to my memory, and at first I wonder why you call him dark. But I decide on thought you are referring to his essence, and the energy of the soul that is lost.'

His words confirm what I already know, but the ceiling is suddenly spinning over my head, as if I've had too much to drink.

'You are there, Joy Miller? This is the one you call dark?'

'Yes, Father.'

'Dear lady, I think you are very much troubled. I am worrying, yes, very much, I am worrying for you.'

'Yes, Father, I'm worrying for me too.'

'Tell me what I must do for you, dear lady. You sound in need of assistance.'

'I'm not sure. No . . . yes.' I try to think. 'Would you please call the FBI office in Lexington, and ask for Agent Russell Woods?'

'Of course, dear lady, and I think this be a good idea. Let me for a moment get a pen. Yes, now, Agent Russell Woods.'

'Tell him that you talked to me. That I'm in a car with the kidnapper on my way to the cave at Highbridge Springs. I'm going to call Woods myself, but I want you to call him too, so he understands that there are two of us who've seen this man and know who he is. Tell him that the kidnapper is driving a white Ford Contour, a rental, with Kentucky plates.'

'You are alone with this him then, dear lady? This man you call the kidnapper—'

'It's him. The one we spoke of. I'm going to the cave with him. Or I'm thinking about it. I'm not sure what to do, to tell you the truth.'

'You must not do this, Joy Miller.'

'He's kidnapped my granddaughter, Father Panatel. If I can get him to take me to her, then maybe I can bring her home safe.'

'Remind your head, please, Joy Miller, what is happening with the postulate Sandbone, who tried to help this man.'

'My head doesn't need reminding, Father Panatel. I know exactly who he is.'

'Listen, please, to what I am saying here, missus. It is not in your power to change the Dark Entity. That can only come from God.'

I don't take the time to respond. I have another call to make.

I take a business card out of my wallet. The dispatch operator at the firehouse answers and I ask to be put through to Captain Reinhardt. He is quick to the phone.

'What's wrong, Joy? You sound unglued.'

'You know how I told you I couldn't have dinner last night? Because I was working on something with the FBI consultant?'

'Goodwin, yeah. How did it go?'

'Not so good. I'm with him now. Only he's not an FBI consultant after all. He's one of the kidnappers.'

There is a moment while Hal takes it all in. 'Can he hear you?'

'I'm in the ladies' room. At a Pilot station. We're in Nicholasville, on our way to Highbridge Springs.'

'But how—'

I explain, ending with the gas can in the rental car. 'I think he's the one who burned down my house.'

'I won't second guess you on this, Joy. Have you called Russell Woods?'

'He's next on the list.'

'You'll stay right there. In the bathroom, right? You won't move till Woods gets to you, do you promise?'

'Hal, he'll take me to the girls if I play this right.'

'You'll be another hostage. Call Woods and let him handle this, Joy. Going anywhere with this guy would be completely insane.'

'Woods is as unpredictable as the kidnappers, Hal. I don't like leaving everything up to him.'

'What makes you so sure this guy is taking you to the girls? And, Joy, I'm sorry, but what makes you so sure they're still alive? Don't make this any worse than it is. Let Woods handle it. Promise me.'

'I don't want to go with him. But I don't want the girls to die because I'm a coward.'

'You're too involved in this, you're not thinking straight. Trust me. Call Woods. I'll call him as well. And then I'll be right behind him. Just stay in the bathroom, OK?'

I shut my eyes tight. Take a breath. Remind myself that a sociopath tells you what you want to hear because it is so effective.

'You're right. You're right. OK.'

I hear Hal's sigh of relief as I break the connection.

Woods answers on the first ring. He has agents at Spindletop, sure that the kidnapper will be one of the faces in the crowd. He wants to know where I am.

'Agent Woods, do you work with a forensic consultant named Jonathan Goodwin?'

'How do you know that?'

'I've met him.'

'No you haven't. Goodwin has been in Singapore the last three weeks.'

'I've met a man who says he's Goodwin, Agent Woods. But I think he's one of the kidnappers. You figured that out already, right? There are two?'

'Where are you?'

I explain for the third time while my cell battery begins to run down.

Woods is professional and quick on the uptake, and for once the two of us are in sync. He gives me the same advice Hal did. Stay in the bathroom. Leave the cell phone on.

'And Joy. If he tries to get you out of there – and he may – scream your head off. Don't go out, don't talk to him through the door, whatever threats he makes, ignore them. He's tricky and he's smart. If you go back out to him you'll only make things worse, and he'll have three hostages instead of two. Go with him and you're lost. You get me?'

'I get you.'

I hear him giving instructions, voices in the background. I feel better. I'm not so alone.

'Stay as calm as you can, Joy. I've got people on the way.'

As soon as I hang up, another call comes through. It's a blocked call, and I answer immediately, thinking it will be Hal.

'Hello, Joy. It's Johnny Goodwin.' I recognize the voice. The Dark Man. 'Joy, I need you to do something for me. For Andee, really. I know you're calling in the cavalry. That's OK. I'm not mad.

'Please understand that if you don't come out right now and get in the car with me to go get your girls, I'll make a call to my partner and you'll never see them again. Cletus has to be handled carefully, Joy. He doesn't leave witnesses. You met him, years ago, in Wal-Mart. You don't want him cutting his losses and moving on.'

THIRTY-FIVE

I hesitate in the doorway of the Pilot station. I don't see Goodwin's car at the pump. But then I spot it. He's parked it by the propane tanks, but I don't see Goodwin inside.

'Did Woods tell you not to come out of the bathroom?'

Goodwin's voice. He is right behind me.

People are getting off work and the Pilot station is a hive of activity. There are people all around. Goodwin puts one hand on my elbow and the other on my shoulder and guides me, smiling, to the car.

He opens the door, tucking me in like a child at bedtime. He is even going to fasten my seatbelt, but I push his hand away. He trots smartly around the back of the car, and in the time it takes me to think about running again he is settled into the driver's seat and putting the key in the ignition.

We are quiet, but soaked in tension. He catches a green light and pulls out of the Pilot station, driving effortlessly, a man without nerves.

'The trunk,' he says finally, with a long drawn out sigh.

'You have a *gas* can in there. A *new* one. You used it to burn down my house.'

'That was Purcell, not me, and he was supposed to have gotten rid of it.' He shakes his head. 'I always let my guard down, around you.'

'So you're not Purcell. You're not Goodwin. And you're not the man I saw on the web cast.'

'I'd like your cell phone, if you'd pass it this way.'

'I don't have it with me. We left in a hurry, remember?'

He snatches my purse, pushes the button to unroll his window and throws it out on the road.

'Just to make sure,' he says.

'My favorite lipstick was in there. My *only* one.'

'I'll buy you a new one.'

'Will that be before or after you shoot me in the throat?'

He says nothing for a while. Just drives.

'I'm Harvey, by the way. Reginald Harvey.' He leans across to shake my hand, shrugs at my rebuff.

'And all that stuff with Purcell's history? I take it that was you?'

He shoots a look at me. 'No, that wasn't me. Everything I told you about Cletus Purcell is true. We're foster brothers, me and Cletus. We both got placed with the Hermans. They specialized in boys like us.'

'But it was Purcell who came up to me in Wal-Mart.'

'Yeah, I always use Cletus when the work requires a face.'

'And Goodwin?'

His face lights up. 'He's at a conference in Singapore, right now. Serendipity, don't you think? It was perfect. You could be completely honest *with* me *about* me. Say what you think to Goodwin, without worrying about a gun to your head. And I could keep track of the investigation.' He sounds amused. 'It was Goodwin, you know, who kept telling Woods you were holding back, that there had to be some kind of connection.'

'And all that stuff about you and Dr Goodwin being in communication?'

'All true.'

'Cletus Purcell was part of that?'

'Nah, it's not the kind of thing Cletus gets into. He's not a big risk taker, and he doesn't like to play. If he knew I was talking to Goodwin, and getting in and out of the computers? He'd take off.' Harvey cocks his head. 'But he'd kill the hostages first. That's why we have to get out there now. Tonight. Agent Woods had just about nailed the location anyway. And now that you've made your phone calls, he and his two teams are going to be squabbling over the big finale. If we let them get there ahead of us, Purcell will damn sure kill your girls. You should have trusted me, Joy.'

'Sure. The guy who set this whole thing up and has a gas can in the back of his car.'

He laughs. 'Goodwin finds me fascinating, you know. He and Woods have been burning up their keyboards, back and forth since late last night.' Harvey flashes me a smile like a movie star. 'These forensic guys, they can never resist. He studies me, I study him. He has some interesting insights on why I am who I am.'

'An apex predator?'

'My *personal* favorite.'

'And what does the real Dr Goodwin say about your quest?'

Harvey gives me a sideways glance. 'That was quite the harsh little e-mail you put together.'

'Don't ask for honesty, if that's not what you want.'

'Yes, but was it meant for *me*, or Cletus? Because it occurred to me that since you know him, and thought he was the guy you were talking to, your answer might be tainted by that.'

'That's possible, I guess. What does Goodwin tell you?'

'You mean about redemption, salvation, that sort of thing?' He looks thoughtful. 'My impression is that it throws him. He can't really make up his mind how serious I am. He is sorely tempted to mark it all down to the usual manipulation. That was his conclusion in his last report to the FBI.' He grins at me. 'I'm in and out of his computer as much or more than he is. As you see, it's the same problem over and over. Nobody takes me seriously about this. Which is why I took the trouble to get your undivided attention.'

'And Darrin Lane? Jimmy Mahan? Gloria Schmid? They didn't take you seriously with a gun to their throat?'

'You tagged it when you gave me that e-mail this morning. I've tried three times already. It just didn't work.'

'They told you what you wanted to hear,' I say flatly.

'Any which way I wanted to hear it, for just a few minutes more of life. And I wondered, thinking about it afterward, if any of them had the right kind of insight, anyway. They went to the same seminary you did, took a lot of the same classes. But they just weren't you. I went to them first because I didn't want things between us . . . getting all snarled up. I wanted to keep things *clean* between you and me. But I couldn't get there, not without you.'

He looks at me, quite seriously. 'I had to motivate you. Make sure you did take me seriously. But I'd never hurt you, Joy. You should know that. You're the one who put me on this path. And I gave you my word, my promise, do you remember? I told you when your husband hired me to kill you that I wouldn't ever hurt you. That as far as I was concerned you'd always be safe.'

'Cletus Purcell gave me *his* word.' Actually he didn't, but I'm not bringing that up.

'It was my word, through Cletus. Purcell doesn't actually *have* a word. He works on a more primitive level. Honor is a concept he does not comprehend.'

'What a team.'

'Not a *team*. Purcell follows orders. For the most part anyway. He has an annoying habit of putting his own spin on things. He makes mistakes. They got a *fingerprint*, from your daughter-in-law's house in Arkansas. How stupid is that?'

'Maybe too stupid, Mr Harvey.'

He gives me a focused look. 'You're right, I set that up. Sometimes you have to throw those law enforcement types a bone. And it's getting a little iffy now, working with Cletus. The neighbor, for instance. Stupid. No point killing him, all he saw was a tall man with a mask. And then there's your cousin.'

'Marsha.'

'She wasn't supposed to be there. Purcell could have waited until she was out of the house. *Should* have waited until she was out of the house.' Harvey sighs. 'I wasn't too pleased when he called and told me he'd decided to kill her, but there was no point in arguing. Cletus doesn't leave witnesses behind.'

'They're still at the cave, though, Andee and Caro? You didn't lie about that?'

Harvey's face wrinkles up, his voice steady and stern. His eyes change like a nictitating membrane and the camouflage of humanity drops. 'I don't lie to you.'

'Are they alive? Caroline and Andee?'

'As of yesterday, yes. That's why you and I are headed for the cave, Joy. To save them. Cletus is a wild card. He's got a natural radar for survival and I think he's beginning to sense the FBI closing in.'

'Then maybe he's killed them already.'

'We're on our way to find out. But consider that as far as Clete knows, this is a straight-up kidnapping, set up to skim off the donation money you've pulled in with your work. And the one thing I made sure Clete understood was that the girls stay alive till we have the money in hand, otherwise, he doesn't get his cut. So he'll see they stay healthy till he gets paid *unless* he thinks the wheels are coming off and decides to cut and run.'

'Scares easy, does he?'

Harvey's tone is gentle. 'You've met him, Joy, you know better than that.'

I look away. It is dark now. Fallen leaves clog the two lane road that takes us the back way to Wilmore, toward High Bridge.

'So let's get on with *our* business, shall we? We're short on time, let's get finished.' Harvey winks. 'Is there salvation, *genuine* salvation, for a guy like me?'

I stare out the window again. It takes willpower not to turn my head.

'Joy?'

Something in the soft way he says my name makes the fear rise up in my throat.

'Answer my questions, honestly, tell me what I want to know, and then I'll take you straight to Caroline and Andee. You'll get your girls back safe.'

'Take me to Caroline and Andee first. Let them go, and do it in a way that I *know* they're safe. And then, and *only* then, Mr Harvey, will I answer any question you want to ask. I won't bullshit you, or say what I think will make you happy. But you get *nothing*, you understand me? Until I know my girls are safe.'

He drives along. He is humming.

'It can't be the daughter-in-law,' he says conversationally. 'Even you must have some kind of limit on what you'll sacrifice for the woman who killed your son.' He reaches into his jacket pocket and I brace myself for the bullet or blade. He rattles something in my direction, a tin of Altoids gum. 'Help yourself.'

I smell the cinnamon when he begins to chew.

'Grandchildren,' he says. 'On the outside looking in, it doesn't make that much sense. You don't raise them. You don't give birth to them. They're a generation removed from your own child.' He taps his finger softly on the wheel.

'You know, of course – you must know, Mrs Miller. That I can *make* you talk.'

There is nothing but kindness in his face.

He tilts his head upward, as if he is trying to remember. '"The world breaks everyone and afterward, many are strong at the broken places. But those that will not break it kills. It kills the very good and the very gentle and the very brave impartially. If you are none of these you can be sure that it will kill you too . . . but there will be no special hurry."'

He smiles at me, as sweetly as a child. 'Hemingway. *A Farewell to Arms.*'

It is the gentleness I hear in the tone of his voice, that makes the hair stand on the back of my neck.

THIRTY-SIX

The road is narrow and meanders from left to right. It is desolate here in the countryside, dark and unfamiliar. The headlights are on high beam, but the darkness hides everything but the next twenty feet of road. I keep my hands twined together in my lap, to hide that they are shaking.

Every half mile or so we pass a house, and I look at the lights in the windows. I see glimpses here and there – curtains, a dining room table. The glow of a television set.

Harvey flips the turn indicator, brakes, and we go left, down a steep gravel drive. At the bottom are three security lights that illuminate the mouth of a monster. The entrance is wide enough that we can drive straight in. The ceilings are tall, a good thirty feet. A metal gate, like the ones that barricade storefronts in the mall, has been raised high enough for us to pass beneath.

Harvey points to the gate. 'I see that Cletus has the jump on us. He is oscar mike to the zone.'

The car slows to a crawl and I open my window. Grit and

gravel grind beneath the tires, and I see the gleam of eyes near a cluster of rocks – a possum, most likely, hidden in the dark. The air pressure changes as we pass through the entrance. Water that seeps from the limestone floors hisses beneath the tires. The quiet and the envelope of darkness swallow us whole.

The primitive part of my brain kicks in. The dark. The unknown. The predator at my side. Pressure builds in my chest and I am humiliated by the tears that run down my cheeks. There is no sign of Hal. Of the FBI. Of anyone but me and Harvey. Are they back there somewhere, Caroline and Andee? Who am I to be afraid?

The car creeps forward.

Modular offices, like temporary classrooms, branch to the right and left. They have little porches on the front, with porch lights. The office windows are dark, employees gone for the day. What will they find, when they come to work tomorrow? Nothing will ever be the same.

I get a glimpse of a conveyor belt and machinery behind a metal partition to the right. The bottling operation, no doubt. Harvey bears right and the illumination from the security lights cuts away. My chest goes tight. I feel like I'm being smothered, and I take deep, panicked breaths.

Harvey turns yet again, and we creep along, and I am already unsure of finding my way back. I see a lake of water; it looks deep. We turn again and I am completely disoriented. I dig my fingernails into the palms of my hands and think about Andee. She is here in this cave, and I will not leave without her. It is that, finally, that keeps me from going over the edge.

Harvey eases the car alongside a wall and turns off the engine, leaving the headlights on. He leans across the front seat and opens the glove box.

'Flashlights,' he says.

There are two of them, small and black, and he hands one to me. It is startlingly heavy.

'In a minute I'll turn off the headlights.' His voice is low and I have to bend close to hear. 'People get kind of freaky, back in the dark like this, when the lights go out. You need to hang tough, OK? Stay quiet and calm. We're close to the

RV where Cletus and the girls are. If you scream or call out, he might hear us. I don't need to tell you that wouldn't be good.'

He flips the switch of his flashlight. 'Here's how it's going to work. You wait here and let me go on ahead. *Don't* wander off. If you get lost, no one will find you. There are miles of unexplored passageways back here. And if Cletus spots you, Caroline and Andee are dead. You understand me? You're clear?'

'I understand you.'

'I'll tell Cletus that we're blown, but that I've got the money. That the FBI is on to us and we need to close up shop.'

'What money?'

He shakes his head at me. 'There *isn't* any money, but Cletus thinks there's a ransom. He's not doing this for fun.'

'OK. I'm with you.'

'I'll take the girls with me. We'll regroup, you, me, Caroline and Andee, and head back out in my car. Then we'll drop the girls at a house somewhere where there are lights and somebody's home, or if not that, then some gas station somewhere. That way you'll know they're safe, and you and I can sort things out.'

'I get to pick the spot where we drop the girls. So I can be sure it's not some prearranged drop.'

He gives me a second look, then nods. 'If that makes you feel better. Fine with me.' He scoots to the door of the car. 'Time for me to get going. Hang right here, just for a minute, and get ready for the lights to go.'

He pushes the button beneath the dash, pops the trunk and disappears. I hear him rummaging through his luggage. I think about Caroline and Andee. I want to believe what Harvey has told me. That they're close and we'll bring them out safe. But why will Purcell let Harvey take the girls, if he doesn't have his half of the imaginary ransom? This man who never leaves a witness alive?

Harvey appears suddenly beside my window and motions for me to get out of the car. 'Just stay behind the car. Sit down, so when Clete and I come up, he won't see you, and blow this whole thing.'

He reaches a hand in the open window. Says 'Ready' and shuts off the lights.

It's like being buried alive.

I don't mind dying so much; it's the getting there that worries me. I flip the switch on my flashlight and focus on the circle of illumination. There is nothing to see but damp walls, a crumbling limestone floor and shadow.

Harvey's voice is barely a whisper. 'If you hear gunfire, stay away from the walls. Bullets tend to travel along walls.' He salutes. 'Wish me luck.'

His light bobs, marking his progress, and I can hear his footsteps and their small echo. The light disappears suddenly, as if he's turned a corner. I listen, but he's disappeared. It occurs to me that he could be standing a few feet away, watching to see what I'll do.

It is chilly in the cave. Maybe fifty-four degrees. I fold my arms, huddled in Harvey's sweater. He has worn it recently. It has his smell. I hear the faint sound of water dripping, and notice the smallest caress of an air current on my cheek. The question is, do I stay where I am?

The psychopath is not your friend.

Harvey will know if I follow too closely. But I could wait a few minutes, then start out in the direction he went. I wonder – what are my chances of finding the girls?

It is the easiest thing in the world to become lost in a cave. Harvey said this one has over a million square feet. Mammoth Cave, further west, is still being mapped, with four hundred miles of passageways down, and who knows how many more to go.

Three hundred and fifty million years ago the local countryside was covered with water, resting beneath a shallow sea. Gradually, as the water level dropped, the land formed sandstone layers at the surface, with limestone layers beneath. A labyrinth of passages was sculpted by rivers underground, and the water is still there, four hundred and fifty feet below the surface, popping up in underground springs.

I aim my flashlight upward, trying to keep my mind off cave-ins, a regular occurrence when ceilings in the passageways get too wide to support the bedrock beneath. Jesse James hid out in caves like this. Maybe this one. He made it back out again.

Not everyone does.

Floyd Collins was trapped in Sand Cave in 1925 when the ceiling came down, trapping him in the passageway. He had air but could barely move, one foot wedged beneath a rock. The cave-in caused a media frenzy, while rescuers toiled over the treacherously shifting dirt and rock for all of two weeks. A reporter for the Louisville *Courier-Journal* held interviews with Collins while rescuers tried to get him out.

The reporter won a Pulitzer; Robert Penn Warren wrote the incident up in a novel that became famous. Floyd Collins died.

I see no trace of cave life – no crickets, no bats. No water here, so no blind fish. I would feel better if I saw something. Animals have good instincts when they make a home. A cave can be a safe sanctuary, for man and beast. I am picturing the pillars we passed on our way inside, where the rock was blasted and sculpted to make supports. There aren't any pillars this far back.

There is a scrape of rock from somewhere behind me. I shine the flashlight over my shoulder but can see nothing in the beam of my light.

I poke around until I find a pointy sliver of rock. I scrape it on the wall and see that it leaves a mark.

I'm not going to stay. My gut tells me not to do what Harvey says. And there is zero chance of me finding the girls if I stay where I am. I might not be able to see them, but there's a good chance I can *hear*. I remember what I saw in the web cast, the little kitchen where they cooked, toilets that flushed according to Andee, and light. The RV will have a generator, and generators are noisy. If I go in the direction Harvey went, I'll be able to hear the hum.

I will walk with one hand on the cave wall and scratch an X in the rock every two or three feet, and be able to find my way back. This isn't a Greek legend, and I don't have a ball of twine.

THIRTY-SEVEN

I am counting my steps, and my tally so far is two thousand two hundred twenty-three. I hear scratching noises sometimes, and what I'm sure must be footsteps, but when I shine my light there is nothing there.

The wall drops away and I am at a crossroads. I can go into a chamber to my left, continue straight ahead or turn right and keep following the wall. Heading right and staying with the wall is my best shot at keeping my bearings, but it'll be no good if I'm going the wrong way. I shine the light at my feet, close my eyes and listen. If someone is close I might be able to hear.

I don't want to let go of my wall. I know how dangerous it is, this wandering. Never go alone, take rope, bring three sources of light. Always let someone know where you are and when you'll be back. I choose the wall, making my marks and counting my steps.

It is the echo that saves me, the sound of a generator somewhere close. The noise seems to come from my right, but behind me as well. I stand still and there's a sudden sound, like someone has shut a door at the bottom of a well. I backtrack, one hand along the wall until the damp rock drops away. I don't hear the noises anymore.

Panic comes in a wave. There is no forward, no backward, nothing but dark. I have no idea which way to go, where to find the girls, the noise I heard or the entrance of the cave. I tremble with an overwhelming urge to run. I stand still instead, taking deep breaths.

And then I hear things, small noises that bounce off the rocks before they're absorbed by the walls. There are voices, like you hear in dreams. I feel the presence of people, am aware of tiny smells, a difference in the air pressure where before there was a sensory void. I move toward the voices and hear, again, the generator's tell-tale hum.

There is light ahead, diffused, hazy, strange. It leaks from the edges of small, boarded-up windows. There is a monstrous presence in the darkness. The dark outline of an RV.

I have found it. Caro and Andee's prison.

The hinged door opens abruptly and voices of men drift toward me. I can hear an undercurrent of continuous sobbing, my granddaughter's exhausted cry. So she is alive, my Andee. She is well enough to cry.

I drop and lie flat on my belly, crawling slowly, with such care, inching closer to the RV. The floor is dry and cold and gritty. I stay flat and silent, lurking to one side.

'They don't go anywhere till I get my cut. After that, you can take them with you, if you want to do it. Smartest thing be to leave them with me.'

I am held by the power of that voice. It takes me back to the afternoon where Cletus Purcell sat across from me over coffee and I faced the flatness, the odd lack of reflection in his eyes. It is Purcell that I remember. I have dreamed of him for years.

'That's fine.' Harvey's voice. 'But we need to head out. We have to wind this up *now*, Cletus.'

'I don't like it.'

The tension is strong between them, strong enough that I can feel it out here.

'Look, just lock them back up.' Harvey's voice. 'We'll go to the car together – it's not that far. Let's split the cash and decide what to do from there.'

I hear layers of meaning in Harvey's words. *Let's go get the money, then I'm out of here, and you can do what you want with the hostages.*

But, of course, there is no money. Just twists, turns, more games ahead.

Purcell makes a sound that I take for agreement. Evidently he reads Harvey's subtext the same way. Harvey is an expert, after all, at being whoever he needs to be. Salesmen are vulnerable to pitches from other salesmen. Maybe serial killers affect each other the same way.

The RV shakes as the two men come out, the weight of them rocking the steps. Neither speaks to Caroline and Andee. I wonder what it's like for my girls inside, being discussed like a carcass of meat.

The door clicks shut, followed by the sound of a heavy plank of wood sliding into place. I can free the bolt of wood from outside the door, and hope rises inside me like helium, only to sink when I hear the chirp of a keyless lock.

I wait until I can no longer hear the murmur of Harvey and Purcell's conversation, and the sound of their footsteps fades. I look out from my hiding place, but they've been swallowed by the dark. I stand very still, I hold my breath. I count to one hundred, slowly, three times. It is disturbingly quiet inside the RV.

I shine my light in all directions. There are damp spots and puddles, but I can detect no one watching from the surrounding dark. I turn the light to the door. A two-by-four of lumber has been placed to bar it shut, cradled in a newly installed metal hasp. There is a back-lit keyless entry pad installed by the door, and a warning sticker that says **STOP – Protected By – Flagship Sentry™ Digital Security System**. The wood plank is awkward, but no trouble once I set my flashlight on the front step. I glance over my shoulder, not that it does much good. It's too dark for me to see.

The keyless entry pad is a problem. The light in the panel means it's working. I can smash the lock with a two-by-four, but I am worried it will set off an alarm.

I knock softly on the door. '*Caro. Andee.* It's Joy, can you hear me?'

'*Joy?*'

The voice comes from the window by the steps, and I see the tips of Caro's fingers. She has dug out behind the wood boarding up the opening and it gives her a peephole so she can see. I can hear Andee as well, but I can't make out her words.

'Where are they?' Caroline asks.

'They're headed out to Harvey's car – we drove it into the cave. Listen, Caro, there's an alarm on the doorway. I can break the lock with this plank of wood, but the alarm has to be wired up to a battery somewhere inside. If you can disconnect it we won't have to worry about some kind of siren going off and bringing the men back.'

'Don't you have the police with you?' her voice squeaks. 'You can't be here *alone.*'

'It's just me, for now. Look, it's complicated, I'll explain later. But the FBI is on the way. In the meantime, we need to get the two of you out. Purcell—'

'Don't say it,' she warns me, and I think of Andee. 'He's let us see him. He's not wearing the ski mask today.'

So Purcell will come back to kill them, unless Harvey kills him first.

'The alarm battery isn't in here,' Caroline says. 'I've already gone over every inch of this place. I think it used to be hooked into the closet light, there's a place where it looks like they took it out. The battery's got to be outside the RV, and it can't be too far away. Look underneath for wires.'

I crouch beside the RV and shine the light, walking all the way around. On the other side I see wires. I pick them up in one hand and follow them, nearly tripping over the twelve volt battery that sits about twenty feet away. There are two leads of double stranded wire, and I unwind and disconnect them both.

I run back to the front of the RV and knock hard on the door.

'Joy, did you find it?'

'Yeah.' The entry pad is dark now. Success.

I unbolt the door and use the two-by-four to smash the lock. The first two blows are off target, The wood is awkward and hard to aim. The third time I clip the lock hard and bend the hasp. It takes a serious effort to yank it free of the wood, then the lock slides off and hits the ground.

The door flies open and Caroline stares at me, blinking, bathed in light. I take a step forward and see Andee, huddled behind her mother.

There is the strangest moment, infinitesimal and surprising, where the three of us freeze – me at the door, Caroline just inside and my little granddaughter, Andee, huddled under a built-in table, arms wrapped tightly around her legs. The smell inside the RV reminds me of the unique scent of a newborn and mother, the first hours after birth. Later I will remember all of it, a color-wheel of detail, as if my mind were a sponge of sensation, going from bone dry to drenched.

It is surprising how new and nice it is inside, and there is a certain sense of wonder, with this compact home on wheels. I remember beige – the carpet, the walls, the upholstery on the couch and chairs. The appliances and counter tops are of stainless steel and granite and I suspect this little prison cost somebody more than my house.

And then we all move at once, coming together in the entrance. The music of our voices and our tears send echoes into the dark. The bond that connects the three of us, that silver cord of love, brings us together in a rare harmony of feeling we will only know again in the memory we retain. We embrace our life and the imminent possibility of our death.

Caro smiles at me. She does not seem afraid anymore. She is young, still.

I hold Andee up high in my arms and settle her snugly upon my hip. She feels as warm as a tiny coal fire. She traces my tears with a slender, grubby finger.

'They'll be back,' I say to Caro.

She nods quickly. 'Do you know the way out?'

I frown, making the impossible judgment. 'I think I can get us out, but we'll have to go slow.'

She bites her lip. 'Hide then? Till they're gone or we're stormed by the cops?'

'The FBI is on the way and Harvey knows it.'

'Which one is Harvey? The new guy? Do they think you have ransom money? Are they crazy stalkers from your old cable show?'

'We can talk this out or we can hide. Later, OK?'

She nods.

'Nina, why are you wearing tennis shoes with a pretty dress?'

'Andee,' Caroline says. 'Go get one of those plastic garbage bags out of the kitchen, and put in three water bottles and the candy bars in the cabinet by the sink. We're going on a big adventure, just the three of us girls together, and you have to do your part.'

'What's my part?'

'To listen when Nina and I talk to you. To do exactly what we say. And to be good.'

Andee's eyes are little circles of exhaustion, but her mother's words ignite a spark. 'But Mommy, after the adventure, can we please go home?'

THIRTY-EIGHT

C aro and I disconnect the generator. The silence is eerie after the hum. We make sure to keep Andee snug between us, with the flashlight on, from the moment the lights go out.

Andee is shivering. She wears a thin cotton shirt, long-sleeved, and a worn, wrinkled pair of brown corduroy jeans. She and her mother had dressed in a panic the night they were kidnapped, grabbing the clothes that came to hand. I know that Caro must be cold as well, in blue jeans and a short-sleeved tee. I take Harvey's heavy sweater off and pull it gently over Andee's head.

We stand together for a moment in front of the dark RV. We've replaced the plank of wood, bolting it across the door. It is Caro's job to count our steps, and mine to find the way. I take the lead and Caro brings up the rear. We keep Andee between us. We have told her that we're all a train and must stay connected by holding hands *no matter what*.

'Nina,' Andee whispers after we've gone a way. 'I want to hold the light.'

I hear the fear in her voice, which I balance against the time we have and our need to move. I wonder if the batteries in the flashlight are fresh.

Caro's voice floats up from behind. 'Nina is the leader, so she has to have the light.'

'You have three turns when you can hold the light,' I tell Andee. 'Don't use them up too fast.'

'I need one *now*.'

Caro starts to protest, but I say OK. If Andee gets hysterical from the dark and the closed-in feeling, her cries will echo and draw the predators close. A few moments now may save us panic on down the way.

I place Andee's small fingers around the flashlight and guide her to the switch.

'I want to hold it myself, Nina.'

'That's against the rules.'

Andee shines the light beneath her chin. 'Don't I look like a skeleton, Nina?'

But now I can hear men's voices. Purcell and Harvey are back.

'Shit,' Caro says.

'Do you hear them, Nina?' Andee whispers.

'It's quiet time, baby. Tiptoe.'

We move quickly and the wall gives me nothing more now than balance. I don't have time to think things through, to keep any kind of track of our path. It's the distance that matters now. The darkness will swallow us and keep us safe.

In the background, I hear masculine voices that fade as we turn a corner. Just as I think we have a chance, a shattering of sound echoes everywhere. Gunfire. Spurts and flashes of light, the smell of cordite, the sound of running feet.

Andee's screams are like breaking glass inside my heart. Caro shouts 'Run', and instinct takes over. Fear keeps us moving and we whip together holding hands, a human chain of fear. I keep the flashlight pointed ahead so we can see where we go. Knowing that if we can see our path, so can others.

And then my light catches a reflection. Water. A lake rises up like a miracle. Is it the same one I saw on the way in, I wonder? Are we close to the entrance of the cave?

'We can hide here,' Caro says. She swings into the lead and wades straight in. We're ahead of the men, but they're close. If we float quietly and duck under the water, they may simply pass us by.

The water is an ice cold shock. It hits me right at the waist, and my dress billows and rises. My legs, exposed in thin nylons, go numb with cold. It is noisy, all the splashing, and we have to slow down, to keep it quiet. Caro pulls Andee along behind her and I bring up the rear. My teeth are chattering hard, but Caro keeps us on the move. I keep expecting Andee to cry, but she stays very quiet. We are absorbed in the energy of fear.

My next step finds nothing, and I go down. It is like falling through a trap door. I am under water, plummeting deeper and deeper into darkness. I don't know which way to go.

Something tugs my left hand. It is Andee, still holding tight. I'm pulling her down with me, and I need to break the grip. Just as the thought comes I find myself being yanked hard and now it is not just Andee, but Caro, who has hold of my arm. Then I am being dragged until my head is out of the water, and my ankle hurts, but I can breathe again. There is air, and noise, and hair plastered in my face, and nothing makes any sense.

Caro is crying and calling my name, and someone lifts me up. It is Reginald Harvey who gets me back on my feet.

I sputter and choke. I am alive, but we are discovered. Cletus Purcell has a gun in his left hand, and in the other shines a light.

The look he gives Harvey is puzzled. 'Should of let nature take its course.'

'Hostages,' Harvey says. He shakes his head at me. 'The FBI is swarming the place. We didn't make it back to the car.'

'Plan C,' Purcell says, matter-of-factly.

And Harvey agrees. 'Plan C.'

'There's another way out of here,' Purcell tells us. 'It's not too pleasant, but it'll do the trick. Anybody starts to making noise and I'm gonna snap me some necks.' He reaches out suddenly, scooping Andee up. 'You ladies can come along or stay. But I'm taking the kid with me.'

Andee kicks and squeals like an outraged pig, and Purcell clamps a monster hand across her mouth. 'Give me trouble, little girl, and I'm gonna twist your Mama's head till I break it right off.'

Andee freezes in his arms. If I had a gun I would shoot him just for the pleasure. I look at Caro and see she'd do exactly the same, except she'd take the time to torture him first.

All the guilt that has compressed my heart for the last fourteen years melts away. Just like that. I remember now, what it feels like, when you have to do what you do. I know what many before have discovered. It is not the good who survive.

THIRTY-NINE

We slog through the water. I am electrified. Alert. Purcell leads the way, with Andee riding piggyback on his shoulders. I see Caro reach out and stroke her daughter's back. I walk behind her, shivering hard, teeth chattering, and Harvey brings up the rear.

I am changing and adapting and Joy Miller the evangelist is gone. I am a survivor with a mission. I will do whatever I must. There is freedom with my fear. I am ready.

I lost my flashlight in the water, but both men are shining their lights. It takes all of our energy to stay on our feet, but I am keeping up. I think of being warm again; somewhere I am not afraid and can see the light of day.

Purcell stops. We have come to a sheer wall of rock and boulders.

Purcell knows where he's going. He is long-legged and wiry, and he scrambles up a cluster of boulders, one arm clamping Andee to his side. He climbs a good twelve feet, stopping on a narrow ledge. I can't see where he plans to go until his light catches a small opening, eighteen inches high and two feet wide.

My mouth goes dry. I know that I cannot follow. Claustrophobia rises, and I'm not even aware that I'm moving backward until I bump into Harvey, who clamps me tight in his arms.

Caro is already climbing, and Purcell stops and shines his light at me. I know I'm not impressive, hair wet and plastered to my head, skin blue with cold, torn dirty silk dress that clings like a second skin.

I shake my head. 'No.'

Purcell points his gun. 'Suit yourself.'

'*No, no, Nina.*' Andee's wail echoes, and the sound of it makes the hair stand up on my neck.

'Shhh, little girl, shhh.' Harvey sounds confident, even friendly. 'Nina's just a little scared, that's all. You need to be brave and show her how it's done.'

It's illogical, this mix Harvey always engenders, this gratitude and rage. A moment of kindness to my granddaughter, while manipulating her to what may well be her death.

Caro is up on the ledge now. I can tell she is looking down at me, but I'm pinned in the light. I can't see her face.

'Come on, Joy,' she tells me. 'You can do this, I know you can. We need you. We need to all stay together.'

I take another step backward and Harvey holds me harder, keeping me in place.

'I'm sorry,' I say. And I am. Very sorry. But there is no way I can go into that passageway.

I turn suddenly and try to run, but Harvey is ready, and doesn't let me go.

A voice booms from the darkness, and all of us freeze.

'Cletus Purcell. Reginald Harvey. This is the FBI. There are three SWAT teams in position around you, and we have an army of agents posted at every entrance to the cave.' A flood of light breaks the spell of darkness, and I squint and use a hand to shade my eyes.

'We have hostages,' Purcell shouts.

Harvey turns me to face the floodlights, using my body to shield his own. He puts the muzzle of his gun against my throat. I remember the pictures of Jimmy, Darrin and Gloria. He's a throat man, is Harvey.

'*Go,*' he says to Purcell, behind him. He is the only one who is calm.

'Nina,' Andee cries. '*Nina.*'

'Hush, baby,' Caro says. 'Mommy's right here.'

Harvey pulls me backward, and he has to drag me. I am dead weight, though it doesn't slow him down.

'I'm not going,' I whisper. Only Harvey can hear what I say.

'Think about this, Joy.' He sounds appallingly kind and only slightly out of breath. 'You don't go, I don't go. You're safe, but what do you think Cletus will do without you and me there to keep control? What happens to Caro and Andee then?'

'I *can't.*'

'You can. You can if all you think about is Andee. Just Andee, that's all you keep in your head.'

I tell myself I am dead already, and there's no reason my corpse cannot go into those rocks. But I'm dealing with phobia. Logic doesn't hold much sway.

'Ten feet, Joy. That's all. Go ten feet into the passageway and then it opens up, and there's a little chamber on the other side that leads right out. Ten feet and you're free. You'll be through before you have time to think about it.'

It is this that finally moves me. That and Andee. I will do what Harvey tells me and keep my mind on her.

The FBI is back on the bullhorn, trying to talk Purcell and Harvey in. It is clear there is little to bargain with, other than a promise not to shoot them on sight, and even the agent behind the bullhorn doesn't sound convinced. I think about SWAT team snipers and wish they'd take their best shot. If they hit me by accident I promise to understand.

'Kill the lights,' Harvey says. 'Do it *now* or she's *dead.*'

And I am she. I am she who will be dead. *Don't, please*, I will them. *Don't kill the lights.*

But the agent in charge is cooperative. I flash on Agent Harris in Arkansas who doesn't cooperate no matter what.

The lights go out and my stomach sinks in the darkness. I am cold. I want it to be over. I am tired of being afraid.

Harvey nudges me forward, giving me a hand and hauling me up the hill of rock, while my feet scrape and slip. Once I'm up on the ledge, he does not give me time to catch my breath. He pushes me toward the passageway, keeping me off balance.

'On your back,' he whispers, his breath a warm tickle on my cheek, and I scratch like I've been bitten by a bug. He lifts my right hand. 'Hold this arm up over your head and keep your other arm down by your side. Remember, Joy, ten feet, and then you're out of the cave. Get along as fast as you can, but be very careful of your head. I still have my flashlight, and as soon as we're out of range of the Feds, I'll pass it up to you.'

How long will it take, I wonder, before the FBI figures it

out? How long till they send agents creeping into the darkness to find out where we've gone when we disappear? Will they be delayed, thinking we're hiding in the water? How much time will it take before they find the narrow opening in the rock?

That is my last thought as I lie on my back, right arm raised over my head. I squirm along on my back, deep into the heart of the wall.

FORTY

I push myself along, listening. The others are not far ahead. I see the occasional flash of their lights and hear the echo of voices ahead.

It is warmer, just a little, in this passage of rock. My heart pounds and I am shivering, but still I sweat. I hit my head and groan softly, wiping a smear of wet grit and blood from the top of my scalp.

Harvey taps my foot. As promised, he shines the light.

I feel the stir of panic build as I see how the rock presses so close. It gets smaller, this passageway, and I begin to wonder if I will fit.

Think like a predator, I tell myself. Beat them at their game. But thinking gets me a throat full of hysteria. I take deep breaths and let the image of Andee safely tucked in her bed fill my head.

A scream echoes from inside the rock. I'm disoriented before I realize it is Andee I hear. I move quickly now, going forward, and I hit my head again, and something scrapes a layer of skin off my cheek. She screams again and again.

I sob, pushing myself along, and I hear Caroline's murmur. Harvey grunts and pushes close to my feet and I think then how much larger he is than the rest of us. I wonder he does not get stuck.

And then I hit a foot. It is Caroline, wedged into the passage ahead of me.

'Joy?' she says, loud, so I can hear her over my grand-daughter's cries. 'Andee's stuck somehow. She won't go.'

'*Cletus*,' Harvey bellows. 'Cletus, are you there?'

'He's gone,' Caro says. 'Andee stopped and he dragged her. Then she got stuck, and I think he went ahead.'

He's left us behind, I think, this man who does not leave witnesses. He must think we can't get out. I know we've gone further than the ten feet Harvey described.

'*Caroline*. Can you see what she's stuck on?' Harvey sounds so calm. The echo of his voice is eerie.

'No, that son of a bitch took the light.'

'We've got one,' I say quickly. 'Tell Andee we'll get it to her, but she has to stop screaming.'

Caro murmurs and Harvey pushes the light as far as he can up the top of my leg. I tell myself to move slowly. I push away the thoughts that come into my head, how Floyd Collins stayed wedged in a passageway much like this one, talking off and on to his would-be rescuers till the moment of his death.

'Caro? I've got the light here. Can you feel it on your foot?'

'Yeah.' She sounds breathless. 'Nina is here, Andee, I promise. And look, she's brought you a light. She says it's your turn again.'

Andee finally winds down to tiny sobs and hiccups. The silence is a calming, blessed relief. I can finally breathe.

'How's she doing?' Harvey asks.

'She's OK,' Caro says. 'She just panicked. I don't think she's really stuck, but I can't get her to move.'

'Caroline? Is there any chance you can get around or over her?' Harvey says.

'Yeah, it's wider here, thank God. Still tight, but I think—'

'Just make sure to take it *slow*,' Harvey says. 'Test it out so you don't get wedged. Joy? Once Caroline gets ahead of Andee, she can hook her toes under Andee's armpits. She pulls while you push Andee's feet, and that way we can move her along if she's still too scared to go.'

I want to ask him how much further, but can't see how the question will help matters as much as it could hurt.

'Ready,' Caro says.

'Andee, it's Nina.' I try to touch Andee's slender ankles and instead get a handful of cold mud and rock from the bottom of her shoes. 'I'm going to push and your Mama's going to pull, and we're getting you out of here, OK?'

Andee speaks so softly I'm not sure I actually hear what she says. *I love you, Nina* may be nothing more than wishful thinking on my part.

I hear Caro groan and we're moving again. It works surprisingly well, Harvey's plan. It's a relief just to move again. And soon I feel a rustle of air, distinct, upon my face.

'*Oh God.*'

'Caro? What is it?'

'A chamber, Joy. Hang on. Be careful, Andee. Joy, stop pushing, just for a minute. Let me maneuver out.'

Now that I know we are almost there, I feel another panic, and it's all I can do not to push and fight my way through. I concentrate on breathing, listening to the noises Caroline makes. Andee inches forward, moving easily now, without any help from me.

'Joy, it's an exit. It's dark in here, some kind of chamber, but I can see the moon.'

I can hear Caro's tears, even if I can't see them on her face. The light disappears, but it's back again in seconds, and Caro lights my way.

And suddenly my arm dangles out into nothing. I feel the caress of fresh air.

'Are you there? Caro? How far down is it?'

But even as I'm asking she takes my hand. 'Five or six feet, but I've got you.'

Two small hands join the larger ones. 'I've got you, Nina,' Andee says. 'You're safe.'

I flop like a hooked fish on to the ground, but I am not hurt. Caro and Andee have made sure to break the fall. We are in a round little chamber, twelve feet wide, maybe ten feet high, and no more than a few steps away from a door-sized opening into the night air. Even from here I can see the stars.

'Purcell?' I ask.

Caro shakes her head. 'Don't know.'

I glance back to the passageway. Bend close to Caroline so

she can hear my whisper. 'It's going to take some time for Harvey to push his way out.'

Caro gets it immediately. Harvey is a big man. It will take him some time to maneuver. We have our chance to escape. But even as she gathers Andee into her arms and moves for the opening, the moonlight is blocked, and Cletus Purcell rises, gun in hand.

'Glad to see you made it,' Purcell says.

Caro shines the light in his face, and he blinks and points the gun straight at her.

'*No.*' A scream. My own voice.

A scraping and tearing is followed by the thud Harvey makes as he pushes his way out of the passage, like the survivor of a difficult birth.

Harvey and Purcell face each other, two predators in a small chamber. I press myself into the rock, and see Caroline and Andee do the same. They are closer to the entrance but, close as they are, Purcell blocks the way. And Purcell has the gun.

If a lion faces off with a tiger, which predator will win? A lion is heavier, and not as fast. A tiger is longer, has a face full of cunning, and superior skills for the hunt. Still, a lion's days are filled with constant fighting, deflecting the challenge of other males who want to rule the pride. And hunting and fighting are different skills entirely.

Cletus Purcell moves swiftly, one glance over his shoulder, aim and fire.

But in the end, it is the lion's capacity for calm analysis and appraisal that rules the day. Harvey takes the slug in the meat of the muscle below his shoulder, but does not flinch. He is moving steadily, deliberately. He takes Purcell's neck in a windpipe lock with one huge hand, deflecting the gun with the other.

And here it comes down to bulk, bone density and tensile strength.

Harvey slams his head into Purcell's temple, a blow that shatters bone. It is a death blow, ensuring that Purcell will be dead in just under two minutes, but the tiger does not have even that long to live.

Harvey is graceful. He arches forward and bites Purcell's

throat in the vulnerable mid center, ripping flesh and carti-
lage, and crunching the delicate butterfly of Purcell's hyoid
bone.

We do not scream, Caro and Andee and I. We run. Fueled
by instinct, we tumble out of the chamber into open air and
a cliffside, landing at the top of a trail. In the split second it
takes to catch our breath I hear a distinctive click, and we are
suddenly bathed in light.

'*Man-bears*,' Andee shrieks, catching sight of the SWAT
team, bundled in helmets and Kevlar.

I put my hands in the air. '*Hostages*. Don't shoot.'

A dog yelps and growls and I hear a shout. I expect nothing
less than a tide of gunfire from the FBI that has hounded me
since this nightmare began.

Instead I am knocked backward by Leo, who licks my face
and snuffles my neck and whimpers while I hear someone
give the order to stand down.

Andee flings herself at Leo's neck, and he is happy to
knock her over as well. Caroline is laughing insanely, and
sinks down beside me, and Leo stands between all of us and
the rows of men in Kevlar, and growls at anyone who tries
to come close.

More orders, and bulky soldiers stream into the chamber
entrance while three men stand near us, one of them scratching
his head.

'Can somebody give us a hand here with this idiot rescue
dog?'

I hear the crunch of footsteps.

'I might be able to help.'

I know that voice.

'Ma'am, you're going to have to get that dog under control.'
Hal bends down and smiles at me. He shoves Leo sideways,
without a second look. 'Down,' he says firmly.

'I am down,' I tell him. Somewhat out of breath.

He grins and looks back over one shoulder. 'This one must
be OK. She's making fun of me.'

FORTY-ONE

Andee has been clamoring to see the burned-out wreck of my house. I refuse her request to go inside, so instead we wander in circles in the yard. The scorched shell seems to fascinate rather than upset her. Leo has retrieved three balls hidden in the grass. He has managed to stuff two in his mouth and trots beside us, immensely pleased with himself. He maintains a two foot perimeter around us.

Either that, or Andee maintains a two foot perimeter around Leo. It is hard to know. I watch Andee for signs of trauma. I know that she will not sleep without Ruby in her bed and a light on.

I do not know if it was luck or design that compelled Hal to go to my hotel room and demand they let him in to retrieve Leo. He says that he had some notion of using Leo to find us, if things went badly. If there was a need. I do know that having Leo to hug made all the difference to Andee. How much she saw of Harvey's teeth ripping into Purcell I do not know. I do believe that the unconditional love and balanced energy of a dog is healing. Hal says that Leo washed out of the rescue program because *he is a dog with his own agenda.* He also says he thought Leo and I would be a perfect match, because Leo has the best heart of any dog he's ever worked with. So perhaps Leo was meant to be my dog. I like to think that I am Leo's agenda.

'Mommy finally told me what happened to Daddy.' Andee is holding Leo's soccer ball, and I've got his Frisbee and rope.

'She did?'

Andee jumps up and down three times for no particular reason. 'She said most of the time he was a good person. Look see, I can play jump rope without a rope. Mommy

says Daddy had some sad past that made him scary sometimes. Is that true?' Andee's eyes are wide, her air deceptively
casual.

'Yes, that's true.'

'Mommy says one day Daddy scared her so bad they had
a big fight and Daddy got dead.'

I wait for her to ask me the details of *how* her father got
dead, but she doesn't. Perhaps she's not ready to know.

'She says she feels sad about what happened, and sometimes she thinks it's all her fault. Do you think it was
Mommy's fault, Nina? Are you mad at her because Daddy
died?'

I pick Andee up and settle her on my hip. She'll be too big
for me to lift by this time next year, but for now she is even
lighter than she was last summer. Those were long days in
the cave.

'No, Andee, I was never mad at your mother. Your Daddy
had troubles in his heart, but he was in charge of how he acted.
Do you understand what I mean?'

'You mean it was Daddy's fault.'

I have to smile. Nuances and seven-year-olds never mix.

'Mommy's boyfriend is coming to pick us up.' She
looks at me intently. 'His name is Sanderson. Do you mind,
Nina?'

'Not if he's a good driver.'

'Do you think Daddy minds?'

'I think he wants you and your mom to be happy.'

'How do you know?'

'Because I'm a wise old lady.'

Andee nuzzles her head in my shoulder, combining affection
and practicality by wiping her nose on my sweater. 'You're
not *old*, Nina. Not creepy old. You'll be fine if you stay out
of caves.'

'From your mouth to God's ear, little darlin'.'

FORTY-TWO

The rain is falling in fat-bellied drops and brings in a whinge of chill. There are lights on inside my home, and I know exactly which ones – the faux twenties floor lamp beside the corner book case, and the Tiffany ceiling fixture in the hall. I manage the lights in sequence, changing the pattern every four days. Yesterday was the last day for the kitchen.

It is not the casual intruder that has me worried, of course. It is Reginald Harvey, who never came out of the cave, not to the knowledge of the FBI. Certain eager members of the SWAT team shed their padding and made their way through the labyrinth, thinking Harvey went back out of the chamber the way he came in. They found a place where the passage forked, but of Harvey himself, there was no sign.

The light behind the shutters of my windows beckons. Hearth, home and safety. I will turn on the fireplace and sit with Leo in my Beatrix Potter bungalow, which I own outright with the money from the insurance settlement on my house. My new home is long on charm and short on maintenance and needs a lot of work, but was amazingly inexpensive. Real estate prices are a bargain in this small Kentucky town where I live now.

There is a good regional university nearby, and I teach classes in comparative religion, part time. My students are bright and curious, some of them hard-working, and it's a pleasure to watch them find their way.

As is usual in old houses, there is a particular knack to getting the key to turn the lock. I have to twist, then pull the knob toward me and hold my mouth just so. Leo is in his bed by the fireplace, ears back, and waits for me to call him to my side.

My phone rings. Calls from numbers I don't recognize make

me nervous, but a lot of things make me nervous these days. And this is a number I know by heart.

'Home safe?' Hal asks me.

'Yes. Let me set my stuff down. Hold on.'

I leave my purse and the book I've been reading on a drop-leaf table just like the one that Caroline has. I found it two weeks ago while out antiquing and I've tucked it beneath the windows. It is usually covered in stacks of mail, but is handy for those rare occasions when Hal and I sit indoors instead of out on the porch.

'Listen, Joy, my rotation's been changed. I go off at midnight tomorrow. How about Sunday morning breakfast? I'll pick you up at nine, unless you want to sleep late, in which case we'll make it ten. Do you mind if I pack a bag? I've got a few days off. Save me the long drive back.'

'I'll clear out a drawer.'

'Let's bump it up a little. I'm ready for a two drawer commitment.'

I ring off, smiling, and Leo follows me into the kitchen. I fill his water bowl, which is bone dry. Leo brings me a tennis ball and I toss it absently, wondering if my favorite black sweater is clean, making grocery lists in my head. Leo dashes back into the kitchen with the tennis ball and drops it into the bowl of fresh water before he takes a drink.

I fill the tea kettle and light the gas stovetop, and it isn't till I'm rummaging for tea bags that I see a puddle of dried yellow liquid on the floor. There are snout marks on the window and I see that Leo's toenails have made new inroads into the freshly painted kitchen door.

I peer out through the shutters, which are mounted slightly crookedly, discount ones I've installed myself. There is something taped to the window of my kitchen door.

The FBI is no longer looking over my shoulder, so I don't have to worry about fingerprints and forensics. Leo butts my leg with his head, trying to get out on the little porch, while I peel a familiar brown envelope off the glass.

Moths circle the base of the porch light and I look up and

down my quiet street. People are home from work now, many of them eating dinner. There is light in my neighbors' windows, a glow from the living rooms and kitchens. Their cars are tucked into driveways and little detached one car garages. Little orange carts crammed with paper and plastic are out on the curb. My neighborhood is prone to recycling, and most of us are environmentally correct.

Nothing looks out of place. I see no signs of the predator.

I close the shutters and lock the door. Prop myself against the wall. I have no way of knowing if Reginald Harvey is watching, but I feel his eyes at my back. Even as I pull the flap open on the envelope, tearing it as I go, I can feel the stiffness of a photograph.

I don't want to do this. I don't want to look at this picture and go back to the bad places inside my head.

I put the envelope on the counter top. I give Leo his nightly ration. I tell him what a good guard dog he is and pat him on the head.

The publicity from the kidnapping has only just blown over. There is still an avalanche of photographs on the Internet and in the newspapers, showing the outside of the cave and the RV. The articles themselves have died down, news stories obsessed with details. The mattresses with pillow top cushioning and memory foam where Caro and Andee slept. The shower stall with a wide angle water head that gave the illusion of standing in a rainstorm, though that was due more to a lack of water pressure than particular design intent. There were estimates of the initial price of the RV, though these were only guesses. The owner of the RV has been blessedly reclusive and uncooperative. But even with imprecise figures, it is clear it was more expensive than my little house.

A newspaper in England offered a large sum of money for an RV tour and unlimited photographs, and Caro and I were relieved when the request was refused. Some details are too personal for the world to chew over. The thought of strangers pawing through our private moments once again is almost too much to bear.

The next wave of attention was predictable. An onslaught of congratulatory editorials and opinion blogs that sang the praises of everyone involved for standing up to the appetite of the media, thwarting the kidnappers' hunger for attention. In truth, neither Harvey nor Purcell seemed to crave the limelight, preferring to go about their twists and turns in the shadows and the dark. I believe that if anything could turn Harvey worse, it would be a breaking story of his search for redemption and inner peace.

I turn off the tea kettle, and reach instead for the wine. I give Leo a rawhide bone, turn the gas logs in the fireplace to low flame. I take the envelope and a file from my office and Leo and I settle companionably, me tucked up on the couch, Leo at my feet.

The file arrived via e-mail, sent at three in the morning the day after Cletus Purcell was killed and Reginald Harvey disappeared in the cave. According to the e-mail address it came from the *real* Dr Goodwin.

I take a sip of wine and set my glass aside.

Dr Goodwin wrote in something of a hurry. I get the impression of a man of intelligence, masculine sensitivity and a careful integrity that compelled him to send me information, though his mind was on other things.

Dear Mrs Miller,

Russell Woods gave me your e-mail address. I understand that you have something of a conflicted work history with him. I hope it is OK that I got in touch.

I've attached a picture file that will interest you. Formatting is JPEG. If you have problems downloading, let me know. Included are copies of photos from a police file regarding death of Harvey's mother, and Harvey family photographs that have just come to light. In particular, please study the shot of Harvey's mother and Harvey himself, aged approximately thirteen months.

Mother's photo should be of particular interest.

Run down of Harvey's parents: father beat Harvey's mother to death when Harvey four years old. Harvey found curled up next to mother's body by neighbor who heard crying and became concerned. Approximate time spent with mother's corpse – twenty-eight hours.

Father died in jail. Paternal grandparents turned Harvey over to foster care age eleven.

Neighbors at time report mother, Cecily Jenkins Harvey, kind loving parent. In process of divorcing Harvey's father, who at time of her death on unauthorized leave of absence from temp. construction job as steelworker in Detroit.

Regards,
Dr Jonathan Goodwin
Forensic Consultant

There are two pictures in the file, saved to JPEG format as promised, which I have no problem downloading or opening. The first is from a police file and shows Harvey's mother curled sideways, her head half on and half off a braided wool rug. Her facial features are a blur of caked blood and displaced flesh. She wears a dress of French blue, belted, with large covered buttons down the front. The third button has been ripped away, and the dress is a color wheel of blue and the red brown of dried blood. A heart-shaped locket hangs sideways from her neck. One long narrow foot is bare, the other half in and half out of a black, embroidered shoe. Her hands look delicate, fingers slim. The ring finger of her left hand, encircled by a thin gold band, has been bent backward and broken. Though it is hard to tell from just a photograph, there is no clear sign of swelling. My guess is she died within moments of the break.

It is the second picture, a happy moment with baby Harvey, that makes me gasp out loud.

Harvey's mother is wearing the same blue dress she died in, though here it is crisp and freshly ironed. She is smiling and shielding her eyes from the sun. She balances Harvey on her left hip. He is just round enough to be cuddly. He has been tucked into a long-sleeved white tee shirt that snaps at the shoulder, and matching little overalls made of the same blue material as his mother's dress. He squints in the sunlight, smiling like he has just been tickled, a wide open, pink-gummed grin.

It is his mother who draws my gaze. His mother, who looks enough like me that she could have been my twin.

A second e-mail from Goodwin says he believes the uncanny resemblance between myself and Harvey's mother at the time of her death is what triggered Harvey's obsession, and made sense of his need to come to me for absolution.

I have e-mailed Goodwin with my questions. I'd like more detail on this line of thought. Goodwin has yet to respond. I wonder if Harvey is privy to our communication. I wonder if he lurks over our shoulders, aware of every message we send.

In the end, it is not Goodwin's insight that connects the dots.

There is one picture in the envelope Harvey left taped to the window of my kitchen door. Along with a slip of yellow notepaper, torn from a legal pad, written in the familiar green ink.

GOOD EVENING, JOY. YOU LOOK HAPPY THESE DAYS. YOU AND HAL GETTING ON?

NICE BUNGALOW. NEEDS WORK, OF COURSE, BUT WHAT CURB APPEAL!

I HAVE NOT BEEN INSIDE.
LEO WAS NOT VERY WELCOMING, AND I HOPE

IT WILL NOT BE NECESSARY TO INVADE THE
SANCTUARY YOU HAVE FOUND.

WE NEVER FINISHED OUR CONVERSATION. YOU
OWE ME THAT, AT THE LEAST.

MEET ME AT OUR FAVORITE BRIDGE IN
KENTUCKY. TOMORROW NIGHT, DUSK, WHEN
THE TOURISTS LEAVE.

MAKE SURE YOU WAIT UNTIL DARK.

The note is taped to the picture, and I peel it away.

My fingers tremble. I take slow, deliberate breaths. Leo
materializes at my elbow and nudges me with his bucket-
sized head.

A minute ago the idea of meeting Harvey would have been
ludicrous, as inevitable as it suddenly seems. It is the picture
that convinces me. We will have to meet.

And what, exactly, will I tell him? That we live in a dark
and wounded world? That the nature of sin is tied to the
nature of life, and I'll have to get back to him later when
I figure out how?

I press the picture to my heart. Leo snuffles the tears on
my face.

'Look, Leo. See this? The pregnant lady is Reginald
Harvey's mother. And that sturdy little three-year-old with
the big smile? That's Harvey before his life went bad. And
that pretty lady? The one holding Harvey's hand and smiling
so radiantly? That's my mother. Look how young she is.
How happy.'

Leo tries to lick the picture and I pull it away. 'We should
go to bed,' I tell him. 'Tomorrow's going to be a long day.'

I fill my glass full of the wine, hoping it will help me
sleep.

FORTY-THREE

There is little light left in these late afternoons, before the darkness falls. The sun goes down early in November, and December is a mere two days away. So much is in my mind as I climb the familiar steep path up to Natural Bridge. I was raised in Kentucky, and like most who grew up here, I've walked this trail before – with my parents, with Marsha, Aunt Cee and Uncle Don, with my first love from high school, with Joey, my son.

Leo is swept away by the kaleidoscope of smells and the feel of sandy soil and dry leaves on the pads of his feet. He is torn between guard duty, the need to keep me in sight, and the puppy inside who wants to run.

Leo carries a saddlebag style dog pack strapped to his belly. I have tucked two flashlights, my cell phone, dog treats and water bottles in the pockets of the pack. It only occurs to me now, as he bounces ahead on the trail, to worry about what might happen if he wanders into a creek.

I am no longer shivering inside my hooded pullover as the climb warms me up. Leo, a cold weather dog, is tireless on the path ahead of me and wanders on the trailside, following his nose.

I do not want to think. I focus on the crumble and crunch of dead, dry leaves, the reddish soil, the trees. My stomach pulses with nervous flutters. I long for this night to be over, and to return to the comforts of my new home. I picture myself curled up on the couch with Hal, fire logs glowing, Leo and Hal's dog Cindy Lou stretched out beneath our feet.

Leo and I arrive, at last, at the base of the arch, and pass through a narrow section between two sheer walls before we make the final ascent. The bridge is a natural sandstone arch, seventy-five feet long and sixty-five feet high, and there is always a wind blowing when you stand at the top. As claustrophobic as I am, I dread high places more. I watch Leo anxiously, relieved but not surprised to find him sure-footed and unafraid.

I hesitate before I step out on the bridge, feeling the wind that blows the hair gently from my face. I am early, but Harvey is waiting.

He stands on the opposite side and lifts a hand to acknowledge my presence. I can see from here that he is leaner by a handful of pounds, comfortable in worn blue jeans and hiking boots. He wears a thin, high-necked black sweater beneath a powder blue denim shirt that hangs tails out, unbuttoned down the front.

I walk out with little stops and starts of hesitation, and he meets me halfway across. His eyes light up as soon as he sees me up close, and for just a moment I know him as Goodwin, the man who understands everything I've been going through, who will help to keep my granddaughter safe. I gut the feeling the minute it comes, reminding myself it is camouflage. I look for the tell-tale nictitating membrane, the predator who lurks in his eyes.

'Hello, Joy.'

'Mr Harvey.' My throat is quite dry.

'Thank you for trusting me enough to come up here tonight.' He holds a hand out to Leo, who studies him with eerie shepherd focus and no inclination to make friends.

'I'd like to know about the picture you left.'

Harvey nods. 'It's the kind of thing you have to talk about face to face. And I wanted to make sure we could talk without interruptions from people like Russell Woods.' He tilts his head, smiling. 'And, to be completely honest, I just wanted to see you. I feel better when I'm around you, Joy. Like I'm homesick, and you're the home.'

I wonder if this is part of the manipulation, another layer in the role he plays. And yet, haven't I wanted the exact same thing? To be like I was before Carl died? To be free of the things I have done?

'Home for a killer is nothing less than who you used to be and can never be again. We both know that, I'm afraid.'

'I wouldn't put *you* in that category, Joy.'

I sit carefully in the center of the bridge. 'Do you mind if we sit? I feel nervous standing out here in the dark.'

Harvey smiles from the side of his mouth and settles about two feet away. Leo stays on his feet watching Harvey, no more than an inch from my back.

'So tell me, Mr Harvey. What magic wisdom is it you expect me to have?'

Harvey gives me a puzzled look, as if I haven't quite caught on. I turn away and watch the final flare of the sun, the way the sky goes purple, then pink. It is almost like a fountain of fireworks, sunset at the top of the mountain. It flares intensely for a handful of moments, then drains like lightning into clouds. An instant ago the sky was washed in color; now it is full-on dark.

'Tell me, Joy. The truth, please.'

It is mesmerizing the way Harvey looks at me, how casually he sits, how utterly relaxed. And the thing I look for passes over his eyes, giving me a glimpse into the lion, the serial killer, the predator at my side. I feel my fingers trembling, the beginnings of sweat.

'You kept it up, after Carl died. The ministry, your faith. But then when Joey died, you stopped. Did everything turn upside down when your husband died? Did the murder of your son just finish the job?'

'Are you really looking for redemption, Mr Harvey, or are you wanting validation instead?'

The tiniest frown shows in two groove-like wrinkles over the bridge of Harvey's nose. He runs a thumb along the edge of his teeth. 'Would you say it's true that God is responsible for evil, if God is responsible for me? Isn't it possible that Dr Goodwin's theory is correct and I'm nothing more than an apex predator, fulfilling the necessary destiny of the bad?'

I rub my forehead. 'The laws of balance hold that your capacity for bad is matched by your capacity for good, and it's simply a choice you make.'

He laughs explosively. 'Are you saying I've got the makings of a saint?' After a while his smile fades and he tilts his head. 'Expert opinion holds that my brain is abnormal. Which means I *don't* have a choice.'

'Scientists and priests are dangerous, Mr Harvey. I have a

book for you to read. Written by someone who's not only trained in psychology, but someone who's been in the mess.'

I unzip the left saddlebag of Leo's pack and hand the book to Harvey.

He holds it close in the dark. *'Man's Search for Meaning.'*

'Written by Viktor Frankl,' I say. 'Like I said, he was a psychiatrist. He also survived the Nazi death camps. There's a section in there I've marked. The story of a certain Dr J., also known as the mass murderer of Steinhof.'

'My kind of guy?'

'Just listen. He was on staff then, in the largest mental hospital in Vienna. His job was to carry out the Nazi euthanasia program, the *final solution*, as they used to say. And he was a fanatic. No mercy. He personally made sure that every single psychotic patient was gassed. After the war, he was snatched up by the Russians. They put him in the Lubyanka – a notorious prison in Moscow.'

Harvey is watching me as if he is memorizing every word I say.

'And there,' I continue, 'he was a model prisoner. Moral, kind, caring toward all the other prisoners, a good man from that time forward until the day that he died.'

'And the moral of this story?' Harvey says.

'He changed. He had practiced evil. He then chose good. It's proof for you, Mr Harvey. Every human being has the freedom to change at any instant. You are not the victim of your genetics. You have a choice.'

His eyes narrow. He is considering.

'One more question, Joy. I know that when you talked to Cletus that day in Wal-Mart, he told you he and your husband were supposed to meet up here on the bridge. That's where he'd arranged to get the final payoff. Scheduled for the night after you were supposed to be killed. I know your husband supposedly committed suicide that same night, jumping off this bridge. But what I want to know is what happened that night. I understand how personal my question is. But I'm curious to find out how much you might be like me after all.'

I wonder what I should tell him. I decide upon the truth.

FORTY-FOUR

'The night I was supposed to be killed, as you say, I didn't go home. I took Joey to a friend's house, made sure she understood he was to stay there till I got in touch and that he was not under any circumstances to go to school or to call his dad. And me? I headed straight up here, to the bridge.'

'To kill your husband,' Harvey says.

I shake my head. 'To find out if it was really true. That he'd hired a hit man to kill me. That's what things were like in my world back then, Mr Harvey. I had trouble believing, no matter how much evidence there was, that my husband would pay for my death.'

He studies me. 'So you laid low that first night, so he would think that Cletus did the job, and you were dead.'

'Exactly. I was here, at the lodge, the night I was supposed to be killed. I drove up while Carl was busy establishing his alibi, moving boxes with his good friend, George. It took me almost four hours to get here. It was a dark drive, once I got off the Interstate, and there was nowhere it looked safe to stop and ask for directions. I'd been here before, but it had been years, and I couldn't remember all the turnoffs. By the time I made it to the lodge that night, it was already after midnight.

'There was no one behind the desk when I walked in the lobby. It was the middle of the week, the off-season, fall heading into winter. There were only three other cars in the lot. I remember thinking about the last time Carl and I had been up here. Joey was only eighteen months old, and we took a long weekend in early June.

'When the desk clerk finally showed up, he apologized for keeping me waiting and said if I wanted to pay a little extra he could get me a room with a view. I gave him cash and registered under the name Cindy Farmer – a girl in my kindergarten class, my best friend. Her name just popped into my head. Because I was afraid that if the story Cletus told me really was true, and Carl was coming, he might ask for a room. I didn't want the clerk asking him if he was with the other Miller who had registered the night before, or noticing that we were using the same credit card account.

'The next morning I hid my car in a parking lot at the bottom of the mountain. My plan was to hide somewhere up near the bridge, where I could watch and see if Carl actually came. I wasn't going to say anything or try and confront him. I just wanted to know if Purcell's story was true.

'Carl was never a punctual person, but I figured if he was meeting someone like a hit man, he might actually be on time. I left the lodge at five p.m. and started up the trail. I'd forgotten how steep it was. I hadn't been hiking in years, and my knees were aching halfway through the climb. And I didn't have any socks. I meant to bring some, but I was a mess that night I left the house. I didn't even have a jacket. Just my good blazer, the one that went with the skirt I'd worn the night before.

'When I got to the top of the bridge, I hid behind that boulder where you were standing tonight, on the other side. It's a perfect place to wait, as I'm sure you already know. By the time I got settled, it was already starting to get dark. I looked out over the mountain watching the sun go down, just like I did tonight.

'I heard him before I saw him, the slide of stones on the path, footsteps on the rocks. I was huddled down low, looking out from behind the boulder, and the first thing I saw was Carl's boots. I recognized them. And that's when I knew for sure it was true. He'd really wanted to have me killed. He was carrying a backpack. He'd brought the money.

'He kept looking over his shoulder, and from side to side, sometimes even in my direction. A couple of times I thought he'd seen me, then I realized he was just scared. He looked down over the trail behind him a couple of times, then started to come across the bridge.'

I exhale a long slow breath. It is so dark I can barely make out the edges of Harvey's face. Leo is sitting now, but I can feel his tension and his warmth at my back.

'All day, alone in my room, I thought that if I actually saw Carl up here, and knew without a shred of doubt that he'd hired someone to kill me, I would fall completely apart.'

'It wasn't like that, though, was it?' Harvey says.

'Just the opposite. Not knowing for sure was the worst of it. Once there was no doubt at all that Carl had actually done it, that he'd set me and our son up to die, that life as I knew it was over – it was powerful, in a weird kind of way.

'So I watched him. Wondering how long it would take him to realize that Purcell wasn't coming. I had this over-whelming urge to talk to him. I just wanted to know if he'd ever really loved me. To know how it could come to this. To know why.'

'You talked to him?' Harvey says. 'That was a mistake.'

'A big one. I should have waited until he left. I should never have let him know I was there. He was a few feet away from my hiding place, still out on the bridge, when I stood up. He sees me immediately, of course, and freezes.

'"No, Carl," I said. "I'm not a ghost."

'It was so mundane. I'm dusting off the seat of my jeans, and he's just standing there, with his mouth open. So I walk toward him, out on to the bridge.

'"Joy?" He calls my name out, sounding incredulous. His voice drops off at the end. Just for one quick second I wonder if I hear relief. Maybe once Carl thought that I was really dead he had regrets. But no, I tell myself. That's called denial. Time for me to be smart. I had Joey to look out for. I couldn't forget about Joey. Carl would have let him die.

'"Aren't you going to say hello?" I ask him.

'"What are you doing up here? Where have you been? I've been worried sick about you."

'"Really, Carl? Did you call the police? Report me missing?"

'"I called . . . friends."

'"What did you tell them?"

'"Just that we'd had a fight, and I was worried about you."

'"But we didn't have a fight, Carl. Did we?" He seemed afraid of me. I liked the way that felt.

'"What are you doing here, Joy?"

'"The question is what are *you* doing here, Carl?"

'He shrugged the backpack off his shoulders and let it rest at his feet.

'"Eleven thousand three hundred dollars in cash is heavy, isn't it?" I said.

'After that we were both quiet. There wasn't any sound up there but the wind.

'"How did you find out?" he asked me. His voice was flat and weird.

'The question took my breath away. There was no pretense, no explanation – he was just curious about how I'd found out. That's when he took a step toward me. That's when I started to feel afraid.

'"I have my spies," I said.

'That stopped him. "Really?" he said.

'"I've been having you followed, Carl. I hired a private detective. He's got pictures of you with some tall dark man in a painter's cap. Pictures of you and your girlfriend. You'd better hope I make it safe and sound down this mountain tonight, if you don't want to spend the rest of your life in jail."

'I'd made all that up, of course, but the way he stopped and regrouped, physically, brought it home. I wondered what he'd been going to do – push me off the bridge?

'"Why, Carl?" I asked him. "Do you hate me that much?"

'And he shrugged. Like it was no big deal. And he's happy to explain.

'"All those donations," he says, "coming in by the carload, and you take a pissant little salary and give it all away. So I started helping myself, just a little. And then a little more. It got *tedious*, having to be so careful, and I knew that sooner or later you were going to find out. And we know what a straight arrow you are, don't we, Joy? You'd want to ferret out every last cent and put it all back. Make restitution to the all-important Joy Miller Ministries. Who knows, you might even have turned me in."

'"*What money?*" I asked him. It stunned me, that there was more to this, that it wasn't just the eleven thousand that was missing, that there were still things I didn't know.

'He stared at me, and then he smirked. "Don't play dumb, Joy. All your little hints and jokes about my secret accounts, all your fussing and fuming and wondering where all our money was going."

'"I take it then that you didn't lose the retirement money selling short on the stock market."

'"No, *dear*. And I haven't paid the mortgage or the car payments or the IRS for the last three months. All those times they called? And I told you there was an account screw up? And you believed me?"

'And suddenly I became a tornado. I attacked him, punching his stomach, his shoulders, kicking him as hard as I could. He swore and pushed me away. I slapped him and his glasses came off his face.'

I stop for a moment, catch my breath. 'It's so stupid, you know, the way these things happen.'

'Go on.' Harvey is patient. 'What happened next?'

'Carl grabbed for the glasses and lost his balance. He fell. Backwards over the edge of the bridge. And no, before you ask, I didn't push him.'

'And then?'

'I screamed. He screamed too. And then I was the only one screaming. I could hear it echoing down the mountain. And then I stopped screaming and it got very quiet.'

'Then why all the guilt, Joy? He lost his balance and fell off the bridge and died. He *was* dead then, right?'

'I don't know. I don't know when he died.' I put a hand on Leo's head and he licks the inside of my wrist. 'I felt dizzy and I was afraid I was going to fall too, so I sat down. I didn't scream anymore. I didn't cry. I just listened.' I take a breath. I need a moment. Harvey is quiet, patient, which is just what I need.

'I'd left my flashlight behind the rocks where I was hiding. So I hung on to the side and peered over the edge. It was dark by then, and even shining my flashlight later I couldn't find him, couldn't see where he fell. I didn't think there was any way he could have survived a fall like that, but there was no way I could be sure.'

'You left him,' Harvey says flatly.

'My first instinct was to go down to the lodge and get help. I grabbed the backpack, and it was so heavy. I opened it, I couldn't stand not to see. And sure enough, it was full of money. And that started me thinking. Because how was I going to explain all this, me being up on that bridge with Carl? Even if I ditched the backpack or hid it in my room, how would I explain being registered under the name Cindy Farmer? And I started to add everything up.

'I'd told my friend, the one I left Joey with, that I thought Carl was having an affair. Which, as it turns out, he was. My cousin Marsha would tell them about the missing money. What kind of proof did I have that Carl was taking it? What if they thought it was me? If Carl hadn't paid the bills in three months, that was going to set off all kinds of alarms. Especially since we'd just taken out a big insurance policy, which in hindsight, he was obviously planning to cash in.

'What was I going to say? That I was warned by a hit man that Carl had hired him to kill me? That the hit man had a change of heart? I wouldn't have believed it, and I didn't think Cletus would come forward and say "yes, I'm a hit man, but I'm currently trying to reform."

'I'd counseled enough families through domestic crisis to have a certain experience with the police and how their minds work. Stay within the bounds of the norm, do what's expected, and usually there won't be any problems. Drive a nice car, live in a nice house, dress well – you get judged by those things. But behavior out of the box like this? Not a chance. And once that legal ball was rolling there would be no stopping it. I wasn't going to take the fall when *I'd* been the victim. It was as simple a decision as that. I decided to do the smart thing, instead of the right thing.

'I left him there. I strapped the pack of money to my back and hiked back down that mountain. Crawled, actually, is more like it. It took hours, in the dark, with just a flashlight. Then I went to my room, packed up my stuff, threw some towels on the floor and rumpled the bed so it would look like I'd spent the night. I'd paid cash in advance so I left the keycard on the dresser.

'I was home, waiting, when the police came. And they told me that Carl had taken his own life, by jumping off Natural Bridge.'

FORTY-FIVE

I can hear Harvey breathing steadily, though he hasn't said a word. I reach behind me and stroke Leo's head.

'Look, I have something for you, too. Something for you to read.'

I sense his motion rather than see it. He turns on a flashlight and shows me a worn book, four inches by six, stained, baby blue.

'It's a diary,' he says. 'Did you bring the picture I sent you?'

I nod, take it out of Leo's saddle pack. Hold it up to the light. 'Our mothers knew each other,' I say.

'Not exactly.' He points. 'Me. Mom.' His fingertip touches the swollen belly of his mother. 'And you. Yes. She was pregnant with you in this picture.'

I catch my breath. '*Me?*'

'Her name was Cecily Jenkins and she was my mom. We have different fathers, Joy, but Cecily Jenkins was our mom. Look, she wrote you a letter. I've got it right here.' He opens the diary to a dogeared page and holds it up to the light.

Dear Little Girl, I write this to tell you how much I love you, now that you are gone. And to remind myself that the decision I made was wise. But oh, little baby. I did not know how hard this would be.

I picture you reading this someday, when you're all grown up and beautiful. If your mother and father choose to tell you the circumstances of your birth.

I was an unwed mother at the age of fifteen. I will say

little of Reggie's father, only these two things. One, he had no desire to marry me. And two, I have no regrets. I could not be sorry for what happened when it gave me my little boy.

Your grandparents did not see it that way, and when I refused to go to a home and give Reggie up, I was no longer welcome in their house. And so I married rather quickly. Rather unwisely as well. Little girl, your father is a dangerous man.

He is more cruel than you can imagine to my little son, and please, I do not want you to imagine it or think of such things. I only want you to know that I have made my plans for the best of reasons – to keep both of my children safe.

I do not think little Reggie and I would be alive today if not for my brother, Henry. You will know him as your father, my dear.

Henry was only seventeen when I was kicked out of the house. We kept in touch, in secret. Henry worked a paper route all year round, and selling Burpee seeds in the summer. He gave me every cent that he earned. And it was Henry who appeared on my doorstep less than one year ago, to take me and Reggie away while my husband worked a long shift laying brick.

Little girl, your father suspected my pregnancy, no matter how hard I tried to convince him otherwise. I knew that you, and your brother and I would never be safe in this world if he had another child to hold over me.

So when Henry came, we disappeared.

When my labor pains began, the night that you were born, it was Henry who took me to the hospital. I checked in under the name of his wife, Marion. By then Henry had been married for two years.

Oh, little baby girl, Marion is the best sister to me. You went home, perfectly legally, as her child and Henry's, because it was the only way I could keep you safe. Because he hunts for me, your father. I don't know what would happen if he found me with you. It is bad enough for me and Reggie. He can never know that you exist.

As much as I want to keep you close to me, it seems this was meant to be. Henry is convinced that the mumps he had at thirteen made him unable to father any children, and it is true that in the time he has been married, Marion has not been able to conceive. And not for a lack of trying, is what Henry always says!

So now, please understand that I love you enough to keep you safe. Please know that I am proud to be your mother, and that you have brought me, and Henry and Marion, nothing but absolute joy.

If I have any doubts, it is this last line that convinces me. Harvey reaches to touch my shoulder, then changes his mind.

'And that's why they named me Joy?' I say.

'Be grateful they didn't call you Absolute.'

I am laughing. With hysterical overtones.

Harvey takes the diary and tucks it back in his shirt. 'I wanted you to know. So you wouldn't be afraid of me all the time. So you could believe me when I say I would never hurt you.'

'But why didn't my father go and get you when your mother was killed? Why didn't he raise you with me?'

'You mean Henry? My uncle? Because after your biological father murdered my mother, his parents came and got me. They found him the next day, by the way, with her blood all over his shirt. Drunk. Idiot. But I was legally, if not biologically, his son. At the time, I wasn't aware of any of this. I don't remember it, to be honest. I just remember growing up in their house.

'But they had the diary. Our mother's diary that she wrote. I found it in a box of her stuff up in the attic. They used to lock me up there all the time, and sometimes I'd get bored and go through all the stuff. I was eleven years old when I found our mother's diary.

'It was a dream come true, at first. My father wasn't my father, and my evil grandparents weren't my blood. I confronted them. As it turns out, your dad – Henry, I mean – did try to come and get me, but the grandparents wouldn't allow it. They blackmailed him. They said that his daughter, you, had been born while Mom was married to their son, and that he and his sister and his wife had committed fraud. They said if he didn't leave me there they'd take *you* away from him as well. He wasn't allowed to have any contact with me, or they'd take him to court. And they said they could prove you weren't really his daughter because they knew he was sterile and could never have fathered a child.'

'That's horrible. They were horrible.'

'Oh, I made them sorry. For the sake of my mother, and for me, and for you. Sorry enough that they dumped me in foster care. They made sure that I could never be adopted and that I got labeled really well. So I went straight to a couple by the name of Herman, who specialized in boys like me.'

'And that's how you met Cletus Purcell. You were foster brothers.'

'That's right. I knew, of course, that I had a sister somewhere. I read about the car accident that killed your parents. Marion and Henry. You were what, about twenty when they died?'

'Nineteen. But why didn't you come to us then? After you got sent to the Hermans'?'

Harvey rubs his forehead. 'I got told to leave it alone. Same deal as your dad. Then later, when I read about your parents' accident in the paper, I knew it had to be the Marion and Henry who were my aunt and uncle. That's when I tracked you down. I used to watch your show, did you know that? I didn't tell anybody you were my sister, not even Cletus, but I was pretty proud. And then one day Clete comes to me and says there's rumors of a hit out on evangelist Joy Miller. He'd been with me long enough to know I'd been following your career. My weird obsession, is what he called it. Cletus worked a lot of jobs that were murder for hire. He was a hit man for years. You'd be surprised to know how good certain kinds of bars are for drumming up the hit man kind of business.

208 Lynn Hightower

'Anyway, Clete lets me know all about it. He owed me. I used to look out for him when we were foster brothers, and we worked jobs together from time to time. So I asked him to make sure he and I got the job to take you out.

'Clete was all for just killing your husband – and turns out he was right, don't you think? But at the time I didn't know what *you'd* want, and I didn't want to hurt you by doing things my way. That's when I first decided I'd take the straight road for a while, and see how things would shake out. For all the good it did you or me.

'But I'm your big brother, you know? I didn't want to get you tangled up in my mess, I just wanted to keep an eye out. Make sure you were all right.'

'Are they still alive? The grandparents?' I don't say our grandparents. I'm not there yet. Not quite.

The inhuman quality comes into his eyes. 'Long dead.'

'And I'm really your sister.'

'That you are.'

And so we face each other, in the darkness, on top of that beautiful and terrible bridge. We stand, I dust off my jeans.

'I still kind of taking this all in,' I say.

'I guess I've given you a lot to think about. I appreciate you coming up here. I just want you to understand you're safe from me. So.' He shrugs. 'Bye, sis.'

Harvey sounds so nonchalant and uncaring. But I feel his yearning crackle in the air.

'Goodbye then.'

Can I do this? He starts to turn away, but I open my arms. I give my brother a hug.

We are careful with it. It does not last long. He is sweating or crying. In the dark, I cannot tell.

'Start fresh,' I tell him.

'I'll try.'

I listen to his footsteps as he walks away, as if I can determine his future by the cadence of his step.

FORTY-SIX

T he next morning, I oversleep.

It was no easy thing, coming down off that mountain. I felt numb, and cold, and strange. Flashlights can only do so much on a steep mountain trail in the dark. There were times I did not think I would make it back.

Still, I had the advantage of experience. I had inched my way down that trail in the dark fourteen years before.

And this time, of course, I had Leo, using his magnificent nose to find the way. And just as I had fourteen years before, I covered the steepest parts of the trail on my backside, sliding down the rocky path after my dog, who returned to nose me often, intrigued to have my face on a level with his.

I am sleeping, tangled in blankets, when my front door buzzer rings. I stumble out of the bedroom in a tee shirt and sweat pants. Hal is on my doorstep, well worn overnight bag in one hand. He kisses my cheek and I am flustered by how I look – hair wild, eyes groggy with sleep. Hal is freshly showered, in a vanilla bean sweater and olive cargo pants. Cindy Lou is nosing the rosebush and the 4Runner is parked in my drive.

'Am I early?' he asks.

'I could be late.'

I open the door and Cindy Lou rushes in. Leo yelps and leaps and the two of them begin the intrusive sniffing that I prefer not to watch.

I haven't had time to guest-proof the house, and Leo's toys are strewn from one end of the great room to the other, including four well chewed tennis balls, strands of a doggie rope toy and the gutted remains of a stuffed monkey. I settle Hal in the living room with a newspaper and a fresh cup of coffee, and Leo and Cindy Lou to keep him entertained.

I stand in the shower, eyes shut tight, feeling the blessed

heat of the water that plasters my hair to my head. I can't quite believe my life.

I take my time. Put on my favorite khaki trousers that make me look slim and the black sweater I particularly like. I take trouble over my makeup. Blow dry and fluff my hair.

We leave the dogs wrestling in the kitchen and head out for a brunch.

Hal, in the way of men universal, is content to be silent in the car. I close my eyes. I know that when he and I walk into the restaurant people will see a fireman and a part-time teacher of religion, happy to be together, content to share a meal. They won't see an evangelist haunted by a killer, a woman who lost her son in a terrible moment of violence or a wife that a husband hired a hit man to kill.

We are all of us an accumulation of our histories – the ups and downs, the dramas and tragedies that are not our particular fault. We think we make choices, we think we're in charge. But the older I get, the more I wonder if we are not just dancing to music that was planned long ago, and have as much control over our lives as we do the stars. We are not so much the sum of all the things we have lived, as the person who made the journey and survived.

This I define as happiness. I am swept away with the thought. It will fade, as all things do, and eventually I will take it all for granted, the simple pleasures of a normal life.

I look forward to that.